STAGECOACH

OTHER FIVE STAR WESTERNS
BY MAX BRAND:

In the Hills of Monterey (1998); The Lost Valley (1998); Chinook (1998); The Gauntlet (1998); The Survival of Juan Oro (1999); Stolen Gold (1999); The Geraldi Trail (1999); Timber Line (1999); The Gold Trail (1999); Gunman's Goal (2000); The Overland Kid (2000); The Masterman (2000); The Outlaw Redeemer (2000); The Peril Trek (2000); The Bright Face of Danger (2000); Don Diablo (2001); The Welding Quirt (2001); The Tyrant (2001); The House of Gold (2001); The Lone Rider (2002); Crusader (2002); Smoking Guns (2002); Jokers Extra Wild (2002); Flaming Fortune (2003); Blue Kingdom (2003); The Runaways (2003); Peter Blue (2003); The Golden Cat (2004); The Range Finder (2004); Mountain Storms (2004); Hawks and Eagles (2004); Trouble's Messenger (2005); Bad Man's Gulch (2005); Twisted Bars (2005); The Crystal Game (2005); Dogs of the Captain (2006); Red Rock's Secret (2006); Wheel of Fortune (2006); Treasure Well (2006); Acres of Unrest (2007); Rifle Pass (2007); Melody and Cordoba (2007); Outlaws From Afar (2007); Rancher's Legacy (2008); The Good Badman (2008); Love of Danger (2008); Nine Lives (2008); Silver Trail (2009); The Quest (2009); Mountain Made (2009); Black Thunder (2009); Iron Dust (2010); The Black Muldoon (2010); The Lightning Runner (2010); Legend of the Golden Coyote (2010); Sky Blue (2011); Outcast Breed (2011); Train's Trust (2011); The Red Well (2011); Son of an Outlaw (2012); Lightning of Gold (2012); Comanche (2012); Gunfighters in Hell (2012); Red Hawks's Trail (2013); Sun and Sand (2013); The Double Rider (2013)

STAGECOACH

A WESTERN STORY

MAX BRAND®

FIVE STAR

A part of Gale, Cengage Learning

Detroit • New York • San Francisco • New Haven, Conn • Waterville, Maine • London

LIBRARY OF CONGRESS CATALOGING-IN-PUBLICATION DATA

Brand, Max, 1892–1944.
    Stagecoach : A Western Story / by Max Brand. — First Edition.
        pages cm. -- (Five Star Western)
    "Stagecoach first appeared as 'Sammy Gregg's Mustang Herd' in Street & Smith's Western Story Magazine (10/3/25)."
    ISBN-13: 978-1-4328-2711-3 (hardcover)
    ISBN-10: 1-4328-2711-1 (hardcover)
    I. Title.
PS3511.A87S73 2013
813'.52—dc23   2013024231

First Edition. First Printing: December 2013.
Published in conjunction with Golden West Literary Agency.
Find us on Facebook– https://www.facebook.com/FiveStarCengage
Visit our website– http://www.gale.cengage.com/fivestar/
Contact Five Star™ Publishing at FiveStar@cengage.com

Printed in Mexico
1 2 3 4 5 6 7 17 16 15 14 13

ADDITIONAL COPYRIGHT INFORMATION

CHAPTER ONE

Someone who knew what he was talking about said that no man should go into the West—the real frontier West, that is—unless he was capable of inspiring some measure of awe. Perhaps by his personal dignity, which is, after all, the best way of keeping a man out of trouble. Or through physical strength or mere size, or by dauntless power of eye, or through fighting skill—any or all of these attributes would be most serviceable. But Sammy Gregg did not have any of them.

He wasn't a whit more than eight inches above five feet, and he did not stand straight enough to take advantage of all of those meager inches, even. He walked with a slight stoop, as a rule, leaning over like a man about to start from a walk to a run. He looked as though he were always in a hurry, and, as a matter of fact, he usually was. His weight was about a hundred and thirty pounds, or a trifle more in winter, and a little less when the hot weather of the summer began to set in. It was not tough, well-seasoned muscle, either. It was quite flabby. And he had small bones, and little, narrow, nervous hands. His eyes were pale, and rather near-sighted, so that he had a half frightened look, when it wasn't simply wistfully inquiring. His pale forehead was constantly contorted with a frown—which was not a frown of bad temper, but of eagerness.

The only truly remarkable thing about Sammy, indeed, was that same eagerness. Like the eagerness of a hunting ferret—if you can imagine a ferret without teeth. But one felt about

Sammy a vast earnestness, rooted as deep as the roots of his soul, a singular intentness in which he was absorbed. That was the secret of the bigness that was in Sammy, for some bigness there was. The trouble was the West, and the people of the West, were not fitted for understanding this small man.

I suppose, for that matter, that he was a rarity in almost any climate. He had the simplicity of a child mixed oddly with some of the guile of a serpent, I am afraid. It was always very hard to understand Sammy. I, for one, never could pretend to hold the key to his complex nature. I can only describe him as he was.

In the first place, he did not come West to raise cattle nor horses, or to ride herd on the cow range, or to dig gold for himself or any other, or to start up as a storekeeper in one of the new towns. He came West with $5,000 in his pockets and a desire to invest it. Choice he had none. He was ready for anything out of which he might make money.

You will think that he would have been wiser to sink that sum of money in a bank rather than expose it, naked, to the air of that climate where gold turned so quickly to bloody rust. But I must add one more thing to my character of Sammy Gregg. He was not afraid. There was no fear in him. Fear did not interest Sammy, but dollars did.

Not from a blind love of coin, either. The impelling motive was love for a girl who kept house for an uncle in a Brooklyn flat and waited for word from Sammy from the wilderness. Sammy had found the lady of his heart long before he ever got on the train that brought him to Munson. Oh, unromantic Sammy. He had fallen in love with her not suddenly, and not from any exciting meeting, but simply because this fair-haired girl had been known to him during his entire life. She had grown up in the back yard next to his. He had made faces at her when he was five years old, peering at her through a hole in the board fence, and that day she ran crying into her house for fear of him. Afterward, he walked to school with her at his side, regardless of the other boys who pointed their fingers at him.

Sammy had no time for the opinions of outsiders. If you consider it from the most logical point of view, you will see that we indulge ourselves in a luxury when we spend energy to conciliate the good will of our neighbors. And Sammy never had any extra strength to spend. He was not, in short, interested in public opinion, and that was why he was such an oddity as I, for one, have never seen the like of.

For instance, he was known as a coward in the schoolyard for years, simply because he did not think that it was worthwhile to fight back and have his face smashed up by the fists of another. But when the legend of his cowardice made the schoolyard tyranny too uncomfortable—when his schoolfellows could not let him alone at any recess but had to pluck at him like sparrows at a strange bird—then he changed his mind. He decided that the time had come to end the persecution. He deliberately selected the largest boy in the yard, picked a fight, and had the satisfaction beyond his fondest hopes of planting the first two blows upon the other—one hard little fist on either eye of the tall youth. Afterward he received a tremendous thrashing from the capable fists of that same boy, but thereafter he was left in peace. If it cost the best fighter in the school two black eyes to handle Sammy, the others decided that they wanted none of his medicine. So he was allowed to go his way, no longer pointed at, even when he wheeled out his infant brother in the baby carriage, or when he packed the books of the girl next door to school and walked beside her going home. It was taken for granted even thus early that Sammy was to marry Susie Mitchell. Their own parents pointed out that there was even something in the names that fitted them for one another. Sammy and Susie. Like two names picked out of a book and linked together in fiction.

I should not say that Sammy loved Susie with a devouring passion as he grew up. But she was a part of his life. He cared for her as he cared for himself, I might say. He had admitted her into his life and she had grown into it like a graft into the trunk of a tree. He thought of her as often as he thought of himself. And if he were not passionately unhappy when he was away from her, he was certainly worried and irritated and confused and ill at ease. When he was at her side, he did not want to kiss her or fondle her or say foolish things to her, or even hold her hand. But he was satisfied—as a cow is satisfied when it is in its own pasture, near its own red barn.

I do not want to cheapen Sammy. But I want to point out that his steadfastness in his love was not the result of overwhelming passion. It was rather the result of weakness. He had not room for many hearts of others in his life. There was no strength or space in him for that. For his own mother or father, or brother or sisters, he felt not the slightest emotion. And when brother Charlie died, Sammy went to sleep at the funeral. More than that, he was not ashamed of his sleep.

"Why not?" he said to his outraged mother. "The room was so hot and stuffy with the smell of all those flowers."

After that, the members of his family scorned him. Their own hearts were so tender, so true, and their own sentiments were so noble and so pure. But Sammy simply went on busily with his affairs, doing the things that counted most practically for his own ultimate happiness. And, among others, he worked as often as he could and he saved every penny of his earnings.

Because he knew his weaknesses. He knew that he was not brilliant or wise or studious or profound, or physically powerful or nervously dynamic. He was simply a little bit weaker than everyone he knew—except the cripple on the corner—and he realized that the only manner in which he could make any progress would be to attempt to do only a few things, but to do those few things very well. And, to increase his own strength, he must have some other allied power working for him as soon as possible—the power of money.

So he saved and scraped and lived cheaply and labored earnestly at his jobs. He was out of school at fifteen and he was constantly contributing to the savings bank on the first of every month until one day in his twenty-fifth year when he had a little talk with Susie Mitchell.

"When are we to be married?" asked Susie.

"Oh, someday," Sammy answered. "When I get enough money to live on right. . . ."

"I'm twenty-five, the same as you," said Susie. "That's not so young."

He looked askance at her in wonder. But her pretty face was very grave and her blue eyes—as pale and gentle as his own—were fixed firmly upon his face.

"Besides," Susie said, "I don't go in for style. You know that. I don't mind working. I don't mind a small house to live in. I don't aim much higher than what my mother got when she married. But I think that it's time we married, and had some children . . . and things like that. Jiminy, Sammy, you've got a lot more than *most* young fellows have. And look what a swell salary you get . . . fifteen a week. A regular position, I call it, down there at the paper mill . . . where you'll be raised, too, after four or five years more. The manager certainly told you about that himself."

Mind you, this was long before the day when carpenters got as much a day as Sammy worked for in a week. In the time of which I write, $60 a month was enough for an office man, with many other men under him, assistants, and all that. Those were the days when the boys pointed out the man who lived in the big corner house, because it was said that he got $125 a month.

So $60 was quite a bit, but it was not enough for Sammy. He

said: "Let me have a chance to think this over." Then he went away and reviewed his position.

In the first place, he had to marry Susie, there was no doubt about that. And he had to marry her quick. He would as soon dream of going on through life without her as he would dream of going on through life without a leg—or without two legs. Susie was simply a part of his spirit and of his flesh, too. But he was afraid of marriage. He had seen other youths attempt marriage and he had seen children and accompanying doctor bills and ill health break down their savings, ruin their nerves, keep them awake with worry, and fill their lives with gloom. Sammy would not stand the chance of such a disaster, because he knew his own strength and he knew that it could not endure through sleepless nights. He felt that he could never marry unless he could marry comfortably. And he had established as a goal a sum of $15,000. With that amount working for him at interest, he would be safe. Even if he lost his health, he could support his family on that same interest until he was well again. A goal still $10,000 away—and Susie wanted to get married.

He came back to Susie. He said: "I am going away for six months. Will you wait that long?"

"Going away!" cried Susie.

"To make ten thousand dollars."

Susie laughed, at first. But when she saw that he was in earnest, she was filled with a sort of religious awe. It seemed hardly moral and decent for a young fellow to speak of hoping to make $10,000 in a mere half year. It had never been done in her family. It made her almost think of enchantment—certainly it made her think very strongly of crime.

She could almost see her little Sammy Gregg with a black mask tied across the bridge of his nose and a snub-nosed revolver clutched in his hand stealing up behind the back of some florid banker. She could almost see it, and the thing gave her a shock of horror.

"Don't go, Sammy," she breathed to him. "Don't go, Sammy."

He did not listen to her. He hardly heard her voice. He was filled with his own thoughts, which were already in a far-away country where dollars grew more readily than they grew in Brooklyn. He was thinking of the accounts that flooded newspapers and magazines from time to time of great fortunes scooped up by a single gesture of the wise men.

In crises we are apt to stop thinking and fall back upon superstitions, religion, fairy tales. So did young Sammy Gregg. He decided to follow his new vision. It was a hunch, and for the first time in his life he was about to do a risky thing. I had to explain all of this because without understanding a little of the background of Sammy, it would be quite impossible to make head or tail of him as he was when he appeared before the grinning populace of Munson, that rude little city in the Western hills. But if Sammy performed at times feats that seemed well beyond his strength, you must remember that there was a spur driven constantly into his soul—the loss of Susie. He was in constant misery. For he was away from her. He could not hurry home from his work and wave out of his window and see her waving back from hers. He could not walk through the little park with her in the evening. Her flesh was three thousand miles away. Her spirit was three thousand miles away. And Sammy was maddened by the sense of loss.

CHAPTER TWO

I have called Munson rude, and it was still something more than rude and rough. It was self-conscious. The worst and the toughest town that ever existed on the cattle trails or in the mining districts in the very early days, when murders punctuated every day of a community's existence, could never equal for concentrated viciousness the towns of the later periods of the Western frontier—the periods of which I am writing now.

In the early times, when a man committed a murder it was, nine chances out of ten, because he had been blinded and poisoned and maddened with bad whiskey. Or else, he was simply a brute and a bully, and as such he did not last long to murder others. A noose was fetched around his neck and he was yanked up to the limb of a tree and left to wriggle there.

But in the later days the real bad men began to crop up. They were bad with a capital B. The reason was that the Easterners and the foreigners and the bad actors of the cities—the rooks and the gamblers and the yeggs and the safe-crackers and the gunmen decided to move two thousand miles West and start life over again wearing two guns openly, instead of one gun hidden. And they went West with a rush and right away they started in being "open and spacious" and "free and easy" and "silent" and "noble". Oh, yes, there were hundreds of men out there being dignified and noble as fast as they could load their guns, you might say. And they were the ones who made all of the worst trouble, I can tell you.

Were they tenderfeet? No, they weren't. No man who has done his stretch or his fiver is a tenderfoot. Any man who has done his bit of time up the river has acquired a skin thick enough for all ordinary purposes of wear in any part of this globe. Those fellows went West with their guns. And they started right in begging for attention.

They were the boys who began to kill not because they were drunk, or because they were stupid bullies. No, they were intelligent, cunning, cruel men, and they killed because they wanted fame—or that article that will do for fame on the rough frontier—notoriety.

Think of it from a point of view of advertising. A man who could shoot straight might buy himself a dozen headlines for the price of one loading of his six-gun. That's what you might call something for nothing. And so, when you trace it back to the beginning, it was the wonder and the shuddering and the worship of the coddled, comfortable East that created the real Western bad man who would as soon kill as light a cigarette. So, after a little time, you began to have your real outlaw—your fellow with a list of twenty deaths, say, established on his record and as many more not proved. And still the bad men lived.

Not so in the old days of the first frontiers. No, the bad boys were taken out under a tree and their necks were stretched like the very deuce, and they were left hanging there to stretch all the crimps out of their souls. Amazing what a lot of good one hanging like that would do in a whole big county the size of the state of Maine.

Well, the fashion changed. It became admirable to shoot straight—at other human beings. There was always the plea of self-defense. What a ghastly lot of crimes were attached to that pair of words.

I have gone on at some length to give you an idea of just the sort of place Munson was—Munson, to which our thin-skinned

Sammy was being swiftly whirled by the train. And that is why I say that Munson at this era was tougher than tough—because it was self-conscious.

The train stopped, and Sammy swung down from the steps and reached for a platform, but unfortunately he found none. The sight of that swinging, pawing foot of his, and his skinny leg, was enough to catch half a dozen wicked eyes. He was already being laughed at before he dropped down to the ground and presented all of himself for the first time to the eye of Munson.

Before he had well landed, Lawson himself was in charge. The first thing he did was to let out a yell that so startled young Sammy that he almost leaped backward under the wheels of the slowly moving train. Sammy, however, was perfectly lacking in the very thing of which Munson was full—self-consciousness. He did not dream, after a moment of reflection, that that yell had been meant for him. So he simply picked up his heavy grip and stepped forward toward the crooked little dusty street where the sign said Hotel. He stepped forward, and as he walked, he settled his hat more firmly on his head.

Alas it was a derby hat. I cannot tell what made an iron hat, as the derby was called, a mortal offense in the West, but it was. It required an almost presidential reputation to enable a man to keep one on his head. And what reputation had poor Sammy Gregg?

Before he knew it, Lawson had loosed off a couple of bullets that struck the ground in front of Sammy and covered him with a stinging shower of dust and flying gravel. He jumped, of course, straight up into the air.

It brought a shout of willing laughter from everyone. Because Lawson never appeared without his gang. I wish I could give a thorough picture of Lawson, but I can't. Words become weak, speaking of the poisonous evil of such natures as his. He was that most gruesome combination—weakness and wickedness combined. He was a coward, a bully, a tyrant, a sneak, a moral wreck of a man, but he was a hero, in Munson, because he could shoot straight. And the consciousness that he could shoot straight always made him brave. Cowards always make the most horrible tyrants simply because they are so familiar with the emotion that they wish to inspire—fear.

Now the weak mouth of Lawson stretched in a grin. And his little, close-set eyes gleamed under the shadow of his sombrero. He put another bullet neatly in the ground just where the feet of Sammy were about to land, and when they did land, Sammy naturally bounded into the air again.

"Dance, confound you!" yelled Lawson.

But Sammy stood still. He said nothing for a moment, but when another bullet struck the ground at his feet, he said calmly: "I don't think I'll dance."

Lawson was staggered, for suddenly he saw that this little man was not afraid. Then he broke out in a savage roar: "When you speak to a man, take off your hat, tenderfoot!"

He did not wait for Sammy to obey. His gun spoke, and the bullet tore the hat from the head of Sammy. It was very close shooting, no one could deny that. It brought another roar of applause and laughter when the crowd saw Sammy instinctively duck. But then he leaned and picked up his hat and settled it, dusty as it was, upon his head once more.

"You'll come and liquor with me, kid," said Lawson. "I'm going to see how your insides act when you get some of Mortimer's poison inside of you. And bring the other dude along with you, boys."

Sammy could not keep the center of the stage very long. Not with such a counterattraction as had dismounted from the same train. It was a tall man, a tall, wide-shouldered, handsome man of thirty, perhaps, dressed in a fashion that Munson could not tolerate for an instant, in those days. He wore riding boots, to be sure, but the boots were not *under* his trousers, and that was a sin, of course. And above the boots rose neat whipcord riding breeches. And there was a well-fitted gray coat, and a gray shirt with a shining white stiff collar and a natty little bowtie, and this gentleman was finished off with a small gray felt hat on his head. And he carried a suitcase of large dimensions with **C.O.F.** stamped in big letters on the side of it.

He made the counterattraction. He looked just as much of a tenderfoot as Sammy did, and there was more of him. The crowd surrounded him in an instant, and he and Sammy were huddled off toward Mortimer's saloon in a trice.

Huddled off with this difference, that whereas many hands were laid upon Sammy, urging him along, beating his derby hat down over his eyes, cuffing and pawing him, there was not so much as the tip of a finger laid upon the tall man. I cannot tell why. Perhaps it was the calmness of his face and eye. Perhaps it was the wrinkle of his coat between the shoulder blades, telling of ample muscles there. At any rate, although they milled about him, yelling and cursing and laughing, no one touched him and so the procession burst into Mortimer's.

He was the headquarters for such affairs, was Mortimer. He was also the gambling partner and the partner in secret murders who worked with my friend, Lawson. And he was only just a trifle less savory than Lawson. He greeted the new victims with a veritable yell of delight and instantly the glasses were set chiming upon the bar. And the big black bottles were spun out.

Lawson stood at one end of the bar and gave directions. "To the top, kid. To the top, both of you. Fill up them glasses to the top, I tell you."

Sammy set his teeth and obeyed. He didn't like it, but neither did he throw away his life for such a small affair as this. And so he filled as he was ordered.

But, after that, a deadly hush fell over the barroom, for it was seen that the tall man, in spite of the order from Lawson, had not touched the waiting bottle to pour his drink. He spoke before the wrath of Lawson could descend upon him.

"Gentlemen," he said, "I shall be charmed to drink with you, but first I'd like to give you my name, if you don't mind."

CHAPTER THREE

He spoke so mildly that they could hardly help but misunderstand him, and the snarl of mockery awoke instantly. However, Lawson appeared to scent an opportunity for further mischief than usual, and he raised his voice to control the murmur.

"All right," he said. "Let's hear your name, and damned if I don't think that it ought to begin with Percy."

A poor jest, but Lawson did not have to invent very witty remarks in order to win the applause of his fellows. While the laughter was still ringing, however, the big stranger sauntered to the stove. It was a raw spring day with a whistling wind from the snow-tipped mountains of the north, prying through the cracks and sending long chill fingers of draft waving through the rickety saloon. The stove was packed with wood; the stove itself was red hot, and the door was open to throw out a greater draft. In that open door the poker lay, just as it had been dropped when the wood was last stirred and replenished. To this stepped the tall man and drew forth the poker and with it in his hand he approached the bar.

He raised it, and with the white point he began to write upon the wood. He had half completed the first word of his writing before Mortimer intervened, for this audacity had paralyzed our saloonkeeper with rage and wonder. When his voice returned to him, it was like the challenging bellow of a bull. He clapped the muzzle of his revolver on the edge of the bar. Then from the ample throat of Mortimer throbbed a stream of cursing that filled the room with storming echoes.

The tall man calmly laid down the poker—where it burned a deep gouge in the wood. His left hand glided out, unhurrying, but swift as the flick of a whiplash. It laid hold upon the barrel of Mortimer's gun, so that the bullet of that gentleman hummed idly under the arm of the tenderfoot. And, at the same time, with his right hand he drew forth a hidden Colt revolver, long and heavy and black, and placed the muzzle against the breast of Mortimer, and fired.

Mortimer, dead before he struck the floor, collapsed in a pool of crimson behind the bar.

The silence that followed was so intense that the crowd could hear the ticking of a clock in the back room—and the hissing of the wood beneath the hot end of the poker as the tall man wrote the rest of his name upon the bar. *Chester Ormonde Furness,* he wrote, and stood back and dropped the poker to the floor while his name still smoked upon the bar.

"That is my name, gentlemen," he said. "I trust that you are glad to see me. Gladder, at least, than I am to see you. Because I have been over a considerable section of this little world and not even in Singapore, where the scum of the world is dropped after it has been skimmed from the pot . . . not even in Singapore, or in Shanghai or the New York slums . . . from which I think a good many of you have come . . . have I seen such a worthless lot of cowardly, sneaking riff-raff . . . fakers . . . sham giants . . . cur dogs wearing lion skins. And about the worst in this very bad lot seems to be Mister Lawson. Will you step out, Mister Lawson?"

Lawson had not turned white. His complexion did not permit that color. But he turned a very pale greenish-yellow. He did not step forward. He whirled, instead, toward the door, and tried to spring through it. But, just at that moment, a gun fired behind him, and a .45-caliber Colt bullet cracked the door from top to bottom. Lawson did not make the mistake of imagining that it was a missed shot. He stopped in his tracks and turned slowly back to face Chester Ormonde Furness.

"Do you know my name?" said the stranger.

"Yes, Mister Furness," said Lawson.

"Why I don't finish you," said Furness, "I hardly know. I suppose it's because there is a sporting instinct in me and I like to have a little *fun* with my shooting. I like to give the game a start. So I am going to give *you* a start, Lawson. Go through that door and start up the street. I'll follow you . . . with my gun."

Lawson did not wait for a second invitation. He sprang back through the door and Furness glided after him. And then the rest of awe-stricken Munson had sight of the terrible Lawson sprinting with all his might down the street while a tall dude stood in the road behind him and emptied a Colt—missing him by neatly calculated distances that the crowd could appreciate, for every time Furness fired, Lawson leaped to one side or the other with a wild howl until he found a corner to dodge around into safety.

When Furness finished his shooting, he put away his gun, swiftly and neatly, so that no lump showed where it rested. Then he turned upon the gaping crowd—a tamed, humbled crowd, now grinning sheepishly in anticipation at him.

"I detest trouble," said Furness. "I always strive to avoid it. And I want you to remember what I say. I want you to remember it and repeat it to your cronies wherever you may meet them. Tell them that I expect to stay for a considerable time in this town. I expect to become well acquainted with Munson and the neighborhood around it. And I expect to live here in peace. When I say peace, I mean it. I intend to rent a house and to live quietly in it on the edge of town. I do not wish to have my sleep disturbed at night. And, if there is a noisy riot, I shall come out and put an end to the good time if I can. If a stray bullet from a brawl happens to find its way through my window, you may trust that I shall find the man who fired it. Beyond this, I wish to say that I desire to have my name handled gently. If there is any vicious talk, I want you to know that I possess an exceedingly sensitive nature, and I shall find the vicious talkers, gentlemen, and I shall kill those vicious talkers, gentlemen, if I am able. I am well aware that there is no law in Munson, at the present moment. And I hereby give notice that my own laws I shall enforce with a gun. And now, gentlemen, I want you to understand, finally, that I quite sympathize with the error into which you have fallen concerning me. To you, I looked rather soft. If you have found that I am not soft, and if you desire to be my friends, come back with me into the saloon and have a drink at my expense."

Not a man held back. They were afraid to, perhaps. Or perhaps there were so many of them that they were not ashamed. Because crowds are usually devoid of all noble feeling—even of shame. They went back with the tall man, and he went behind the bar and served them, stepping over the body of the dead man that lay on the floor, while he passed out glasses and bottles. He drank with them most cheerfully, and they noted that he put down the red-eye without blinking an eye and without a chaser. They noticed, too, that he paid punctually for the drinks, leaving a bright new gold piece shining upon the bar as he passed out.

The crowd remained behind to chat about this new wonder, to lift the body of Mortimer and give him a dog's burial just as he had died a dog's death.

In the street the tall man met the little tenderfoot. He smiled down at little Sammy Gregg and he found the steady, unshaken, pale-blue eye of Sammy Gregg surveying him gravely.

"Does a man have to be like you to get on in this part of the country?" asked Sammy.

"Not a bit," said Furness, "but it's a good thing to be able to take care of yourself. Have you a gun?"

"I never fired a gun in my life."

"There's a store. You'd better go buy one, the first thing you do."

Sammy Gregg shook his head. "I'm no good at a bluff," he said. "If I wear a gun, it's a sign that I pretend that I can use it. But I can't. And I never could afford the time to learn. I'm pressed for time, you see."

The tall man did not smile. He began to regard the little man more seriously. "May I ask what your business is?" he said.

"I have no business," said Sammy, "except to make ten thousand dollars in six months out here. Do you think it can be done?"

"That depends," Furness replied.

"Honestly, I mean."

"Ah," said Furness, "that is another story. No . . . frankly I'm afraid that you can't."

The ferret gleam of eagerness came into the eyes of little Sammy Gregg. "I think that I will, though," he declared.

"Finding a gold mine, then?"

"No, I don't know what I'll find. All I want is an opportunity . . . not a gold mine. And fellows like those"—he gestured toward the bullet-cracked door of the saloon—"are liable to leave a whole lot of opportunities lying around loose without anybody really claiming them." He added: "I ought to thank you, though, for getting me out of that mess."

"Don't say a word about it," the big man said genially. "I was fighting my own battle, and not yours. Affairs have come to such a horrible point around here that a man has to take a killing on his hands whenever he enters a new town . . . or very nearly that."

He said this in rather a jesting tone, but still there was something in his manner that made little Sammy open his eyes, and he thought he knew now what he had only guessed in the barroom—that Furness was the veteran of a hundred hand-to-hand encounters. And awe and dread filled Sammy, and, with it, a certain instinctive dislike.

Others were to feel that same dislike for Furness later on, but Sammy was the first man to sense the danger and the evil in the big fellow. He said good bye rather briskly and swung away down the street.

Opportunity: really and truly to turn $5,000 into $15,000 in six months.

But one could not examine such country as this on foot. And there must be horse and saddle procured at once. He went to the store for the saddle and got a second-hand one, a badly worn and tattered one.

"It won't give you none too comfortable a seat," the storekeeper advised him frankly.

"I'm not looking for comfort," Sammy Gregg said. "Now, where can I get a horse and what do I have to pay for it? I hear they have ten-dollar horses out West?"

"Texas is what you mean," the storekeeper said. "But around here they gobble up everything in the shape of a horse for fifty dollars. And up at the Crumbock mines they'll pay seventy-five."

CHAPTER FOUR

That was enough for young Sammy Gregg. He was looking for an opportunity and here, it seemed, was one shoved under his very nose.

Horses cost $10 in Texas—in Crumbock they cost $75. The difference would be $65 in clear profit. Allow $15 a head for transportation, and the profit was still $50 a head. Very well. For the sake of caution, suppose that he invested only half of his available capital and turned $2,500 into horses. That would give him two-hundred-and-fifty head at $10 a head. But fifty times two hundred and fifty was $12,500! That was $2,500 more than the profit he needed and already at hand.

Fire began to burn in Sammy Gregg, but he masked it carefully from his face. "I should think," he said, "that a lot of people would be in the business of buying Texas horses and selling them in the Crumbock mining region."

"You *would* think that," the storekeeper said, nodding, "unless you *knowed*."

"Knew what?"

"Knowed what Texas mustangs is like, for one thing."

"Well?"

The storekeeper closed his eyes in strained thought as he reached for a superlative. "Keeping hold of a herd of mustangs," he said at last, "is like trying to keep hold of a handful of quicksilver. The harder you try to hold it, the farther it spurts away."

26

"They're wild, I suppose."

"You suppose, son, but I know. I've rode 'em . . . I've broke 'em . . . and then they broke me!"

"Really?"

"I got a hip smashed as flat as a pancake. That's one thing. My ribs is mixed up worsen a mess of eggs scrambled in a frying pan. And my head is set on crooked. All from mixing too long with them mustangs."

"But if one just herds them along . . . ?"

"Herded the devil!" said the storekeeper with a weary sigh. "I herded six of them twenty miles, once. It took me a month."

"A month!"

"And then I only delivered seven of the twenty."

"Good heavens!" Sammy Gregg gasped. "Did you lose the way?"

The storekeeper stared at him. "Lose my way traveling twenty miles? Son, I ain't that kind of a fool. Not me. I pack a sort of a compass in the back of my head. But lemme tell you about a mustang . . . that everything that you want to do is just what the mustang ain't got any idea of doing."

Sammy was amazed.

"They stampede," said the storekeeper, "from hell to breakfast and back ag'in. That's their nature. Promiscuous and free and easy. Where they want to be is always just over the edge of the sky away from where you want 'em to be. You can write that down. Besides, even if a herd was drove up here by good horse hands . . . like some of them Mexicans are . . . still what chance would there be of it getting safe to Crumbock?"

"I can't see why not."

"You're young, son, but I'll make you a little older in a minute. Lemme tell you that this ain't no open level plain around here."

"I can see that," Sammy commented seriously.

27

"It's all gouged up and criss-crossed by gullies and cañons every which way, ain't it?"

"It is."

"And them gullies and ravines is all slithering with horse thieves, old son."

"You don't mean it," Sammy said.

"Don't I, though?"

"But why doesn't the law . . . ?"

"The law is a thousand miles away, son. Didn't I lose eight head of good horses six weeks back?"

"And you never could get a trace of em?"

"Trace of 'em? Sure I did. I bought four of 'em back."

"Good heavens," Sammy said. "You knew the men who stole them and didn't . . . ?"

"Didn't what? Try to chase them?"

"Perhaps . . . with help."

"Where would you get the help? Besides, you chase these crooks away into the hills and they're plumb gone. You could hide twenty thousand head in any square miles of them badlands. And then, after you've got back home, somebody all unbeknownst sneaks up to your window and puts a bullet into the small of your back.

" 'Murder by men or man unknown,' says the jury.

" 'Poor old Bill,' says my friends. 'He wouldn't let well enough alone.' "

"No, sir, the best way is to keep hands off of them thieves. They's too many of 'em, and they got this advantage . . . they hang together and work together, and the honest folks don't."

"But suppose that one hired a strong guard to herd the mustangs across the hill country . . . ?"

"Herd it across a hundred miles of mountains? A guard for a few hundred mustangs? Son, you're talkin' mad. You'd need a whole company of soldiers to watch every mustang, and even then you'd come in with only the tail of your horse in your hands. Them thieves are that slick that they would steal your horse right out from under your saddle and leave you ridin' along on a one-eyed maverick that you never seen before."

By this time Sammy began to wonder not that the price of horses in Crumbock was $75 a head, but that it was not $175. He went off by himself and sat down for a cigarette and a think.

The first idea is as good as the last, Sammy thought to himself. *As good as the last, most of the time. So lemme see what I can make out of the horse idea.*

He turned it back and forth.

In the first place, it was plain that Mr. Storekeeper had exaggerated somewhat. According to him, a man was a fool who tried to drive horses to Crumbock, and yet horses were certainly there—great numbers of them. Some people, then, were making money by sending livestock there. How did they manage it? Simply by doing what his friend the storekeeper swore could not be done—guarding their horses through the mountains, and herding them successfully across the great Texas plains.

And what others could do, Sammy could do—if he only knew where to hire the right men—the right Mexicans, if they were the best.

The thought of large profits will lead on like the thought of a Promised Land. And so it was that they led Sammy. For two long hours, with the map in his hands, he made his calculations. He knew that $10,000 is a great deal of money to make. And six months is a short time to make it in—and the penalty of failure, as he saw it, was the loss of the hand of pretty Susie Mitchell. It was, indeed, a great deal. And when he thought of Susie, he vowed to himself that somehow he would find the inspiration to carry him through—the inspiration to handle even such devilish brutes as Texas mustangs.

Besides, he was beginning to feel lucky. He had never played even in thought for such stakes as these. To win or lose all was a great thing; a fever was beginning to burn in Sammy and how could he tell that it was the gambler's world-old fever?

Before that day ended, he was on board a train away from Munson, and the next morning he had changed trains and was shooting in a roundabout way toward the southland of cheap horses.

Six months to go when he left New York City. Five months and three weeks when he left Munson. Could he make it? Yes, confidence arose in Sammy as he computed the distance. A month, say, to gather the herd. That left four months and a half. Then an eight-hundred-mile drive. Suppose they journeyed only twenty miles a day. Still, at the end of forty days they would be at their destination.

It seemed simple. Allow a month for mistakes. Allow another month for unknown bad luck. Still he would have time to get back in Brooklyn under the wire of the six months with some $20,000 weighing down his pocket.

He was in San Antone now. He spent five desperate days trying to interview Mexican cowpunchers and getting no further than: *"Sí, señor. Mañana."*

Always, they would meet him tomorrow, but tomorrow they did not appear. What was wrong with him?

Finally, in a San Antone hotel, he confided his troubles to a sharp-eyed man with a fighting face. A man too stern to be trivial.

He said to Sammy: "You're bound for a losing game if you're bound to drive horses to Crumbock. But if you want a man to handle your herd . . . there's one now." He pointed to a dark-faced man in a corner of the room.

"He!" Sammy gasped. "He looks like the king of Mexico more than like a cowpuncher."

"You go talk to him," said the stern-faced man. "And tell him that I sent you. He's a crook and a scoundrel. He'll either rob you or else he'll see that you don't get robbed. It's six of one and a half a dozen of the other. If you can trust Manuel, you can put your life in his hands with perfect safety. But if he decides to trick you . . . well, as good be done by him as by a dozen others."

So thought Sammy, and, sitting beside the handsome young Mexican, he poured forth his plans and his desires, while Manuel, stiff with gold-laced jacket and collar, listened, smiling, and dreamed over the idea through a thin blue-brown cloud of smoke.

He said at last in good English: "I hire the right men . . . men who can ride and who know horses. I buy the right horses for you. I drive those horses to Crumbock. You pay me five hundred dollars. But if I can't drive those horse to Crumbock, you don't pay me a cent. Do you like this idea, *señor*?"

The thought of $500 in wages to a single man was a staggering thought to Sammy Gregg. And yet, the more he pondered, the more it seemed to him that this was his only solution for the problem.

So he closed with Manuel on the moment, and went up to his room and wrote out a careful contract and offered it to Manuel.

"Ah, no," Manuel said, still smiling through a mist of smoke. "I do not wish it in written words. If I fail . . . so! But if I succeed, then I shall trust *myself* to get the money . . . not a piece of paper."

CHAPTER FIVE

There was only one fault that Sammy was inclined to find with Manuel. He was everything but swift in his motions and in his appearance, but nevertheless he accomplished a great deal. He spent three days sorting over his acquaintances until he picked out a pair of villainous-looking rascals—in the eye of Sammy Gregg—of the roughest peon class. However, they could ride anything and anywhere. They could shoot well, and they were willing to obey orders from the mouth of Manuel. Also, they knew horses.

After the assistants had been chosen, a central corral was picked out and toward this, presently, Manuel and his men began to drift horses by the score and by the fifty. It was all Manuel. Very soon Sammy Gregg found that he might as well stop worrying and simply submit to the thorough management of Manuel, who went straight ahead doing what he wanted to do, and if Sammy made suggestions, Manuel received them, always, with a beautiful smile that showed his flashing white teeth. That smile might have meant anything, but before Sammy was through with this Mexican, he knew that it meant: *You are a fool and all of your ideas are worthy of a child only.*

This did not trouble Sammy. He was not interested in the scorn of Manuel. He was only interested in the speed with which he gathered horses.

And what horses they were. At first, when he saw a section of the brutes driven in, Sammy threw up his hands in despair and asked Manuel if it were not a joke. Manuel assured him that these were selected animals. Selected from what? Lump-headed, roach-backed, thick-legged, pot-bellied creatures were these, with Roman noses and little wicked eyes that glared tigerishly out from beneath a shag of forelock. One could believe nothing about them, at first glance, except tales of evil temper. But when Manuel saw that his boss had no opinion at all of the purchase, he simply had the most tractable of the lot saddled and gave it to his boss to ride. Although Sammy had already learned to ride, he spent three days struggling with this "well-broken" animal, but after that his eyes were opened. He discovered that the ugly little monster could rock along all day at an easy canter that ate up mileage as swiftly as the gallop of a wolf. The bronco could stop in his own length while going at full speed, turn his body faster than a man could turn his head, and be off in a new direction. He found that the body of the mustang was like his temper—as tough as rawhide, than which there is nothing tougher. He discovered, too, that there was no gentling these creatures. They remained to the end enslaved barbarians always hungering for the moment when they could plant their heels in the stomach of the master and then knead his body soft and small with their sharp hoofs while he lay on the ground.

These were the animals that Manuel and his two assistants collected, but not at $10 a head. The price had risen. It was almost a $12 average that Sammy had to pay, so he contented himself with a herd of two hundred, and with these he started out with the three cowpunchers on the long trek north toward the mountains.

They had luck enough across the great Texas plains. For mishaps they had half a dozen stampedes that lost thirty horses and cost them altogether a good additional three hundred miles of going. But by the time they got to the hills, the herd was in fairly good shape for traveling. The running edge had been taken out of their temper and they had learned to troop along obediently enough. Manuel had turned out to be the king of herdsmen, and his two assistants were masters of the same work—delicate, delicate work indeed. Whoever has ridden herd on a bunch of wild mustangs knows that above the mind of the brute there is the mind of the whole mass of animals, blind and deaf and enormous, and sensitive. Ready to stampede straight over the face of a cliff at a moment's notice, or just as ready to trample down a town.

Sammy had come to be of a little use before the trail was ended. And he was even trusted with the dangerous work of riding night herd on the horses, which is that portion of the work that requires the most skill.

By this time they were looking forward to the end of their trail. Munson was a scant march of thirty miles away. Beyond Munson was another hundred miles of mountains, and then the end of their labors. So Sammy, from time to time during the day, could not help letting his thoughts run ahead of him. A hundred and seventy horses at $75 a head made $12,750.

Just enough, just enough. And so to return to his Susie Mitchell not in six months, but in two. He would appear before her startled eyes like a hero, indeed. He would be invested with a veil of glory. Yes, even in his own eyes.

They had bedded down the herd in a sort of natural corral. It was as though some great hand had scooped a basin among the hills. There was a broad, flat-bottomed meadow in the midst, and around the sides half a dozen throats of cañons yawned black upon the little amphitheater. They could not have found a more ideal location, and to make perfection a gilded wonder, there was a little shallow stream of water, glimmering in the starlight as it trickled musically along over a bed of hard gravel. No danger of broken legs on steep banks—no danger of horses bogged down in quicksand here.

"We won't even need to ride herd tonight," Sammy Gregg observed. "This place is so made to order."

"Ah, *señor*," murmured Manuel, "you are full of trust. Perhaps it is well in some places, but not here. Here . . . even the mountains are watching you and hating you, *señor*."

That was a sentence that young Sammy Gregg did not forget. And, that night, he prepared for riding herd as a token that he was willing to take advice. But Manuel was also in the saddle.

"Why?" asked Sammy Gregg. "Surely at the worst, one man is enough here."

"If they should shoot off up one of those cañons. . . ."

"They are not as restless now as they used to be. . . ."

"They are always restless . . . in their hearts . . . no matter how tired and how quiet their bodies may be."

Before that night was over, Sammy had to agree with this hired man. A nervous devil seemed to have possessed the herd. Once, at the hoot of an owl, every one of the beasts started to their feet. There they stood poised and ready for everything. But the voices of the men soothed them.

They rode clockwise and counterclockwise around the edges of the herd, and their voices were never still, talking, talking, or singing softly all night long—a weary work. And, at length, the herd sank down again on the ground as though at another signal.

When Sammy reached Manuel on the next circle of the herd, he paused to ask: "What could have made them jump up at the same minute?"

"There is something in the air, tonight," said Manuel. "You and I cannot tell, but the broncos certainly can tell."

For his part, Sammy was willing to believe. He had seen enough of these wild animals to begin to have an uncanny respect for them. In a way, they seemed to be as full of wisdom as they were filled with meanness. So he rode on in his work, still singing—it did not matter what, so long as the song was soft. As he passed, the pricked ears of the prone horses would flatten in recognition of the human voice that they hated, but which nevertheless reassured them.

Give a horse something to occupy his mind and you can do anything with him. If it is only a bit to chew on and champ and worry while you are giving a colt his lesson. But don't try to occupy the whole attention of a dumb beast with your teaching. Sammy was beginning to understand this, too.

After all, there was something charming about this scene. He had a vague wish that Susie Mitchell might be riding by his side, here, looking at the black, gaunt, treeless hills, or watching the faint shine of the running water, with the lumpy forms of prone horses dimly silhouetted against it here and there—and always the broad, bright beauty of the stars overhead. The alkali scents and sharpness were taken from the air now that it was night. The wind was cool, almost cold. It touched the hands and flowed across the face like running water. It brought peace to the heart of Sammy Gregg.

Day was not far off now. There was no coming of light, but there was a change in the air, which Sammy was beginning to know as the forerunner of the sunrise. And just when he told himself, with relief, that there would be only another hour of darkness to watch through, the horses leaped suddenly to their feet again.

There had not been a sound this time—not even the hoot of an owl, and yet here were the horses bolt upright, heads raised, and all turned toward the west where the black mouth of one of the cañons yawned wide upon the meadow land. Out of that cañon, at last, Sammy heard a noise like a far-off clapping of hands. Then he heard a thin sound of a horse neighing, and after that five horses shot out of the blackness into the light of the stars—five horses with a man on every back—and the crash-

ing of the flying hoof beats rang and echoed in the ears of
Sammy.

The thieves—the horse thieves of whom Manuel had spoken
so often—of whom the storekeeper had warned him.

There was a shrill, universal squealing that broke from the
herd. Then they whirled and fled at lightning speed from this
sudden horror that had leaped out of the heart of the dark
night. They ran with heads stretched forward, ears flattened,
tails streaming straight out behind them—they ran blind with
speed. And in an instant the meadow was swept as bare as the
palm of Sammy's hand. And on the heels of his disappearing
herd, five riders were spurring along—not mounted on broncos,
but upon tall, long-legged blood horses that sprang across the
ground with a tigerish grace and swiftness.

Sammy himself spurred wildly in pursuit. Up to his lips rose
a harsh cry—such a sound as he had never uttered before. Here
was Manuel close beside him, his teeth glinting, but not in a
smile. Sammy reached across and tore a Colt from the saddle
holster nearest to him. Another weapon gleamed and spoke
from the hand of Manuel.

For answer, there was a blasting volley from the scurrying
shadows far up in the ravine—first the brief, wicked humming
of bullets, wasp-like, in the air about the ears of Sammy, and
after that a rattling of long echo above the thunder of the flying
herd.

But what was that to Sammy? They had missed him. He felt
that he had a charmed life—that it would be given him to ride
through a steady rain of bullets until he came up with these villains, these robbers. He raised his Colt and with the heavy
weapon wobbling in his weak, untrained hand, he fired, and
again and again.

There was no more shooting from the riders before him. No,
they were drawing farther away at every moment, and now they

rushed around a corner of the ravine and were beyond his sight. But what was this beside him? A riderless horse—the horse of Manuel.

The madness was brushed from the mind of Sammy Gregg, and suddenly he saw himself as he was—a foolish child riding down on a band of five practiced warriors of the frontier—warriors as cunning and as merciless as Indians, if indeed they were not Indians. Here in this fight in which poor Manuel had fallen already, how could he, a tenderfoot, hope to succeed? He drew rein.

And Manuel?

He galloped back as fast as he could and he found that Manuel's two Mexican friends were already at the spot. It occurred to the bitter heart of poor Sammy that these fellows might have been riding on the trail of the thieves rather than waste their time here. But no, they squatted beside Manuel, not in any agony of grief, but calmly smoking their cigarettes. Manuel himself had his head pillowed upon a rock, and he was trying to smoke, but his fingers were thick with numbness, and the cigarette kept falling from his hand.

He greeted his employer with a flash of his eyes.

"Why do they try to do nothing for you, Manuel?" gasped Sammy. "Where is the wound?"

There was so little breath in Manuel that he had to collect it through a long and deadly pause before he could answer: "I am shot through beneath the heart. I have not long to live, *señor.*"

"A bandage . . ."

There was a slight motion of the hand of Manuel. It denied all aid. It mocked at the possibility of assistance. "Nothing can be done, *señor.* Only, to make me sleep more easily, if one of them can be found . . . and sent where I am going . . . it would be a great comfort to me, *señor.* It is a place where one needs company, eh?"

38

He began to laugh, but the laughter died off into a weirdly bubbling noise, and Manuel stiffened himself, and died.

Chapter Six

When Sammy Gregg had seen to the burial of poor Manuel and then suggested to the two remaining Mexicans to begin a pursuit of the thieves, the latter merely shrugged their shoulders and held out their hands for their pay. They declared that one dead man was enough and that the two of them were not prepared to fight with five who were as well armed and shot as straight as did these thieves.

After all, they had a good deal of reason on their side, particularly since Sammy himself would not be of much use in a battle. So he paid them in haste, and then mounted and rode as hard as he could pelt for the town of Munson.

He was glad of one thing, and that was that the flight of the thieves with their stolen horses had been in the same direction. They had driven on toward the very spot from which he would receive his succor. Indeed, they kept on that straight way until they were a scant ten miles from the town, and then the track of the herd diverged and turned to the left up a branching cañon. And Sammy Gregg pushed on and on. And by the midmorning his foaming, staggering horse come into Munson town, with Sammy shouting from the saddle the news of his loss.

When they heard him, people ran out of shops and houses and listened, but when they understood the news that he brought, they shrugged their shoulders and turned back. Sammy began to see more backs than faces, and those who did turn toward him were, most of them, plainly laughing at him in his distress.

Suddenly Sammy understood. They smiled at him because they simply did not care, these hard-hearted fellows. They did not care for the hundred and seventy mustangs that he had bought at such an expense and that he had driven with labor and money, both, into the mountains so near to his market place. What was it to them that the savings of ten years were represented in this holocaust? They merely shrugged their shoulders and were glad that the loss had not fallen upon them.

He went into Rendell's store and sat down on top of a barrel of dried apples and dropped his chin on his fist and stared at the dust cloud that trailed down the street behind a passing horseman, and wondered at the brilliancy of the sun as it flashed and burned and turned that fine dust into powdered diamonds. Rendell, even, did not offer sympathy. However, neither did he say: "I told you so."

He merely said: "Are you down-hearted, kid?"

"No," Sammy said truthfully. "But I'm surprised. That's all. They don't seem to care, you see . . . these people don't seem to care."

"Not their horses that were stole," Rendell pointed out.

"Yes," explained Sammy, "but if they let these things happen, their horses *will* be stolen next, you see. And they'll suffer because *I've* suffered. Don't they see that the only thing is to stand together and fight the thieves off?"

Rendell shook his head. "Maybe about half of them would sort of like to be thieves themselves," he said.

That afforded a ray of dazzling light to Sammy, and he gaped at the genial storekeeper.

"Sure," expanded Rendell, "you can't trust nobody. Nobody that likes a quiet life is up here, and you can depend upon that. Everybody you meet might be a crook. I might be a crook. You

41

never can tell." He added: "Some is made to understand these here things and prosper pretty good around here in the West. And some ain't made to understand these things, and then they'd better go back to where they got a cop on every corner to watch out that the law is obeyed."

The hint was very pointed. But Sammy was really not frightened. He simply said: "I know what you mean. But they haven't taken the heart out of me yet. I got something left. Only . . . I didn't know how they played the game. That's all. Now I'm beginning to understand, and maybe I'll find a way to fit in with this sort of thing."

He went out into the street and the first thing he heard was the sharp whistling of a flute around the corner. He turned that corner and found a slender youth sitting on a broken apple box, with his back against the wall of the saloon that had once been run by Mortimer. He had the flute at his lips, and with eyes half closed, either from laziness or from love of the music that he was making, he blew forth sweet showers of sound.

"Have a drink, kid," a burly cowpuncher said, lounging past and pausing a moment to listen to the tunes.

The musician shook his head with a smile and continued his work. He merely nodded at his hat, which lay on the ground at his feet.

"*Bah!*" said the cowpuncher. "He's a half-wit, I suppose. Rather eat than drink?" And the cowboy strode on with a snort and disappeared within the door of the saloon.

Others seemed to be of the same opinion. Perhaps they could not understand why a white man who was sound of body had to sit and beg on the streets in that land of golden wages for either industry or rascality. But Sammy, feeling that he must more and more pause to study every strange feature of this strange land, stood nearby and watched the youth.

He was dressed in what might have been called splendid rags.

For his shirt was silk and so was his bandanna, and his boots were adorned with beautifully long-arched spurs, and the boots themselves, battered and tattered as they were, had evidently once been shop-made goods. The sombrero itself, which lay upon the ground to receive any random coins that the passers-by chose to drop into it, was now merely a relic of a former glory, for around the crown young Sammy Gregg could see a shadowy network that had once, no doubt, been left as an impression there by interlacing metalwork—silver or gold.

He was a brown-eyed boy, this player of the flute—a handsome, lazy-looking, sleek-looking fellow, and the more Sammy looked upon him, the more he seemed worth beholding. For it seemed to Sammy, as he stared, that for the first time in his life he was looking upon a man who had never felt the sting of the universal curse of Adam. He had never worked.

Aye, that accounted for the girlish smoothness of that cheek, the brow as clear and as placid as standing water, the eye so calmly open that one could look a thousand fathoms deep into it, as into the eye of a very young and simple child. Yet he was not simple, either, this player of the flute. And indeed, the more Sammy looked upon him, the more he felt that he was beholding something unique.

Not so the others in Munson. They were too filled with their own affairs. Besides, the music was not to their taste. It consisted chiefly of wild improvisations, swift and light and eerie playings of the fancy, and there were none of the downright jigging tunes that the rough fellows of the mountains were apt to like, swelling the beat of the rhythm by the heavy beating of their heels. They shook their heads at the more refined music that the young stranger made. It annoyed them, more than anything else. And the only money that the labors of the stranger had gained were a few coppers and a few small silver coins. It seemed to Sammy that there was enough to this young man to be worth a more liberal reward, and so he stepped closer and dropped the broad bright face of a $10 gold piece into the hat.

The flute player picked up the coin from his hat, rose to his feet, bowed slowly and with much grace to Sammy, placed the hat on his hand, the flute under his arm, and sauntered deliberately off down the street with the laziest step that Sammy had ever remarked in a human being—a stride in which he rested with every step.

And that was all that Sammy's $10 had bought him—in place of the interesting conversation that, he was sure, might be made to flow from the lips of the boy as readily as the music had come.

Sammy had lunch at the hotel, and he was wandering back down the street to the door of Rendell's store, in fact, when he saw a thing that made his heart leap. Straight down the street toward him came half a dozen tired mustangs driven along by a tall, wild-appearing fellow with long, sandy mustaches. He, however, was not the chief object of interest to Sammy. His horses were what held Sammy's attention. The instant he glanced at them, he knew them. They were a fragment of his newly stolen herd.

He could not be mistaken. At first, each of the hundred and seventy had looked very much like one another. But afterward he had begun to see the distinctions as he rode with them day and night. And now he knew them all. He knew that Roman-nosed roan. He knew very well that blaze-faced brown and the chestnut with the broken ear. He knew all six of them—he could swear to them. And the papers of sale were in his pocket.

He started into the store and called to Rendell: "Here come six of them with one of the thieves behind!"

Rendell ran to the door. "No," he said, "that's not one of the thieves, any more than I am. That's one of the oldest ranchmen around these parts. It's Cumnor, son . . . and he's no thief.

Look yonder . . . they got new brands burned into their shoulders. No, sir, you can depend upon it that Cumnor bought those horses honest."

"What bills of sale did he get with them?" asked Sammy.

"Bills of sale?" asked the storekeeper, opening his eyes as though at some strange new star that had swum into the heavens. "Bills of sale?" Then he added with a rather wicked grin: "Maybe you'll ask him what bills of sale he's got, and he'll show 'em to you."

The troop of horses was already opposite the doors of the store. And Cumnor was waving a buckskin-shod hand in greeting to Rendell, when Sammy ran down the steps. In another moment, Sammy was standing at the head of Cumnor's pony.

"Mister Cumnor," he said abruptly, "these six horses were stolen from me this morning."

"Son," said Cumnor, "dog-gone me if that ain't interesting."

There seemed to be a touch of dry humor about this, but Sammy Gregg was not in a humor to enjoy such wit. He said: "I have the bills of sale, with the register of the brands, and all."

"You have?" echoed Cumnor, frowning a little.

"I'm sorry," said Sammy, "but the thief must have taken you in."

"You're sorry?" echoed Cumnor.

"Sorry that you've lost your money."

"Look here," said Cumnor. "I paid fifty dollars spot cash for each of them six, and I had all the trouble, too, of picking 'em out of a big herd. Now what do you think I'm gonna do about it?"

Sammy shrugged his shoulders as he had seen others do that day. "I'm sorry," he repeated, "but if you want to see my documents, here. . . ."

He reached for an inside pocket, but before his hand got to it, a long Colt was in the hand of Cumnor and the muzzle yawned terribly just before the face of Sammy Gregg. It seemed, indeed, that Cumnor had gravely mistaken the gesture of Sammy Gregg.

"Now, look here," said Cumnor, "I ain't aiming to have any more trouble with you than I can help. But I ain't got any care to see your papers. The papers that I'm interested in is the gold coins that I paid for the six horses that stand here. And outside of that, I bought them six horses from a gentleman that I would trust pretty complete."

"Will you tell me his name?" asked Sammy.

"His name is one that's pretty well known around here in the past few months. Maybe even *you* have heard of Chester O. Furness, young stranger?"

Sammy gasped, and then he shouted: "But I tell you, if that's his name and he sold you those horses, then Chester Ormonde Furness is one of the five thieves who ran off my horses this morning!"

Cumnor lowered his revolver just a trifle. "I'm sort of busy today," he said.

"Ride on," said Sammy. "I'll herd the horses away. . . ."

"You'll what?" Cumnor asked. "Keep off of them six, son."

"Cumnor," Sammy Gregg said, facing the big man without fear, though he saw that danger was before him, "I offer to prove my right to them, one by one."

"I ain't got time to listen. You find Furness and talk to him, first of all. Now stand out of my way."

Oaths were rare upon the lips of Sammy, but now he cried out: "I'll see you damned before I stand away!"

"Then take it, you fool," Cumnor snapped, and fired his pistol full in the face of Sammy Gregg.

CHAPTER SEVEN

Rendell heard the shot fired and saw Sammy fall, and the big storekeeper came hobbling down the steps in haste, moving himself sidewise on account of his stiffened, ruined hip. And yet he had agility and strength enough left in his body to lean and lift poor Sammy in his arms. He carried him to the porch of the store and laid him out in the shade. One side of Sammy's head was running blood, and big Rendell made no effort to bind the wound or examine it. Death seemed only too certain.

But he busied himself fumbling through the pockets of Gregg and at length he stood up with an oath and turned upon Cumnor, who sat his saddle sullenly nearby, keeping one gloomy eye upon the disappearing mustangs down the street as though he wanted very much to ride after them, and yet not daring for shame to ride away from his victim so soon. Such a hasty flight might well turn self-defense into murder, even in the lenient eye of the public opinion of Munson.

"D'you know that he didn't carry no gun . . . d'you know that, Cumnor?" Rendell asked.

"How should I know that?" growled Cumnor.

"By the look of him, for one thing, I should say," said the storekeeper. "The devil, man, you ain't blind."

"I ain't no mind-reader, though," Cumnor said.

"D'you need to read minds to see that he ain't a wild fighting type."

"He was talking pretty big," Cumnor rumbled.

47

"He was talking for his rights," said Rendell. "And nothing more'n his rights."

"Look here," said Cumnor, "who made you the judge and the sheriff in this here county?"

"Why," Rendell replied, "if it comes right down to that, I'm due to prove that I can handle myself as well as though I *was* a judge and a jury. I may've busted up my ribs and my hip, Cumnor, but darned if my gun fingers and my gun wrist ain't about as supple as they ever was."

But Rendell had built up a not inconsiderable reputation in the days before he retired to the quiet of his store, and Cumnor was in no haste to see the storekeeper make his threat good. So the rancher was extremely pleased to see an opportunity to make a change of conversation, and, pointing past the other, he said: "What's all the shouting for, Rendell? Are you talking about a dead man or one that's only been scratched a mite and taught a lesson?"

Rendell whirled about and saw Sammy Gregg, with a hand laid against the side of his head, propping himself up on the other arm. Instantly the big fellow was at work examining and dressing the head wound, and Cumnor, glad to be away from this place, spurred off to look after his mustangs so recently purchased. And he had barely veered around the corner at the farther end of the street when who should he see before him but the tall form and the handsome face of Chester Ormonde Furness, mounted upon a magnificent, dappled-gray horse—a gelding with a stallion's wild eye and crested neck. The heat of the recent scene was still in Cumnor, or perhaps he would not have ventured as much as he did, for the men of that region had not forgotten and were not likely ever to forget how Furness had burned his name in the bar at Mortimer's saloon. Cumnor, however, was in the humor for a hasty action at this instant, and he reined his horse abruptly in front of Furness.

"Furness," he sang out, "when you sold me those six horses an hour ago, did you know that I was buying trouble with them, too?"

"My dear fellow," Furness said, "I have no idea what you're talking about, I'm sure. Except that I know you got the pick of the herd. You paid fifty dollars a head for horses that might have brought sixty-five in any market about here."

"Aye, and suppose that I was to ask you for a bill of sale . . . and the records of the transfers of those horses, Furness. . . ."

"Records?" Furness echoed, frowning like one in pain. "Why, Cumnor, the word of the man from whom I bought those animals wholesale was enough for me, I'm sure."

"What man?" snapped Cumnor. "What man did you buy them from, I'd like to know?"

Furness grew exceedingly cold. And he straightened himself in the saddle. And upon his hip he rested his ungloved right hand. A very odd thing about Furness was that though he never rode forth without his gloves, yet he was rarely or never seen to wear leather upon that supple right hand. Indeed, constant exposure had covered it with a very handsome bronze that made his well-kept fingernails look almost snowy white in contrast.

And he said to the rancher: "I trust that I don't understand you, Cumnor."

"The devil," said Cumnor. "I'm talking English, ain't I?"

Then Cumnor saw that the deadly right hand of Furness *was* resting on his right hip—resting there lightly, as though poised for further movement.

And Cumnor regretted with all his heart that he had been so extremely hasty in making remarks upon the financial principles of Furness. The latter was saying coldly: "Really, Cumnor, this is extraordinary. I don't know that I can tolerate this even from you."

Cumnor saw that he had come to a point in which it was far

better to walk backward than to continue straight ahead, and he remarked gravely: "I think that if you ride down the street, you'll find a man at the store of Rendell with a bullet wound in his head. I wish that you'd ride down there and hear that fellow talk." And he said no more about sale records and deeds of transfer, but he reined his horse to the side again, and spurred away in the pursuit of the six mustangs.

Furness cantered his big gray gelding down the street to the store of Rendell and dismounted there and looked into the store. What he saw was young Sammy Gregg leaning against the counter with a very white face—a face almost as white as the bandage that was tied around his head. And the color of face and bandage was set off by a spreading spot of crimson that was soaking through the cloth.

"And how are you now, kid?" Rendell was asking.

"I'll do fine," Sammy Gregg said. "Ah, there's a man that I want to talk to." He started up and confronted big Furness. "Furness," he said, "I had nearly two hundred head of horses stolen from me this morning. Five men did the trick. They killed my chief helper and they scared two more of them nearly to death. I've seen six of those horses that were stolen. No doubt about them. I know them as well as I know my own hand. On account of those horses I've just been shot down. Well, Cumnor did the shooting, and Cumnor says that he bought those horses from you."

Furness bit his lip and then drew in his breath with a sound that was very much like the moan of wind through thin branches. He sat down upon a stool and he removed his hat and he mopped his forehead. "Stolen horses. Good Lord," Furness said. "No wonder the scoundrels were willing to sell those horses to me for twenty-five dollars apiece."

"Was that what they asked?"

"That's it. Twenty-five dollars. And of course I knew that

almost anything decent in the line of a horse will sell for fifty dollars a head. I saw a quick profit. Heavens, youngster, it never came into my head that the horses might be stolen. You see, I'm almost as much of a greenhorn around here as you are. I paid cash for the horses and landed the whole lot of them."

"I suppose that I ought to be sorry for you, then," Sammy said. "Because I'm afraid that I'll have to claim the entire lot of them."

"I wish you luck," Furness said. "I wish you luck, upon my soul of honor. But I'm afraid that you'll have to do a tall bit of scrambling for them. Not thirty minutes ago three horse traders who were bound north came up with me and looked the lot over and they offered me forty dollars a head spot cash. The profit was too good to be true. A quick turnover better than a long deal, you know. I took that money and they split the herd into three chunks and rattled them off through the cañons to the north."

Gregg clutched his hands together. "North," he said. "They're bound for Crumbock and seventy-five dollars a head!"

"Eighty dollars, my friend," put in the gentle voice of Furness. "The price is going up and up at Crumbock."

Gregg groaned. "Will you tell me what the five thieves looked like?"

"There were only two that I saw anything of."

"Well?"

"They were very well mounted, for one thing."

"Not on mustangs?"

"No, there was a lot of hot blood in the horses they were riding. Long-legged steppers, they were."

"I saw them and I watched them move." Sammy sighed. "Yes, they're fast. But what of the two men?"

"I could pick them out from any crowd for you, Gregg," said the big fellow, "and I should be delighted to do so. Delighted!

51

One was rather young . . . the other middle-aged. Both Mexicans. The older fellow has a pair of scars that look like knife-work on his right cheek. He must have had a fight with some left-handed man. And the younger chap is distinguished for a very long chin and an overshot lower jaw. Unmistakable, both of them. We'll get up some posters to spot them . . . you might offer a reward. Yes, by Jove, I'll put myself down for a hundred on that same reward. I want to help you out, Gregg. I sympathize with you, my friend." And he stood up and clapped a kindly hand upon the shoulder of the smaller man, and then turned to leave the store.

He had reached the door before Sammy had the courage to cry out: "Just one minute, Mister Furness!"

The big man turned with a pleasant smile.

"You see," said Sammy, "a man can't keep the proceeds from the sale of stolen goods."

"I don't understand," Furness said.

"I mean, Furness," Sammy insisted, "that the money that was paid to you for those horses really belongs in my pocket."

Furness laughed, but without much conviction. "I see that you're a wit," he said. "But after all, that's rather a queer joke." And he stepped away from the door of the store and his whistle came blithely back to them.

Sammy, with an exclamation, started to run in pursuit, but the quick hand of the storekeeper caught him and held him back.

CHAPTER EIGHT

It seemed to Sammy, for a blinding instant of wrath, that even big, good-natured Rendell had joined in the conspiracy to drive him mad with persecution. But one glance at the frowning, unhappy face of the cripple convinced him.

"Don't you see, kid?" said Rendell. "It's no good. No good at all. It's Furness . . . that's all there is to it."

"Furness? But Furness simply doesn't understand the law on that point, and he doesn't see that the law will really restore to me. . . ."

"Furness understands everything," said Rendell. "I always knew that from the minute I laid eyes on him. I knew that he understood everything. But I never quite got onto his dodge. I didn't see what side of the fence he was on. But today I see, and I see it mighty plain."

"What, Rendell?"

"Look here, kid. If you run after Furness and stop him with your talk, d'you know that you'll only collect another chunk of lead? Cumnor missed, but Furness ain't the kind that misses."

"You mean he's crooked?"

"He is. But smooth. Crooked as a snake . . . and softer and smoother than a snake. That's all the difference there is between 'em."

"Furness? Why, Rendell, I've seen him. . . ."

"Kill Mortimer and run that cur Lawson out of town. Yes, but a crook can be a brave man, you know. I say, Gregg, that

53

Max Brand

you'll never get a penny out of Furness."

"I remember, now," Sammy said gloomily, "that when he tried to laugh, there was no ring to it, at all. No ring at all. But . . . it don't seem possible that he's a crook. Nobody could suspect it."

"Not until I begin to let the news of this drift around the country," Rendell declared. "Then there'll be a little change in the feeling about Furness. But you, kid . . . what are you gonna do?"

"I'm going back," Sammy said gravely.

"Back to Brooklyn? You're wise, at that. This sort of a country ain't made for your kind."

"Back to Brooklyn? No, sir, I'm going south and buy me another herd."

"Not again?"

"I've got a shade more than two thousand left. And that's enough to get what I need. I got within a hundred miles of Crumbock last time, nearly. This time I may win all the way through."

Rendell was more than impressed. He was frankly amazed and admiring, and he said so at once. Because it was no more his nature to disguise admiration than it was to disguise disapproval.

"Why," he said, "you're a bulldog, son. With twenty more pounds of beef on you, you'd be at the throat of this here Furness, I got an idea. Going south for more horses. Why, dog-gone me, kid, you'll be taking them wet, I suppose, this trip."

"What does that mean?" asked the innocent Sammy.

"Taking them with no papers *at all*. Taking them just the way they're drove up out of the Río Grande. Wet. That's all."

Sammy was interested. He wanted more information and he got it.

"I'm the fountainhead for all the talk you want about the

54

border crooks," said Rendell. "I used to work and run horses in them ranges. And that's where I was used up. Up here, maybe you think that some of the boys is a mite rough. But they ain't rough enough to be called men, even down in my home country. They'd use these here blooming heroes for roustabouts, and don't you forget it. Why, when I come up here, I found that they figured on me for a man, even when I was only no more than a cripple. Well, down yonder on the border they didn't think shucks of me. Not a bit. They used me up so bad that I had to move out.

"Well, sir, down yonder they're all fire-eaters. But right along the river itself is the worst land of all. That's the place where the boys go that ain't got any home. The boys that need more freedom than they can get in this here free country. There's districts down there where they draw a deadline that no sheriff is allowed to pass. And the minute a deputy or a sheriff shows up, anybody is free to pull guns and start blazing away.

"And down in them parts they go in for the horse business pretty frequent. Mostly it ain't Texas mustangs that they're after, but Mexican devils dressed up in the hides of horses. Them boys just ride out in a party twenty strong and they spot a place that's famous in north Mexico for having a good set of ponies, and they kill the greasers that are riding herd, and round up the horseflesh and slide it off toward the river.

"Them that want to buy horses, and good horses, and buy 'em cheap, goes down to the badlands, there, and buys 'em up mighty reasonable. I've knowed three-dollar horses from them parts that looked a pile better than any of them fifty-dollar horses that Cumnor got today.

"But when you buy *them* horses, you buy 'em pretty cheap, but you don't get no papers. I don't have to tell you . . . you take your chances. And the first gent that comes along and takes a fancy to your herd, he can cotton onto them horses of yours, if he's able to lick you. And you can't complain to no sheriff because you can't prove that them horses really belong to you by rights.

"Besides, after you've drove them horses five hundred miles into the country, they're liable to stampede and run all the way back to their own pasture lands on the south side of the river, and then you got a thousand miles extra to ride and considerable hunting to do after you arrive."

Such was the story of wet horses and cheap ones that Rendell told to Sammy Gregg, but Gregg listened with the fire in his eyes once more. The morals of the matter did not trouble him. If it were wrong to buy stolen horses, Sammy did not pause so much as to consider the subject. He had had a herd of horses stolen from him. Therefore the world owed him another supply. And it made very little difference where he got them so long as *he* was not the actual thief.

He went to sleep to dream of $5 horses that night, and the next morning he was on the train once more and headed for the southland. Poor Sammy Gregg, bound for the land where men were really bad. But perhaps you begin to feel that Sammy deserved something more than pity. And I think he did. The storekeeper was right. There was a great deal of the bulldog in Gregg, and there was fire, too—fire that would not burn out.

After he arrived, he spent a week or more learning what he could of the best district that he could head toward on the river. He learned that. He found a bank to which he could entrust his money, and then he set out to see the sights of that frontier town. He saw enough, too, but the thing that filled him with the greatest marvel was the second glimpse he had of his flute player of Munson.

But, oh, how changed! The difference between a dying, tattered moth and a young, brilliant butterfly. He fairly shimmered with gold work and with silks. He sat at a table gambling with chips stacked high before him, and with every gesture he seemed to sweep fresh oceans of money toward himself.

There was little else that stirred in that room, filled with drifting smoke oceans from cigars and cigarettes. No other games were in progress. Men stood about in banks and shoals watching the progress of the campaign of the flute player, studying his calmly smiling face and the desperate eyes of the other four who sat at the table with him. There was a mortal silence while the game was in active progress. It was only during the shuffling and the dealing that any talk was allowed, and in the first of these intervals Sammy spoke to his nearest neighbor: "Who are they?"

The other did not turn his head. He answered softly: "Look at 'em hard, tenderfoot. The chap with the long white face is Boston Charlie. And him with the pair of blond-looking eyes is Don McGillicuddie. The big gent with the cigar stuck in the side of his face is Holcum. I guess you've heard of him, all right. And there's Billy Champion . . . him that made the gold strike in the creek last year. And the one with the chips in front of him is the king of 'em all, poor kid. He's Jeremy Major."

"Why do you call him poor kid, then," asked Sammy.

"You see him now. He's got them eating out of his hand. They're all crooks, and he knows it. They're rich, and he knows that. And he'll trim them out of every cent they got, because he's a slicker and a cooler gambler than the best of 'em."

"Is that why you pity him?"

"No, but after he has a million in his poke, he'll let it drift out again like water running through his fingers. They's a curse on poor Jeremy Major. He's the only man in the world who can't say no. And when he's flush, he hands out the stuff with both mitts. Listen to me, kid. I've seen a gent step up and touch him for ten thousand in cold cash . . . and get it. And him one that Major never knew before that day. Aye, them same four skunks that are getting busted now . . . they know that they can go around to him tomorrow morning and beg back most of what they've lost."

"But if he's so sure of what he does with the cards, why do they play with him?"

"Because they are gamblers, even if they're crooked. And every time they figger that they sure got some new tricks that'll beat Jeremy Major. And so they come and try their luck with him. Why, look at Holcum, there. He's been away in the East, and they say that he cleaned up more'n a quarter of a million there. Besides, he got some new ideas, and he come all the way back West to see if he couldn't be the first man that could say that he had busted Jeremy Major at a card table. And now look! Look at the chips in front of Major. And Holcum has got one pile left. That's all."

Another new and dazzling sidelight had been thrown upon the men of the West for Sammy. He could not tell how deeply this young beggar-gambler-musician was to enter into his life. But he took one more long look at the youth, and then he turned out into the night to find his bed and go to sleep.

He did not like the way his pulse was racing. He did not like the lift and the giddy whirl of his spirits. For the first time in his existence, temptation had deeply entered the heart of Sammy Gregg. He, with the burden of an unmade $10,000 upon his soul—what had he to do with games of chance?

But he slept little that night, and when sleep did come, it was broken by evil dreams in which he saw a vision of a hill of gold toward which hungry thousands struggled. But they got nothing of it, except what coins were carelessly flung to them by a laughing youth who sat on the top of the golden hill with a richly laced sombrero pushed far back on his head.

CHAPTER NINE

All was arranged almost without the volition of Sammy, and certainly without any effort on his part. How the news was spread he could not, of course, guess. But a whisper seemed to have passed around, for the next morning a smiling fellow appeared before him—a brown-faced, good-natured-looking chap who said: "I hear that you're trying to find cheap horses, Mister Gregg?"

"I'm looking for them. Cheap good ones," Sammy Gregg averred.

"Which is exactly the kind that me and my friends handle," said the stranger. "But there's only one peculiarity about 'em."

"What's that?" Sammy asked.

"They got sort of sensitive natures. You see, they don't like to have questions asked about 'em."

Even so green a tenderfoot as Sammy could understand this innuendo. And he grinned with perfect comprehension and raised his hand to adjust the bandage that encircled his head.

"All right," said Sammy. "I don't intend to talk them to death. Their family affairs are their own business."

The other nodded. "How many, and what's your price?" he asked.

"I want about three or four hundred," said Sammy. "What sort of a price can you make me on that lot?"

"Three or four hundred," said the other, and whistled. "Why, that's quite a handful. Suppose we say two thousand for four hundred head . . . all warranted sound?"

Sammy, who saw nearly his entire block of remaining capital involved, and who knew that he needed leeway for herding expenses, fought for a margin.

"Sixteen hundred dollars," he said. "And I'll take my chance on the sort of horses you give me."

The other frowned, but only for a moment. "Is that your top price?" he asked.

"Partner," Sammy said, "I've just lost two hundred head. And I've got to pay heavy for good hands to drive this lot."

"I'll send you three Mexicans . . . born in the saddle. They'll drive 'em north for you at thirty dollars a month. Does that sound?"

It sounded very loud to the ear of Sammy Gregg, and he closed with the proposition at once. The rest was arranged in a trice. He was simply to head for the river at once, and a week from that night, at a named point, a herd of horses would be driven across the Río Grande with three Mexican cowpunchers in their rear. After that, the rest was in the hands of fate and Sammy Gregg. He need not pay a cent until the horseflesh, every bit of it, was north of the river.

So Sammy made his preparations, and on the appointed night he sat in the saddle on a long, lean bay mare as ugly as a caricature and as fleet as the wind, under a little hill of sand beside the river, with a sack of gold tied to his saddle bow and a pair of heavy Colts weighing down the two saddle holsters.

It was well past midnight before anything stirred on the south side of the little stream, so muddy that it would not take the glitter of the stars on its face to show them back to the sky. But when there was a stir it was a sudden upheaval out of the dark and then a noise like a great rushing wind, and after that a volley of shadowy forms that plunged into the water and dashed it to clouds of milky foam. Out of the river, squealing, snorting, neighing like a small pandemonium, the charge continued onto the northern bank and then past the amazed Sammy Gregg and thundering away into the darkness of the northern night. Behind them rode three cursing cavaliers, and, without a word to him, they spurred past on the trail of the mustangs.

But that was not all. For now out of the river arose half a dozen riders and swept around him. He recognized the voice of the good-natured man, not quite so good-natured now.

"Let's have a little look at your wallet, Gregg!"

There was no mistaking the summons. Gregg tossed it across to the speaker and thanked the caution that had made him bring not a penny more than the stipulated price. He saw that money counted out by match light. And then, with a grunt of disgusted disappointment, the case was tossed back to him.

"Sixteen hundred even. It's plain that you ain't paying us for all the fun we're giving you, Gregg."

"I didn't know"—Sammy grinned—"that it would be such a show."

"Well, old son," spoke up another, "all I got to say is . . . . ride them ponies north as hard as their legs will fetch 'em along, because there is folks on their trail that's mighty curious about where they're galloping to."

Sammy, glad to be gone on this hint, turned the head of his mare in the direction of the disappearing thunder across the plain.

"And keep them greasers on a tight rein, Gregg. Don't let 'em hold you up for more than thirty a month."

We all believe in good beginnings, no matter how philosophical we may be. And Sammy, when he contrasted this smooth opening of his campaign with the knotty work that Manuel had had to do the time before, was sure enough that his scheme was due to pan out, at last.

It took an hour of brisk riding before he caught up with the rear guard of the herd. And, when he came up to them, he found the broncos pretty thoroughly subdued. They had had enough running to content them, and it would take a whole thunderstorm to rout them on a new stampede.

Here, there, and beyond, in the rear of the trailing herd, he could spot the Mexican cowpunchers by little sparks of light. That meant that they considered that the worst of this night's labor was completed. They were smoking in content. And Sammy sighed with relief. Next day he would slip into town to get the few remaining dollars that belonged to him, pack up their grubstake for the trip, and swing out again to rejoin the herd. In the meantime, he watched hungrily, joyously, as they drifted through the night time. Four hundred mustangs, and by the manner in which they kept bunched without trailing laggards, he judged that there were no cripples in the lot. Four hundred! He counted them roughly and found that the number was actually exceeded by five.

What noble thieves were these frontiersmen, more than living up to their contracts. Four hundred ponies. Even suppose that a whole hundred of them were stampeded away on the trip, three hundred at $50 a head, even, meant $15,000 in his pocket.

"I am going to be lucky," Sammy said aloud, and fervently. "The bad luck can't hit me twice in the same place." And he went on in a dream about Susie Mitchell and the home that was to be theirs. I think that Sammy had begun to idealize her at last. Perhaps she was ceasing to be so much of a habit with him, and becoming rather a passion. Distance and time are apt to work like that on the mind of a lover.

He reached the town by the dawn. He was back again at the herd by the falling of the night, and he found that all had gone well with them during the day. There had been no mishaps. There had been not so much as a single beginning of a stampede. Not a single horse had gone lame and fallen behind.

In a word, the record of that glorious first day was not marred by a single scar.

And to see those horses in the daylight. They were not like his other herd—those ugly little rascals from the sunburned deserts of Texas. These creatures had come off good grass and a lazy life. They were sleek and round. And they carried their heads and their shining eyes after the way of free, wild things.

"These horses got sense pretty good," said one of the Mexicans in tolerable English. "If we get a few good quiet days, they herd like sheep . . . just like sheep."

And they had good days—three handsome ones. The work was easy. They reached water often enough to keep up the heart of the herd. There was enough grazing grass along the way. And now the herd had become deftly organized. There were certain known leaders that trotted in the van. And the whole procession moved in a great, scattered wedge.

They covered a huge amount of ground. Not during the marching hours, when they were urged along by the riders behind, but in the morning and in the evening when they scattered to feed. And Sammy, staring with delight, would see the rising and the setting sun flash over a whole landscape that was flooded with horseflesh that belonged to him.

And then, on the evening when Sammy estimated a hundred and fifty miles lying behind them—just after they had made camp by a water hole and while the herd was ranging freely to find the best of the bunch grass—just at that quiet time trouble struck them again.

It reminded Sammy horribly of that other night in the mountains thirty miles from Munson, when Manuel had died. But this time the thieves came out of the rolling hills, waving their arms, screaming wildly, and gathering the herd in instant flight before them. Oh, cunning devils. For they turned the rushing mass of horseflesh straight upon the camp. With Sammy's own property they would destroy him and then make off in safety.

He made for the tall mare in a mad haste. No time for saddling. He had a revolver in one hand, and he wound his other hand into her mane and swung himself up with all his might. He just managed to hook a heel over the sharp ridge of the mare's back. Then he slumped into place, and, with a side glance, he saw where one of the herders—who had foolishly tried to saddle—was caught and overwhelmed by the sweeping wave of horses. Even the death shriek of the poor fellow was stifled and lost in the roar of the hoofs that beat him to a shapeless mass.

The forefront of that racing world of horses involved Sammy, and then, in another moment, the mustangs were shooting ahead and he was in the rear—in the rear with the three thieves.

Where were the Mexicans? The last two of them sat their horses at a little distance and tucked their rifles into the hollows of their shoulders. A whirl of bullets began. One struck a mustang in the herd just before Sammy and made the poor creature leap with a squeal high into the air.

Aye, and there was another target. For the robber who was nearest to Sammy suddenly tossed up his arms and lunged from the saddle. Then the first fighting madness of his life came to Sammy. There were two thieves left, whirling in their saddles and dumping hasty bullets toward the two cool Mexicans, and they were fast rushing out of range—and four hundred stolen mustangs streaming before them.

All of this whirled through the brain of Sammy. And then he found himself belaboring the ribs of the mare with his heels and rushing her after the herd. He had no means of guiding her. But, in her panic, she naturally took the direction that the rest of her kin were fleeing, and it so happened that the particular route she selected carried her straight at a red-headed ruffian who bestrode a tall roan. One instant he was shouting and waving at the frightened herd. The next, he was wheeling in the saddle and shooting marvelously close at the Mexicans.

And then he saw Sammy and yelled at his companion: "Hey, Jerry, what's this comin'!"

"A joke, Tom!" shouted the other. "Throw a chunk of lead in the fool."

"I'll do that for us!" And, turning in his seat, he snapped his Winchester to his shoulder again and fired pointblank at Sammy, not thirty yards behind.

He was a good shot, was Tom, and, moreover, he fired this time in perfect surety and contempt of his enemy. But, when he looked back again, Sammy was still coming—coming with a wild yell of rage of fearless battle lust.

For Sammy was a man transformed. It is not the pleasure of the gods that the big men alone can go berserk. Little men can do it, also. And Sammy was literally running amuck. Ordinarily he could never have stayed on the back of that long-bounding mare for a single moment without saddle and stirrups to help him and steady him. But he was thinking of something more than a fall to the ground at this moment. And, riding without self-consciousness, he rode very well, balancing himself adroitly and gripping with his weak knees, and waving above his head one clenched fist and in his other hand the Colt. But he had never shot off a firearm in his life.

He made a weird picture, with that white bandage clasping his head, and his hair flying above the bandage, and his hat blown off, and his unbuttoned sleeves flying up around his shoulders and showing his skinny arms. Have you ever seen a little spindling, nervous weakling of a boy fly into a passion in the schoolyard and make the bigger boys run in sheer terror at the devil that is in him? So it was with Sammy. And big Tom, the horse thief, who had been in many and many a fight, running and standing, before this day, looked back again to see if his odd enemy had not fallen to the ground. And behold, there he was, and now not more than fifteen yards away, and gaining at every leap of his horse. For the mare was a born sprinter.

And fear leaped into the strong heart of Tom. "Help, Jerry!" he screamed, and jerked up the muzzle of his rifle again.

He saw Jerry fire, and he saw the little madman behind him merely laugh, and urge his mare on more swiftly. Even Jerry had missed. Something jammed in the rifle. Tom dropped it with a wild shout of pain and snatched out a revolver.

Time for speed now. For here was Sammy Gregg rushing along not two lengths of a horse behind him. And as big Tom wheeled in the saddle again, Sammy shoved forth his own gun, and set his teeth, and closed his eyes, and fired.

His eyes were still closed when the mare stumbled upon something soft, and went on. He looked before him, and there he saw that the big roan horse galloped, riderless, before him. He glanced behind and there lay a figure sprawled on the ground.

And Sammy Gregg, the mild and the weak, had killed a man with his own hand and in his own right.

CHAPTER TEN

It would have been too much to expect any qualms of conscience from Sammy. Indeed, he was half mad with the joy of the fight. And he could see that his deed had worked an effect upon the two Mexicans, also. They had left off their useless, long-distance firing, which had only served, after the first death, to bring down two mustangs. Now they were running their ponies as fast as they could to get up to the scene of action.

There would be no time for that, Sammy vowed. He himself would settle the remaining thief. For, if a man can be shot with one's eyes closed, cannot another be disposed of still more effectually with eyes open? So thought Sammy. And he wanted blood.

He struck the mare a resounding thump on the side of the neck and caused her to swerve violently to the side and head, indeed, straight for the last of the trio. He had not waited for the charge. He had seen two of his companions fall upon this luckless evening, and he was not the stuff that wishes to fight out stubborn campaigns along one line, even if it takes all summer. In fact, he had had enough, for his part, of firing at a lucky, gun-proofed fool of a man like this wild fellow who rode without saddle or bridle—and who waited to come within arm's reach before he fired his weapon. The third thief, in short, wheeled abruptly away and now was flying for his life.

Sammy would have followed willingly. But when he hammered at the ribs of the mare, it just so happened that one of his heels struck a spot that had already been thumped very sore in that wild evening's ride. And the mare, at that instant, decided that she had done enough for one day. She set about unseating her rider, therefore, and, although she was a clumsy and most ineffective bucker, the first humping of her back and the very first stiff-legged jump snapped Sammy from her back and deposited him in the dust.

To Sammy it was like a drop into deep sleep from which he was awakened by the voice of a Mexican, a changed voice, no longer snarling and sullen, but filled with respect and gentlest solicitude. So Sammy sat up and blinked fearfully around him. What he saw was the herd, which had been headed by his two hired men, trooping back toward the spot that had been originally selected for that evening. Behind them rode one of the men. The other had come to assist the fallen boss.

He had been a silent man, before this. But now Pedro was transformed. Words ran like water from his lips. He himself had guessed it, and he himself had told his companion, Gonzalez, he vowed, that *Señor* Gregg was probably a great fighting man. But to rush on bareback in this fashion straight upon a desperado—this was a thing that even he, Pedro, had not expected. For his own part, he would have been on the heels of the villains, long before, had it not been that his scoundrel of a horse—which he hoped to see die in torments!—balked at the last instant and refused to carry his master toward the scene of danger.

All of this while he assisted the dizzy boss into the saddle on that same balky horse and led him back toward the site of the camp. On the way, they paused to examine the three dead men. Their poor comrade they buried where he lay, but in a shallow grave. As for the other two, coyotes and buzzards could attend to their remains. What was of importance to the Mexicans was that they collected no less than $122 from the pockets of the two thieves who had died. And they took, also, excellent revolvers and long rifles of the very latest and best model. They brought this considerable heap of plunder obediently to the chief.

It turned the blood of Sammy cold to see the gold and silver coins from which the body heat of the dead men had hardly yet departed. "Keep the stuff," he said to Pedro and Gonzales. "Keep the stuff and take the two new horses to ride . . . they're better and bigger and faster than the ponies you have now."

If his feats of war that evening had made him seem a new man in the eyes of those savage followers, this stroke of generosity raised him almost above the level of mere humanity. The wages of two months apiece—two precious horses—and revolvers and rifles fit for a king of the plains. Tears stood in their eyes. They could not thank Sammy Gregg. They could only withdraw to a little distance and worship him mutely.

Gonzales whispered softly to his companion: "Did I not guess it from the first? Did I not say, Pedro, that no man would do business with the river horses unless he were a fighting man with nerves of steel? Did I not say it? How he rode in on them. Like a devil . . . with no fear. As if he were riding a colt in my father's pasture."

The trail from that day was a changed thing for Sammy Gregg. He was no longer allowed to rise and catch his mare and saddle her in the morning. It was done by swift, skillful, willing brown hands. Neither must he soil his fine hands with cookery or with cleaning of pans in the evening. No, for here were abler and happier cooks, in the persons of his devoted servants, *amigo* Pedro and *amigo* Gonzalez. They would have rolled his cigarettes and sung him to sleep if he had wanted them to. In a few brief minutes of one day he had revealed to them the two qualities that, alone, they esteemed—dauntless courage and almost boundless generosity.

Max Brand

Out across leagues and leagues of burning desert now. Day by day, wearily, steadily. They had had weather of only one kind since the start. But on the afternoon of the very day in which the brown of the foothills began to be visible before them, they were treated to a change. Gonzalez saw it first—a haze in the northwest, looking like a distant dust cloud. But, as it drew nearer, they could see that the faint mist extended from the earth to the heavens.

"It is going to storm," Gonzalez said. "Let us get these horses down into that draw. Hurry, Pedro. *Señor* Gregg . . . with your help, it may be done. Ride, ride, Pedro, and head them into the draw. The storm will keep them there. But if they have no shelter, they may scatter like feathers in the wind. Spurs, Pedro!"

Pedro was already off like the wind itself.

The sharp eye of Gonzalez had noted a shadow across the surface of the desert to the right, and he knew that here was one of those hollows that might well serve almost like a barn to keep the herd from the edge of the storm. But unluckily they had come into a region of good grass, and the result was that the younger and more eager among the mustangs had pressed far forward, trotting from bunch to bunch, nibbling here, and then rushing on, while the older geldings and mares lingered in the rear.

The result was that Pedro and Gonzalez had far to ride to get to the head of the column. And, in the meantime, the mist out of the horizon was growing and changing apace. It reached, indeed, to the very roof of the sky and now it was thickening and blackening. The rim of the storm reached the sun. Instantly the sun was reduced to a dim red ball that seemed to be falling swiftly and silently down the arch of the sky. No, it was only the rush of the storm clouds as they shot across the heavens. They neared the herd.

70

A close race, surely, for here was Gonzalez ahead of Pedro and almost at the top of the column of horses at the very same moment that the manes and tails of the leaders of the procession began to fan out to the sides, blown by the first breath of the storm wind. But right behind that wind, came the rain itself. Already the sun's light had been curtained away to sunset colors. Now it was reduced to nothing more than a grisly green twilight. And the storm came head down, reaching level, white, blind arms of rain before it. Flying hands of stinging mist cuffed against the eyes of the mustangs and made them whirl as though they had been struck with whips. They bunched their backs and cowered for a moment, head down.

Sammy Gregg, paralyzed by the violence of the stroke, and stunned by the uproar that crowded against his ears, could only grip the edge of his hat and lean his weight against the wind, and shade his eyes with his other hand to see what was happening with the other men and the horses.

He heard Gonzalez ride by a mere six feet away from him, yelling at the top of his lungs, but in the dreadful screaming of the wind the voice of the big Mexican sounded no louder than a far-off whisper.

"*Señor* . . . and Pedro! Now is the time! Ride into them, for the love of heaven, and start them across the wind a little. Start them across the wind only a little, and they will reach the draw. Courage . . . and help! Away with you!"

He rode at the huddled horses, firing his revolver, lashing at them with his loaded quirt. The animals blinked and shrank away, and then, one by one, they began to edge off across the wind, staggering as blasts of renewed and freshened violence cuffed at them broadside. Here was Sammy, understanding, now, what was to be done, and fighting desperately to save $15,000 worth of horseflesh that he could still call his own. And Pedro, too, had aroused himself and was laboring valiantly.

But here fortune struck directly against them. At the very moment when the whole herd was in a sort of blind, staggering motion across the wind, heads low down to the ground, ears flattened, spirits dejected—at that very moment, the heavens opened and a yellow torrent of lightning flowed down the gash. Then came thunder like the beating of giant horses on a wooden bridge just above their heads. Roaring, rolling, crashing thunder—as though the whole sky was crumbling and showering to earth in vast fragments about their ears. The heads of the mustangs snapped up, and they stood alert with terror. What were the whips and the shouts of the men compared with this tremendous artillery?

The sky yawned again. Again the quivering tongues of lightning licked the heart of the heavens and edges of the earth at the same instant. It was more than enough. The horse herd leaped wildly away. The scourges of the wind whipped them along the path. And they rushed back south and east, south and east, toward the land from which they had come.

CHAPTER ELEVEN

There are two ways to follow a stampeded herd of horses. One is to ride like mad and strive to head them. One is to let them run out of sight and follow at a walk, on the simple principle that a horse will stop running more quickly if he sees that there is no living thing behind him. But when an eighty-mile wind is cutting the hindquarters of a mustang, he is apt to try to run as fast as the wind blows and keep right on as long as the storm and his strength last. So the three riders simply lashed their helms, to speak in naval parlance, and let their craft drift before the wind at its own free will.

They scudded along at a brisk enough rate all the rest of that day, and, when the early darkness came, the rain was no longer with them, but the wind was, and as far as they could peer across the storm-darkened desert there was not a sign of a horse to be seen ahead of them.

They made a silent and desolate camp, that night, wringing the wet out of their clothes before they lay down to try to sleep, without a fire to warm them.

When the sun rose, there was not a cloud in the sky. The wind had fallen away. Before the sun was an hour high, the day was burning hot.

The rain had left the earth in a condition to hold sign deep and well. After a time they found traces enough of the herd. But what traces. Some had run here and some had run there. Like a fleet of merchantmen cruising here and there and everywhere at the sight of an enemy man of war, the broncos each had followed its own will, and now, in flying clusters, they were breaking for the southland, all in that direction, but doubtless on a seventy-mile front.

There was not the slightest doubt as to what they should do. They bore off to the right hand as far as they could go, and finally reached the outermost sign of the mustangs. Along that trail they followed. And for two days they rode before they found a wretched score of animals in a clump of cottonwoods. Twenty out of four hundred.

But they were not done trying. They swung to the east now, and, still bearing south, they drove the mustangs ahead of them as hard as they could. In this fashion they began to pick up some of the rest. In clusters and flying knots, here and there, they found the remnants of that fine herd that had been so well in hand only a few short days before. But some were lost. And some had broken their legs by stepping in the holes of prairie dogs in the blind rush of the stampede, and some had ruined themselves on murderous barbed wire, and some had run into other men who wanted them almost as badly as Sammy Gregg did.

Still, day after day, getting closer and closer to the point at which they had begun their weary trek, they kept gathering in the mustangs. Until, in due time, they counted noses, considered their position, and decided that they had collected as many as they possibly could. Three long weeks had elapsed since the stampede. Three terribly vital weeks to Sammy, whose eye was on the six months' limit now. And they had raked together, finally, two hundred and ninety-odd mustangs. More than a quarter of the herd had returned to the desert out of which it had come.

But Sammy was not down-hearted. He was daunted, but not beaten. And he said to the Mexicans: "Listen to me. My bad luck is used up this time. The pan has been turned upside down and the last bit of that scrambled bad luck has been dumped over my head and shoulders. So the thing for me to do, now, is to push straight ahead. Because we'll have no more trouble with the horses."

He spoke confidently, but Gonzalez sighed and shook his head in a covert despair. He knew horses, did Gonzalez. Not a book knowledge, and not because he loved them, but because he had lived with them more intimately than he had ever lived with men. He had been with them in the desert and in the corral. He had roped and thrown and branded and ridden herd and cared for orphaned colts and dragged foundering broncos out of the mud of water holes. He had been with them for many years, day and night, and he knew horses. Therefore he knew that the trouble with this lot was not over. It was hardly begun. For horses have nerves as much as any pampered women have nerves. There is a grain of madness in every horse, and the better the horse, one might almost say, the nearer that madness is to the surface. Have you seen the thoroughbred come rearing and dancing out of his stable in the morning? Eagerness to go—feeling his oats. A little natural spirit—who wants a dead thing under the saddle?

Yes, and just a little madness, too. A desire to turn himself into the wind and be blowing across the ridges of the hills—a wild passion for speed, more speed, yet more speed. Madness you must call it—madness or nerves.

And those mustangs had nerves, too. They had not led pampered lives, but they had nerves that were quickly developed. And lately they had seen the sky turned into a hell of fire. Yes, and they had heard it, too—heard the crashing of the sky as it smashed down upon the earth.

In the face of this infernal hubbub the human beings had tried to guide them into the teeth of that huge destruction—the human beings who, perhaps, had caused all that wild destruction by their magic.

High-headed and meant for trouble that herd had been when it came across the river, but still good herdsmanship had kept them in hand. But this was a different matter now. They were transformed. They were as filled with quivering and dancing, as full of shying and snorting and prancing as any unbroken two-year-old thoroughbred. Terror was behind their eyes, and willfulness. They had run through the hands of these men before, and why might they not do it again?

A horse is the hardest animal in the world to head, next to a stubborn dog. And, like a dog, he pursues one system. He runs straight at you, head stretched out, tail whipped away in a line. He paralyzes you by driving straight at you, and then, when he is close, he swerves far out to one side and flaunts smoothly away.

Try to catch even one horse—even a tame old veteran of fifteen years' service under the saddle. Try to catch him when he doesn't want to be caught some morning. Try to catch him in a half-acre lot and see how long it takes you—until he suddenly remembers some of the lessons of fifteen years and stands still, rigid, stiff, hating you out of the corner of an eye of fire.

Remember that, and then think of three hundred unbroken mustangs that have recently been frightened almost to death, and who have a hundred thousand square miles to play their tricks in. Then you will have an idea of the problems that lay before Sammy and his two men. Not that the Mexicans were unwilling to work. By the law of their race, having given their hearts to this *gringo*, they would not be in a hurry to recall their faith again. They would work until the flesh was worn from their hands. But mere work will not serve in the handling of three hundred horses shod with the wind and whipped by hysteria.

However, by pains, by slow herding, giving the wild creatures time to find themselves, toying with them, never pressing them, the first three days of the return trip went off smoothly enough. And then, by the ill fortune of war, they came within the sight of a railroad track running glimmering across the desert. For an hour or so they roiled slowly toward that double line of living light. And then something else happened.

From the direction of a patch of shadow on the edge of the horizon—that was a town, no doubt—a streak of thunder began to roll out toward them. Thunder, but coming more swiftly than even the thunder of the storm had come. Here it flew—a long black body running without feet. No, for its feet were the thunder to which they listened. Aye, and it cast before it a murmur of dread down the living lines of light that marked the way that it would fly. And above its reeling, swaying, furious front, there was a great black plume, a mile in length, a glorious plume, forever vanishing at the end and forever renewed just above the head of the monster.

What nerves could stand such a sight? Not those nerves, surely, that had seen the heavens turned to fire so short a time before. The herd tossed up its universal head, and stood and stamped. And then eye flashed to eye. There was a shudder of dread. A sweat of horror started out, glistening upon their drawn flanks.

"Heaven help us . . . here they go," Gonzalez murmured.

And, as he spoke, every horse in that herd whirled about and with flaring manes and burning eyes they stormed away through the hands of Sammy and his men.

The men did not pursue. They sat their horses, drawing quietly together. They did not speak to one another for so long that their saddle horses forgot the thrill of excitement that had run tingling through their very souls the moment before. They were quiet again, stretching out their heads toward the blades of sun-cured grass that were near.

Then Sammy said: "It's a queer thing, Pedro. But why don't the devils ever take it into their heads to run north?"

"Ah, *señor*, because they know that the spur and the quirt and the saddle are waiting for them in the north. However, thank heaven that the heart of the *señor* is so brave that he can laugh."

"I cannot laugh. Gonzalez, you know horses. Tell me . . . can we drive those horses north . . . the three of us?"

Tears of grief stood in the eyes of Gonzalez. "Ah, *señor*, we cannot take them. They are all like children now. They are afraid. What can we do with them? They do not understand our language. And to explain one little thing to one horse . . . does it not take a week of months, *señor*?"

"We'll go for help, then," Sammy said sadly. And he thought of the few dollars in his pocket. "You cut south after them. Follow them slowly, and I'll ride to the town and hire two more men. I've *got* to get them north. I'm facing a time limit, and that limit is almost up."

He turned toward the little shadow out of which the train had rushed. Aye, he must get them north, and when he had them there, he must sell them and collect the money. And then even a fast train East would require some priceless days in addition.

For the first time he thought of wiring to Susie to give him a little extension of time. But he couldn't do it. His strength failed him at that point, because it was a matter of pride with him. Six months to make $10,000.

And here his hands were overflowing with the very prize he wanted, if he could only bring it to the market.

CHAPTER TWELVE

A sharp-sided cañon ran past the town, a cañon filled with trees, and a thin sound of running water from the creek that had cut out this little gorge. There was a gaunt skeleton of an iron railroad bridge spanning that gully, and there was an old wooden bridge, too. A buckboard rattled across it as Sammy approached, the planks flopping up and down, no longer nailed, under the rolling of the wheels. And a thin cloud of dust floated up.

Sammy waved and nodded dumbly to the man in the buckboard. A man of middle age—no more. But with what a face. And when Sammy looked after him, he thought that the bowed shoulders and the bent head made the silhouette of an octogenarian. Was this what this free Western country did to the people who strove to settle in it and wring a living from it with hard toil?

The first doubt entered the soul of Sammy Gregg like cold iron. He began to feel that he had thrown the product of his life's labor into a barren ocean. He would never see any return of his money again. Aye, and while he was away, might not the two Mexicans simply slide away from him and start for the comforts of their familiar Southland? There would be a reason behind them—they had his money, and horses, and guns of his giving.

For the first time in his life, great, cruel doubts began to fill Sammy's mind. It came to him as a part of his thoughts, rather than as a shocking surprise, when a voice from the brush beside the road said: "Hands up, you bum, or I'll drill you!"

Through the shallow screen of greenery, he could see the steady glimmer of the steel barrel of the rifle. Aye, and another rifle beside it.

"All right," Sammy said wearily, and raised his hands shoulder high.

One of the men stepped to the edge of the brush, his rifle at the ready, his guilty eyes glancing up and down the road. After all, they *were* perilously near the town.

"Ride your horse in here, kid, and ride it in quick, or we'll lead the horse in and *drag* you!"

Sammy did not need threats to make him obedient. He was not afraid, either, but he had a foolish desire to laugh, greatly and idly; he was only afraid to give way to the laughter for fear that tears would follow on the heels of it.

The brush switched together behind him. He found his arms clutched on either side, but as a strong pair of fingers gripped him, he heard the fellow snort: "Why, Steve, he ain't got no arm at all. Like a girl, darned if it ain't. Go easy with him."

They guided Sammy and his horse down a steep slope to the bottom of the ravine. There they made him dismount. They stripped off his coat, first, and then, when they had mastered his wallet, they counted out the contents.

"Two hundred and eighty-five dollars! Kid, maybe we ain't in luck."

"And a suit of clothes, too. . . ."

"The devil! What good would that do us? Am I a blackbird, maybe, that I could step into his togs? Not if I shrunk down to what I was at twelve years old. Look at the gats he packs, too. A regular soldier, this bo is. A regular hero, maybe. Hey, kid, did you ever shoot one of them guns?"

He handled one of the Colts familiarly under the nose of

Sammy. But Sammy replied nothing. He felt that he could see to the bottom of his future now.

To return not with $15,000—but with nothing. To go back there empty-handed. To say to Susie: "I've got to start all over again."

And then she would say: "How long did it take you to make the last five thousand, Sammy?"

Ten years. It had taken him ten years to make the money the last of which was now to be divided between these ruffians. They were conferring a little apart, only fixing him with grim side glances. But, as they talked, so great was their contempt for him that they allowed him to overhear them.

"Suppose we tie him up and leave him here?"

"Aw, even if we let him go, he won't have the nerve to come back and make no trouble. Not him. He's scared stiff."

"Take no chances, I say, bring him in and let the chief have a look at him."

"Why should the chief know about it at all? Why not skin out with this stuff? If the chief hears about it, he'll have to come in for his share."

"Why, you blockhead, do you think that not telling him would keep him from knowing?"

"Well, maybe not. He's got ways of finding out. But if we was stowed on the rods and bound East. . . ."

"You *are* batty, Steve. Would you try to get away from him?"

"Aw, I dunno. He ain't a god."

"He's his nephew, then. No. We take the swag in and show it to him. Come along. We take in the boob, too, and ask the chief what to do with him."

They led Sammy Gregg, accordingly, through a screen of shrubbery into a clearing and there he saw a thing that he had read of in books, before, but never seen. A tramps' jungle.

There are few of such jungles in the West now. There was still fewer then. Even for scoundrels, there were easier ways of making a living than to skulk from town to town, robbing hen roosts and pilfering small articles. It was precarious, too, that life of petty thievery. Because one never could tell when one would be hunted down by swift horsemen and queried abruptly at the point of a revolver. But there were always a few to whom exertion of any lawful kind was so mortally uncomfortable that they would risk death itself rather than do an hour's labor for a dollar. There will always be such men. They are the spice of the underworld. Men who would invite death by exhaustion and the tortures of hunger and thirst rather than work comfortably a few hours a day, for three meals, sound clothes, and extra money to spend at their leisure. But they, the floating scum of the world, who exist only because they love freedom, are the only people in the world who do not know what leisure means.

For the first time, Sammy looked upon a collection of tramps not large, but rare. A scant seven or eight were lolling about the clearing with their hands occupied in odd jobs of mending or laundry. They started up when Sammy entered.

Steve stopped their grinning queries at once. "Where's the chief?" he said. "Has he left already?"

"No, he's asleep."

"Well, wake him up and tell him that we got a haul."

One or two hurried into the shade of a tall, wide-spreading tree through which the sun fell and reached the ground in scattered spots and irregular patches of gold. Stretched there, half in sun and half in shadow, with a green heaven of branches above his head, and scatterings of the sweet blue beyond, the chief slept like a happy child, with his arms thrown out crosswise, on either side of him. He was gradually dragged to a sitting posture, reluctant to yield to their hands.

"But Steve and Lew have brung in a bird and some coin on

him, chief," they argued. "And you've been wanting some money."

"Stolen money? Who the devil told you that I want stolen money?" responded a voice that was oddly familiar in the ear of Sammy Gregg. "Take that man away. I don't want to see him, and I don't want to see his money."

"Good," grunted Steve. "You come with us, kid."

But the other tramps now stood about in a close circle. They did not like the idea of two of their compatriots getting away with such a haul, undivided.

"Look here, Lew," one of them said, "d'you think that we're simps enough to let you two get away with murder like this? Shell out, you tightwad. Lemme see the color of the coin that you got off him."

"He had twenty dollars," Lew said. "I'll give you ten and Steve and me'll take the other ten."

"Listen to him sing," scoffed another. "Twenty dollars was all they got, and that's all that they're excited about. Twenty dollars! Look here, Steve, it ain't gonna do."

"Maybe you'll search us?" Steve asked harshly.

"Maybe we will."

"Maybe you'll be. . . ."

"Lew, drop that gun."

"Why, damn your heart. . . ."

"Hello!" the sleepy voice called from beneath the tree. "Bring him back here. You can't whack up square. You have to snarl like a lot of starved dogs over one bone. Bring him back here!"

Sullenly, but submitting to an authority too great for them to resist, Lew and Steve led Sammy Gregg back before the chief, and, stepping forth from the shadows of the tree, Sammy saw a person no other than his quondam beggar and minstrel of Munson, his gambler *par excellence*—Jeremy Major.

And Jeremy Major recognized him. Aye, at the moment, that

was the thing of importance. He did not hesitate an instant, but, stepping forward, he caught the hand of Sammy and shook it heartily.

"Were you hunting for me?" he asked. "And so you ran into this crowd?"

"The devil," muttered Steve. "He's a pal of the chief."

The chief had not waited for any explanation. His voice had an edge like a rasp as he turned to the two captors. "Everything!" he commanded sharply. "Tumble it all out and lay it in that coat of mine. And if he misses anything, I'll come after you and let you know about it."

So, to the utter amazement of Sammy, nearly $300 in coin was scrupulously counted out before this odd leader, and on top of the other pile of loot, finally, the two long Colts were laid, one across the other.

"Is that all?" asked the chief.

"That's everything," said Sammy.

"Nothing else that you want?"

"A chance to go on my way for help . . . that's all," Sammy replied.

"Sit down, then," Jeremy Major suggested. "Sit down and let me hear about it. Because, old-timer, I owe you money, and just now I'm broke."

Broke? Sammy remembered the heaps and heaps of chips that had been stacked before the place of Jeremy Major not so many weeks before, and every chip had meant gold in that million-dollar game. Where had it gone? Suddenly it seemed to Sammy that his own affairs and his own losses were too small for even a pigmy to consider with interest.

CHAPTER THIRTEEN

Now with his money gone, Jeremy Major was chief. But chief of what? If these were thieves, who spiced little household and back-yard pilferings with occasional adventures on the broad highway, and if they called Major "chief", nevertheless Sammy himself had heard the leader tell them that he would not touch stolen money. A strange streak of virtue in one who thought nothing of cheating at cards. But each man to his own gods and his own altars.

"Come," said Jeremy Major. "Sit down here with me, if you please, and let me hear the story. You were throwing away ten-dollar gold pieces when I last saw you, and now you seem rather down on your luck. What's happened?"

He had waved away the others. And the knaves retired, grumbling and mumbling, to sit in corners of the glade and glower savagely at their chief and his friend. Only the horse of Sammy was left standing near them, and the tall mare, glad of the good forage here, began to crop the shade-nourished grasses.

There Sammy told his story. He put in everything, because his companion seemed bent upon hearing every scruple of the tale. He told of the first adventure, and the loss of the horses at Munson, and the encounter with Cumnor, and what tall and handsome Furness had had to say. He went on with the tale of the second disastrous expedition, the storm, and the regathering of the scattered herd, and the new stampede that had broken the spirit of himself and his two stanch allies.

Jeremy Major listened to this tale with a wandering eye that often roved above the head of his friend and rested on the branches of the great pine above them, as though he were more interested, by far, in the squirrel that scampered there than in the words of Sammy Gregg.

"So," Sammy concluded, "I have told you the whole story, because you asked for it. And now I'll ride on into the town to get another pair of 'punchers to help us out, if I can." He stood up, and Jeremy shook his head.

"But look here," Jeremy said, "I don't see that five men will have a better chance to head that wild herd than three would have. It seems to me that what you need is a fast horse that can carry a rider around the herd faster than they can run away from him."

Sammy Gregg smiled a wan smile. "That mare," he said, "is about as fast as any horse you could get. But she can't head the mustangs unless she's within a few yards of the head of them at the start of their run. And even when she does get in front of them, they simply try to run her down."

"Well," murmured Jeremy sympathetically, "I'll show you a horse that they won't run down. Hello, Clancy. Come here, you fat, worthless loafer, and let the gentleman see you. Hey, Clancy!"

In answer to this somewhat peevish call a glimmering black form slid out from the shadows and stood before Sammy Gregg with an inquisitive eye upon his master. And the sunlight scattering through the branches of the tree tossed a random pattern of brightest, deepest gold over the black satin of the stallion's coat. And Sammy Gregg, who was only beginning to know enough about horses to form a picture in his mind of an ideal— Sammy Gregg, staring at this black monster, with a new vision, understood why the stallion as he stood could be worth more than the value of all the four hundred wild mustangs that had been driven to him across the Río Grande—worth more than the four hundred could ever fetch if they were delivered even in far-off Crumbock, where the labor of the mines used up horseflesh hungrily every day.

"I'm going to ride back with you," Jeremy Major explained, "and try to help you to drive those mustangs north. Not that I'm much of a fellow when it comes to handling mustangs. But Clancy, here, is. He has a way of handling them that would surprise you."

"Partner," said Sammy, filled with awe, "I can't afford to pay you what you're worth."

"Thirty a month," Major said, "will do for me. You start on out of the ravine and I'll catch up with you. I have to say a few words to the boys before I leave them."

Sammy obeyed gladly enough, and with every step that the tall mare struggled up the side of the ravine, it seemed to Sammy that his heart was raised that much higher in hope. So he came to the level going above and let the mare canter briskly away. Back there toward the south, Gonzalez and Pedro were doing their best to come on traces of the herd. How long would it be before the rider of the black horse arrived?

A scant half hour, and here he was, swinging across the plain beside him. And how lazily the big black went. Now there is a peculiar vanity in every man that makes him think that the horse he is riding can run a little faster than any other horse in the world—at least for a little distance. And Sammy, who had felt the tall mare take wings under him more than once, could not help slackening the reins a little. She stretched away at close to full speed instantly.

"We might as well travel while we have a good surface . . . without prairie dog holes, you know," Sammy said by way of explanation, and he turned to look back at the rider of the stallion. No, here was the black horse at his side. Galloping how easily—no, simply floating along, wind-blown, above the ground. For each of those tremendous bounds advanced the big animal the length of a long room and yet he seemed merely to flick the ground with his hoofs in passing. There was no lurch of straining shoulders. There was no pounding of hoofs. But like a racing shadow the monster flew across the plain. Not freely, either, but with the hand of the master fixed on the reins, and keeping a stiff grip upon the stallion's head, lest he might rocket away toward the horizon and leave the poor mare hopelessly and foolishly behind him.

Sammy was in deep chagrin. But joy took the place of shame at once. How would this black giant round up the herd of the flying mustangs when they attempted to scatter away across the plains? Aye, there was not long to wait for that.

They reached Pedro and Gonzalez in another hour or so—the mare foaming with her effort—the black untouched by his gallop. And Sammy saw the cunning eyes of the Mexicans flash wide in a stare of wonder as they surveyed Clancy.

They had a hot trail, by this time, and by midafternoon, they sighted the herd—or at least a wing of it. Clancy was off at once. No fencing about to slip past them. He ran straight up on them, and while the three other riders pounded along far, far to the rear, vainly striving to keep up, they saw Jeremy Major go crashing through the herd.

"But now that he is in front of them, what will he do . . . one man?" Gonzalez asked darkly. For Gonzalez knew horses, and particularly Gonzalez knew that herd.

He was answered quickly enough. They saw the mustangs bunch rapidly together, while the shining stallion glimmered back and forth before them like a waved sword. That whole section of the herd abruptly turned and headed north again, and it had been managed in a trice—all in a trice. And only one sound had come to the ears of the rearward three as, in wonder, they spurred to the side to clear the path for the truant ponies—and that sound was the high-pitched neigh of an angry stallion.

"Do you hear?" Gonzalez gasped. "He makes his horse talk to them. Who is this man?"

That was not all. Through the rest of the afternoon the black horse and his rider ranged freely toward the south and east, and while Sammy and Pedro strove to steady the redeemed portion of the herd toward the north, Gonzalez dropped to the rear to pick up the sections of tired ponies as Major sent them flying in with the stormy neighing of the black horse ringing in their rear. The whole assembly was completed by the dusk. They counted heads, then, and found that the last stampede had cost them forty mustangs. Still there were two hundred and fifty ponies to take north, and at a good price all might still be well with Sammy Gregg. Except that the time was pressing, and the end of the six months drew daily closer and closer.

But the daily drive became a different thing, after this. A thunderstorm caught them on the very next morning, but when the herd strove to race westward away from the flying rain, away from the ripping lightning, the black stallion was before them, ranging swiftly back and forth. And much as the herd might dread the wrath of the elements, they seemed to dread the wrath of Clancy even more. For presently their flight was checked, and they turned cringingly back to face the wind-driven rain.

"This thing," Gonzalez said somberly, "was never seen before. And I think that we shall never see it again. See how the black devil goes for them . . . hello! Has he taken the head off that one?"

This as a fine, cream-colored horse showed a nasty pair of heels at the head of Clancy. But only to have the black bound up with him, and take him by the arched crest of the neck in his teeth and shake him as a cat shakes a rat. The frightened pony screamed with pain and terror, and his cry made the last of the rebels turn, shuddering, into the rain. They knew their master and his handiwork now.

"And yet," Gonzalez said, "I have seen the same thing. Now that I remember, I have seen a stallion turn his herd straight back into a sandstorm . . . to get them away from the danger of men that lay in front. But those were wild horses. And this . . . it is very strange."

"But beautiful," Pedro added. "He has saved us two hundred miles of riding, this morning, with his work."

Aye, and the next day they saw the black stallion drive two hundred and fifty terrified mustangs straight at the railroad track, even while a train of cars was thundering across the desert.

What time they made across the rest of the desert, and then over the foothills, while the mountains turned from blue to brown before them.

"If we pass Munson with no trouble," Sammy suggested. "But I think that that is the chief place of the horse thieves."

"We'll do our best," said Major. "But they're not human if they don't attempt to run this herd away. A quarter of a thousand mustangs . . . and prime good ones, too."

They did attempt it. But Sammy and the two Mexicans saw little of the effort. They only knew that it was made in full daylight by half a dozen masked men. They saw, from the rear, how the riders came storming down a ravine that they filled with their shouting. Only the black stallion was near enough to check them, and, to the bewilderment of Sammy and his two Mexicans, Jeremy Major charged straight at the enemy, gun in hand—a bullet for every stride of the black horse. Then one of the strangers ducked sharply over his saddle horn. They saw another slide sidewise to the ground. And then the rest whirled and rushed away for safety toward the head of the mountains.

CHAPTER FOURTEEN

The fallen man was not dead. But he had a broken shoulder from the fall and a bullet through the base of his neck, breaking the collar bone.

Altogether, it was a nasty mess. They could not take him forty-five miles to Munson. They could not remain with him, until the wounds were healed.

"We'll give you your choice," Sammy said to him sternly. "Tell me who was leading that gang and you go free, old son. And we leave you enough chuck, besides, to keep you going here until your pals come back for you. But if you won't tell, you can stay here and starve."

The fellow had the assurance to laugh in their faces, as though he knew well enough that they could not be as good as their promises. "I'll tell you what, though," he said. "The gent that leads the gang is man enough to make the lot of you sweat for what you've done today."

And Sammy Gregg snapped at him: "Is his name Chester O. Furness?"

The eyes of the wounded man widened. "Are you crazy?" he gasped. "But I've talked enough, and you get no more out of me."

They left him enough provisions to see him through, of course, but they did it grudgingly, and then they started on for the last and most arduous part of the trail—the final hundred miles to the Crumbock mines.

They had two hundred and forty-five mustangs when they began that climb. They reached the mines with two hundred and twenty-eight.

But though they were gaunt of belly now, oh, how they were needed at the mines. All that walked upon four legs, indeed, was welcomed there at Crumbock. There were even ox teams moiling and toiling slowly up toward the mines, grunting along the hard grades. And they had horses of every description. And somebody had brought in a troop of Spanish jennies to pack in provisions. For the Crumbock lode opened in the sheer side of a mountain ridge, with a host of other ridges gathered around it on either side. As someone had said, Nature had put the gold here and then started building fences. And what fences they were.

The day was to come when graded roads, at a cost of many millions, would be driven through the heart of those mountains, but that day was far off and for the present the teamsters had to be content with jumping the fences. Up and down the steep-faced mountains, winding in and out among enormous boulders, the wagons wound their way. And the result was that almost one in three of the draft animals were lamed with every trip. The teamsters had to start out with extra spans hitched behind their wagons to splice into the teams to take the places of those who fell by the way.

Nothing but the iron leg and the iron hoof of a mule could stand that labor, and where were they to get mules? They were rarer than diamonds, and almost as precious. And, in the meantime, horseflesh was at a premium. The very news of the coming of the herd was enough to cause a welcome to pour out in advance. Half a dozen eager buyers found Sammy on the way down the hillside, and when they heard that the price was $75 a head, he found his sales so swift that by the time he got to the bottom of the gulch, he was minus a hundred head of livestock and $7,500 in pocket.

"Buck up that price to eighty-five dollars a throw," Major advised. And the thing was done.

But it made no difference. Teamsters were clearing enough in a single round trip to pay for horses and wagons and all, and leave a neat little wad of money over and above. What difference did $10 a head make to them?

Sammy drew back from the hustling and left the Mexicans to handle the deal. And sitting in the saddle beside Jeremy Major, he said: "I got to tell you what that dust cloud and the things inside of it mean to me. It means that I'm going to be able to buy a home, and buy happiness inside of the home, too."

The lazy brown eyes of Jeremy Major turned slowly toward him. "Can you do that?" he asked mildly. "Can you *buy* happiness? I suppose you mean a wife, by that?"

When the idea was presented thus bluntly to Sammy, he hardly knew how to answer, and Major seemed to feel his embarrassment, for he changed the subject abruptly. "Tell me one thing," he said. "What made you ask if Furness were the leader of the horse thieves? Because of what happened to you in Munson?"

"Because," Sammy answered, "I thought I saw a gray horse in the crowd that looked like the horse that Furness was riding when I saw him in Munson."

"Are you sure of that?"

"It was a fine, big, upstanding gray, with big dark dapples all over it. There might be others just like it, but one of the horses in that outfit looked mighty like it to me."

Major began to whistle a soft little tune. "We'll have to have another look at Munson," he said, grinning. "Things seem to be looking up around there. There goes the last of your mustangs, Gregg."

There was counted into the hungry hand of Sammy, $18,280.

It was a golden dream to Sammy—a golden dream edged with a crimson joy. He took $16,000 dollars—$1,000 for expenses and $15,000 to redeem his promise to Susie Mitchell. He gave the remaining $2,280 to Major, to be divided as he saw fit between himself and the two Mexicans. And he did not remain long enough to see Jeremy Major split the pot in two equal parts and present it to wonder-stricken Gonzalez and the awed Pedro. He did not wait to see these things, for south, south, south was the railroad that would carry him to the house of his bride.

He crossed the terrible mountains to Munson in three short days, but in doing so, he well-nigh ruined the tall mare. She was a staggering wreck when he rode her to the station. And when the station agent remarked on the leanness of the poor creature, he was astonished to receive the mare and saddle and bridle and two good Colts that occupied the holsters, as a present from Sammy. For, with a ticket in his pocket, what more could Sammy wish? There were twelve days to the end of his contract time. And in only ten days the train was due in New York. Only ten days!

There was one letter at the post office from Susie—a very brief and unhappy letter that said: *I haven't had a letter from you in a month. What has happened? Write at once!*

What had happened? He lay back in his seat in the railroad coach and laughed softly to himself. What had happened? If she could see the brown hand that was now holding her letter, she might understand. If she could remember as he did, the slender pipe-stem wrist with which he had come West—was it not nearly doubled in size now? What with the bigness of the tendons from pulling at the reins all day long, and the cordage of swollen veins that surrounded the flesh—was it not transformed? And the hand itself, all reddish brown on the back and gray with work on the palm and fingers. Who could know that hand as the hand of Sammy Gregg?

Aye, and the shirt that he wore was uncomfortably tight. It seemed a little short in the sleeves. It clasped his shoulders too tightly. And it nearly choked him at the neck, until he unbuttoned the top hole.

"These infernal cheap laundries in this wild country," growled Sammy Gregg, "they've shrunk my shirts. I'll have to get a new lot of them when I land in Brooklyn."

But it was not the shirts that had changed size, if Sammy could only have guessed.

If she could only know what had happened to him. He was no artist to tell her how the gun in the hand of big Cumnor had looked him in the eye. In fact, the best that he could do would be to hint at a few things and let Susie guess the rest, and, after all, she was usually a pretty good hand at guessing close to the truth.

Trains of those days were not all that fast, but when Sammy walked the streets of New York again, there were still thirty-six hours between him and his time limit. He had not wired nor written from the West, because he felt that he might as well give himself the small extra reward of surprising Susie.

Horse and cab could not rattle him over the streets fast enough. And so he saw the cab turn down the familiar street. He dismissed it two blocks away. He wanted to walk to steady his nerves a little. He wanted to drink in the familiar sights. And, ah, who but a returned wanderer could have guessed with what joy he would notice that the Murphy house on the corner had been recently painted. With what a sense of pain he observed that the tall elm trees in front of Mr. Holden's place had been cut down. They had long been ailing.

And there, poised on the top of the back fence of Mr. Jones, was the same brindled cat that, two years before, had made itself famous by biting and scratching a fat bulldog until the poor dog ran for help. It looked as lean and as formidable as ever as it turned its big yellow eyes upon Sammy.

All of these little details were mysteriously comforting, because each of them added a touch that helped to assure him that he was indeed home at last. How far, far away the West was—and how barren, and how bold, and how filled with wicked, brazen men.

It was Saturday afternoon, and here the good citizens of the town of Brooklyn were out to mend their fences and mow their lawns and trim their hedges. And Sammy, as he listened to the whirring of the watering hose, felt sweet peace sink into his soul.

He turned up the steps of the Mitchell house. He was almost loath to arrive there so soon, for there had been such happiness in the stroll down the old street that he would willingly have extended it another mile in length.

However, here he was. The meal, prosaically speaking, was finished, and only the dessert remained to be eaten. Only Susie to take in his arms. And it filled him with wonder, now, when he recalled that he had never taken Susie in his arms before this day. Not in both arms, strongly, as he meant to do today.

The door opened, and Mrs. Mitchell loomed broad and low in the doorway, like an overloaded barge in a narrow canal.

"Heaven save us!" Mrs. Mitchell cried. "You ain't little Sammy Gregg!"

"Oh," Sammy said, "have I changed as much as that? But I *am* Sammy, just the same. I hope Sue is home?"

Mrs. Mitchell seemed totally overwhelmed. She merely backed down the hall, gaping at him. "I'll send Mister Mitchell to you," she said, and whirled and fled.

CHAPTER FIFTEEN

Sammy walked into the front room and looked at himself with a grin in the gold-gilt mirror between the two front windows. Many a time, in his boyhood, he had seen his frightened face in that mirror when he had ventured into that sanctum of sanctums with Susie Mitchell. And now he could sit here at ease, and admire his new, ruddy complexion. Ah, could this quiet household see the scenes in which that tan had been acquired.

The heavy step of Mr. Mitchell himself approached, and now he entered in the act of settling his spectacles upon the bridge of his nose and smiling with professional courtesy upon his visitor. For Mr. Mitchell was a grocer by trade, and his smile was a noted asset. Furthermore, he had a ruddy, healthy complexion. If he had said—"I use these groceries on my own table."—no one could have resisted the temptation to buy at once and on a large scale. How is it that so many grocers have complexions modeled after the shade of big red apples? Such was the hue of Mr. Mitchell. It was even a little redder than usual as he clasped the fingers of Sammy in a moist, fat oozing palm.

"Little Sammy Gregg," Mr. Mitchell murmured. "Turned into a wanderer . . . and then come home again. After such a steady life, too."

Sammy was a little taken aback. He had hardly expected such a reception from his future father-in-law.

"However," Mr. Mitchell went on mildly, "I suppose that

even the quietest of us have a small patch of wild oats that need sowing. Isn't that so? But I never thought it of you, Sammy. However, I was sorry to hear from the mill people that they have no place for you now."

"No place for me now?" Sammy echoed, turning pale. "You mean to say that in spite of their promises . . . when I left . . . ?"

"It's a shame how people will make promises and never intend to live up to them, isn't it?" Mitchell said sympathetically. "But it seems that the manager had thought it all over. Good, conservative, close-headed businessman, I have to call him. He says that when a young man takes six months in which to turn five thousand dollars into fifteen thousand . . . why, it shows what the manager calls a little streak of foolishness . . . besides a desire to take a gambler's chance."

Mitchell's own opinion was so apparently tucked into this same speech that Sammy was more amazed than ever. He was glad, at least, that Susie remained for him to give him comfort.

The paper mill, however, had closed him out. After ten years of faithful, most faithful service. Oh, all the nights when he had remained after hours, hoping against hope that his bulldog devotion to work would take the eye of one of the upper members of the firm. And now this ambition was wiped away.

"It's a very hard blow to me," he confessed to Mitchell. "I didn't expect that of my employers. They know how I've slaved for them."

"It's always this way," Mitchell said. "Unfortunately the world is so made that one stroke of folly will erase a hundred strokes of good sense and industry. Only one match need be lighted, my boy, to ignite the greatest building in the world."

In the far West, from which he had just come, Sammy was well aware that such talk would cause men to say: "Aw, cut out the Sunday-school stuff, partner." And he had an almost irresistible temptation to say the same thing on his own behalf.

However, he checked himself and remarked: "It's a hard thing, Mister Mitchell, if a young man is not to be allowed to step out and take a chance for himself now and then. Otherwise, how is he to get on?"

Mitchell leaned forward in his chair and pressed his fat hands upon his fat knees, until the palms squeezed out on the sides, white as the belly of a fish. "Young man," he said, "slow and steady is the word . . . slow and steady is the word that builds life in the way it ought to be built. Now tell me, frankly . . . out of the five thousand dollars in honest money that you took West, how much did you lose?"

Sammy closed his eyes to calculate. "Nearly three thousand," he said. For, up to the day of his arrival at the Crumbock lode he had, indeed, been that much cash out of pocket.

Mitchell writhed in his chair. "Three thousand," he groaned. "Three thousand honest dollars . . . thrown away! Why, with that money I could have built a new wing . . . oh, Sammy, this is a thing for which you will grieve in years to come. Three thousand dollars at six percent is a hundred and eighty dollars a year. Many a poor man in Europe is toiling fifteen hours a day for smaller pay than that." He closed his eyes and fairly groaned aloud in the pain that the thought of such waste gave him. "Ah, well," he said, "it is a fortunate thing for Susie that I warned her and opened her eyes."

"Warned her?" Sammy murmured.

"That this would be the probable outcome . . . wild adventures in the West. Fifteen thousand out of five thousand. Stuff and nonsense! Why, young man, even I, at my time of life and with my experience in the business world, would not attempt to accomplish a thing of such a magnitude. It argues a wild brain on those young shoulders of yours, Sammy, my boy. A very wild brain, but I thank heaven that poor Susie will never bear any of the painful results of such folly."

A terrible thought blasted its way into the mind of Sammy. "Where is Susie?"

"Not here," Mitchell said gravely.

"Not here?" echoed Sammy in a whisper. "But she's . . . out shopping . . . out calling . . . she's over at the Johnson house, maybe. . . ."

"Oh, Sammy," Mitchell said, shaking a fat white finger at him, "how I hope that this will be a lesson to you never again to venture all and lose all."

"My Lord," Sammy breathed, "you mean that she has left home?"

"Yes . . . but not alone."

Sammy, perfectly white by this time, stood up from his chair, "Mister Mitchell," he gasped.

"Sammy," said the grocer, "I grieve for you. Upon my soul, I grieve for you bitterly. But I trust that the lesson will not be wasted upon you."

A bright spot of color came back in either of Sammy's cheeks. There was in his eyes such a fire as Brooklyn had never seen there before. And when he spoke, his voice was suddenly rough and harsh. "I hate to think it," Sammy said, "but it's forced on me that you . . . you fat sneak . . . may have advised your daughter to marry another man."

The grocer rose, also, and stood, big and towering and fat as butter, above little Sammy. "Samuel Gregg," he said, "can I trust my ears?"

And those astonished ears drank in the following unholy words: "You can trust your ears, you blockhead. But tell me if I have guessed right? Have you really told Susie to marry another man?"

"Yes!" Mitchell shouted in a voice that Mrs. Mitchell, in the back yard, heard and knew and quailed beneath. "Yes! I have told her to marry another man."

"And the little fool," Sammy said, "the little fool has taken your advice?"

Mitchell raised both fat hands. No, rage and bewilderment had paralyzed him. His thick arms fell with a wheeze to his sides again and left Sammy intact.

"My guess is a good guess, I think," Sammy said. He stepped to the mantelpiece and lifted the picture that stood where his picture had once reposed. And out of the frame he saw the chinless face of young Tom Hooker, the dentist's son—a pleasant, smiling, useless face. "My Lord," Sammy said, "is this my substitute?"

"Young man," shouted Mitchell, "leave these premises! You are a worthless young reprobate. Never return to this place again, or with my own hands. . . ."

"Stuff," Sammy declared. And he dropped his brown fists upon his hips. "Stuff, you fool," he said. "I've killed men twice your size, Mitchell. And men twice as good as you. Why, in the country where I've been, we use fellows like you . . . for grease. Sit down, before I wring your stuffy neck for you. Sit down, while I talk to you."

Mitchell turned flabby, like a punctured balloon, and sank, almost lifeless, into a chair. His pale, fishy eyes beheld Sammy Gregg in the act of taking a wallet from his pocket. From that wallet Sammy counted forth, one by one, fifteen new, crisp, banknotes of $1,000—oh, magic word!—to the note. A treasure—$15,000. And then a handful of smaller currency.

"And another thousand, just for luck . . . another thousand to paint the house, maybe," Sammy Gregg said, thrusting out his jaw. "Luck was with me. And tomorrow I'm going back to the free country. I'm through with you people back here. Why, you choke me. I can't talk and I don't seem to be able to think. I'm glad that Susie has that pinhead. She'd look up to a wooden image, I suppose, and call it a man. And you can pay the bills for the party. I wish you luck. As for me, I'm going back to the West, and roll this fifteen thousand into a couple of million, maybe. And when I get that, I'll have just about enough to marry one of those Western girls. And they're worth it. Mister Mitchell, I hope you have luck." He settled his hat upon his head, he turned his back, and he swaggered deliberately out the front door, and only one sound pursued him—the faint whisper of the grocer, moaning: "Six-teen thou-sand dol-lars!"

Then Sammy found himself in the familiar street once more. But the joy had gone out of it. Only, in the first place, he felt a burning fierceness in his soul. And in the second place, he began to discover that what he had said to the grocer had not been altogether a bluff.

How small, after all, had been his hold upon the life in this street when one conversation of five minutes could suffice to root up all his interests here. But out West—aye, that was different.

Gamblers, hobos, thieves, horse rustlers, miners, teamsters, villains—he felt suddenly that they were his brothers.

And that night the westbound train took Sammy with it from Manhattan.

CHAPTER SIXTEEN

The trip Sammy Gregg took to Munson for the second time was a melancholy affair, by no means comparable with his first excursion to the West. Granted that on the second occasion he had some $16,000 of well-earned money in his pocket, still, there was a difference. The first time, with less than a third of that sum in his wallet, he had come West to find enough money to make his marriage with Susie Mitchell a possibility. And he had come with an outlook on the world that was gay and careless, to say the least. Now he returned with three times as much capital and less than a third as much self-confidence.

He felt like a fish that is half in the water and half on dry land—in a word, he was not at home. He needed friendship, gentleness, and enough comforts to smooth his path before him. Not many months before, when he had started West to conquer a fortune, he had left behind him the consciousness that Brooklyn was his home. Nothing but a wedding ring was needed there to complete that portion of his destiny that usually makes the last chapter in a romance. But now that Susie Mitchell had married another man, Brooklyn was literally wiped right out of his life. There was nothing to take him back to that place, and he was finding, as he sat in the train, that there was very little to make him turn toward Munson as a substitute.

It was simply the only other town with which he had ever associated himself. And yet, as he told himself in the train, what prospects had he there, and what friends? Certainly he could not look forward to establishing a business by bringing up fresh herds of horses from Texas to the mountains, as he had done before. The mere thought of the trials through which he had passed on the desert and in the mountains was enough to make his blood run cold. And he knew, in spite of all the money and the conscientious labor that he had invested in that exploit, that there was only one good reason why it had succeeded, and that reason was Jeremy Major and his black stallion, Clancy. That singular youth had rescued Sammy, and Sammy very well knew it. So he could tell himself that he had won his little fortune by luck, pure and simple.

As for friends, upon whom could he count? There was Rendell, the storekeeper. But was he not rather a conversationalist than a friend? And there was Jeremy Major, to be sure. But Jeremy could not be counted. Probably, by this time, that free-handed youth had been stabbed in the back during some gambling brawl. As for the rest—well, there was no rest. He would arrive in Munson to play a lone hand.

There were half a dozen people at the station when he dismounted from it, suitcase in hand. A brown-faced half dozen who looked at him without recognition and without interest. A brisk north wind was curling about the little station house, keeping the eyes of everyone squinted half shut, and tugging at coattails and bandannas, and covering Munson with a sweeping mist. No, it was not a pleasant picture.

The hills were sunburned and bare at this season, and the more distant summits lifted rocky heads and cliff-like shoulders, as though to say: *Yes, the Crumbock lode lies in this direction . . . reach it if you can.*

As for Munson itself, it had grown even since he had last seen it. Here, there, and again, he saw the white faces of new buildings, all of raw, unpainted pine boards, with cracks between them so wide that they could be distinguished a block away. For no nails in the world could keep the half-seasoned timbers from warping, once this hot sun got in its work on them.

Munson was growing, but that thought brought no cheer to Sammy. He slumped gloomily down the street, ankle-deep in dust. And the dirt that his footfall loosened was combed up instantly and curled like a plume over his head by the wind. He was white with a thick layer of the dust before he got to the store that carried, above the door, the name of Rendell. One thing startled him. New-painted plows—gang plows of two models stood in the vacant lot next to Rendell's—obviously a part of his stock. And Sammy looked at them in amazement. They were painted a shining yellow, and the seat of open ironwork was distinguished with a coat of crimson, and the lower tips of the plowshares were covered with paint of the same color. Very bright, but who under the wonderful heavens could want gang plows in the town of Munson?

He stepped into the door of the store and there he encountered almost the last person in the range that he wanted to meet—none other than Cumnor, whose revolver had fired the bullet that had caused a furrow to be made down the side of his head not many months before. The hair was growing out now, along the scar, and that hair was a white slash in a brown head.

The meeting seemed no more pleasant to Cumnor than it was to little Sammy Gregg. But Sammy looked him coldly in the eye and stepped to one side. Yet Cumnor did not pass. He stood there, ill at ease, combing his long, drooping, sandy mustaches.

"Gregg," he began.

Sammy scowled, but said nothing, and a crimson tide washed across the heavy features of the rancher.

"Gregg," he repeated resolutely, "I got to tell you that I want to apologize for the downright low trick I done to you here a while back. Only, at that time, when you stepped up and claimed them horses that I had just bought from Furness . . . well, it went sort of ag'in' the grain to pay out three hundred dollars twice for the same stock. Y'understand?"

Sammy, watching him in wonder, nodded.

"But here," said Cumnor, "I've had a chance to think things over. I've had a chance to see that you're a man of your word and a square-shooter. And I've got to say that I'm sorry about the shooting, and here's three hundred dollars for those ponies. Gregg, I want to be friends with you."

It would have been a considerable speech in any part of the world, between man and man. But this speech was overheard by an audience, consisting of Rendell and a gaunt cowpuncher who was buying a yard or so of plug chewing tobacco. And in the far West apologies come hard. It is apt to be considered unmanly not to persist, even in error. For that, after all, is the unwritten law of the frontier.

Now Sammy was not a man who forgot or forgave lightly. And during many a month he had taken home the thought of Cumnor to his heart and sworn that someday he would find a means of righting the wrong that had been done him. However, he had seen enough of the frontier and its ways to know that this apology from such a man as Cumnor meant almost as much as bullets themselves could write. And he stretched out his hand.

"Cumnor," he said, "I believe you mean it."

"Mean it?" Cumnor said. "I'll tell you that I do." And he clutched the hand of Sammy. "And the three hundred just to say for certain that I don't lie."

"Keep it for me," Sammy said, "until I need it. Be my banker to that extent, old-timer."

The big man regarded him for a moment in wonder, and then his glance passed over the head of Sammy and toward the rear of the store. "You were right, Rendell," was all he said, and he hurried out from the store.

The cowpuncher, staring at the little man, followed. And Sammy was left alone to shake hands with Rendell. That crippled hulk of a man heaved himself partly up on his counter and sat there grinning down at Sammy.

"Where's the wife?" he asked. "Back in the hotel?"

"I don't know what hotel she's in," Sammy answered. "She married, all right, but she married another man."

Rendell gaped—started to speak—and then busied himself biting off a great corner from a wedge of chewing tobacco. When he had stowed that great quid safely in a corner of his mouth, he said solemnly: "Questions is always foolish things to ask. I'm sorry, Gregg." But Sammy was able to grin. "What the boys will want to know," went on Rendell, "is what queer new dodge you're gonna try on the town this time . . . after driving a few hundred horses clean up from the river to Crumbock."

"I could never have done it. It was a man named Major."

"Oh, he's getting to be pretty well known, now . . . that same gent. But who would have figured that you would know a gent like him to help you out? Well, Gregg, what are you going to do this time?"

"I don't know," Sammy said. "Something big enough and hard enough to keep me busy, hand and foot and brain, until I get over feeling the way I do."

"Something real hard?"

"Yes."

"Start over Crumbock way and try to find the mother lode. That ought to be a job for you."

"It's hard enough to get to the mines, let alone the lode," said Sammy.

"Aye, if you want a real man-size job, start a stage to the Crumbock mines, old son."

"A stage?" Sammy said doubtfully. "Is there money in it?"

"Oh, I ain't serious," Rendell said. "Nobody'll start a stage line in this part of the world while there's so many gents like The Duke, hanging around."

"The Duke?" Sammy said.

"That's Furness."

"How did he get a title. Does he own one?"

"No . . . it's only a way he's got, they say, when he shoves a gun under your nose and tells you to stand and hand over. He gets kind of high and lofty, like a duke would be, if he was a road agent, maybe."

Sammy whistled. "Have they got the goods on him?" he asked. "Is he living out?"

"If there was a sheriff and a decent judge in the county," Rendell answered, "they'd find that they had enough goods to nail him, right enough, but the law ain't more'n a baby around here, and any way that you look at him, The Duke is sure a growed-up man. Young Blythe and Harper was the last pair that started out to get him. We ain't heard from them yet. But there is three other gents in the last three months that has gone out and started to get famous by bringing in the scalp of The Duke, and them three has all failed. Leastwise, they ain't showed up lately, and I don't look, personal, for Harper and Blythe to show up, neither. But nobody'll start a stage and run men and money between Munson and Crumbock while birds like The Duke has got their wing feathers unclipped. Look at the Chadwick City bunch. They've closed down and offered their stages and their whole string of horses for sale. The horses has gone. But who the devil wants a stagecoach?"

"I don't know," Sammy said, "but maybe I'm the man."

"Hey, Sammy Gregg! You ain't taking me seriously about starting that stage line?"

"No," said Sammy. "I'm only thinking."

CHAPTER SEVENTEEN

Chadwick City was only seventy miles away. And it was forty miles farther away from Crumbock than was Munson. So Sammy rode over to find out what he could find out. He found four magnificently built coaches standing out in the open for the wind and the weather to wreck, though so far wind and weather had not accomplished much harm, for these were masterpieces of Yankee craftsmanship in the good old days when there still were Yankee mechanics who were proud of the things that they could shape by hand and hammer and lathe, instead of by machine. Those coaches were built of the very finest hickory, with a generation of seasoning to make it tough. Tough it was—light as dry wood should be, tough as leather, strong as iron.

Sammy knew little about wood, but when he heard that those coaches had actually been used over the rough roads, he was amazed. Certainly there was little sign.

"What might *you* want with them coaches?" asked the representative of the defunct stage company.

"Nothing," Sammy answered. "Nothing, perhaps, and yet the running gear might be useful for something." For Sammy himself was enough of a Yankee to know how to cheapen a price.

"A hundred and fifty dollars will buy the lot," said the other sadly. "And when I think of what it cost to build ary a one of them wagons, it makes me powerful sick, old-timer."

Sammy blinked and then drew a long breath—$150, for all four. "Hold out your hand," he said. And he closed the money in the other's palm. "Now," said Sammy, "tell me if you have had any experience in the staging business?"

"I've had enough," the other said, "to keep me from ever wanting any more. How come you to ask?"

"What broke up this line?"

"There was a sort of a lack of things," said the salesman. "There was a lack of cooks to work in the three eating houses that we had to build along the road. And there was a lack of drivers, too, for the driving of the stages. Drivers that a man could trust, I mean."

"Why," Sammy contradicted, "the country is filled with good teamsters."

"Just so," said the tall man. "But they found that stage driving was sort of unhealthy, by reason that now and then somebody would want the stage to stop where there wasn't no regular station, and the most usual way he took of stopping the stage was to shoot the driver and then one of the lead team of horses. Mostly that would stop up the stage pretty quick. But it got the drivers to feeling sort of restless. We lost two in one week, and after that the boys got sort of sick of the work. Then there was a lack of passengers. They kept coming pretty good for a time, but then they sort of got tired of having their pockets looked into. I knowed one gent that made four trips on our stage and three times the stage was stuck up and he lost his wad each time. He was a gambler, so he took it pretty calm. But he says . . . 'I never sticks in a game where the chances is three to one in favor of the dealer. And the crooks is the dealers in this game of riding on the stage.' Which it sort of looked like he was right.

"But outside of them things, and the lack of a few more, such like as the lack of any kind of a road, and the lack of hay to store in the sheds for the horses at the stage stops, and the lack of horses that was busted for the harness work, and the lack of harness to take the place of the leather that the broncos jumped through their first few times out . . . outside of them few lacks, there wasn't much to keep the stage line from running, except that them that was putting up for it got sort of tired and pretty soon they lacked the money to keep on paying the losses."

To this original relation, Sammy Gregg listened with a smile, to be sure, but also with a falling heart. "Between you and me," he asked, "what do you think of the chances of running a stage from Munson to the mines?"

"I don't think nothing about it. I *know* it couldn't pan out. It'd break the heart of the gent that tried it. Break him inside of a month."

"All right," Sammy said. "I'm thinking of it."

"Then I'm sorry for you."

"Will you tell me why?"

"Your business is your own. But just the same, I got to ask you why a stage would have a chance from Munson when it's failed from Chadwick City?"

"We're forty miles closer, for one thing, and most of the people bound for Crumbock come through Munson."

"You're forty miles closer, but you got a road that's twice as rough. If the freighters can hardly make it at a walk, how are you gonna keep passengers comfortable at a trot?"

"I don't intend to keep 'em comfortable," said Sammy. "I just intend to get 'em there . . . if they hang on tight."

For the first time a light came in the eye of the other. "That's a new idea," he said. "But you're gonna get 'em there with a lot of stops. There's a good hold-up place every quarter of a mile along the whole road from Munson to Crumbock."

There is nothing more stimulating than opposition. The man who is winning at cards is the man who is able to stop play when he chooses. But he who is losing cannot let go. He has to keep on bucking fate. And the more the stage man of Chadwick City blasted the hopes of Sammy Gregg, the more the courage of Sammy rose. We will not believe a picture that is painted too black. Better to throw in some relieving touches. And Sammy, when he heard that there were *no* chances of winning through, began to feel that his companion was purposely making matters worse than they really and truly were.

He hired four men and four spans of horses to drag the stagecoaches across the hills to the town of Munson, and when he arrived, riding proudly at the head of the procession, he had the satisfaction of having the town turn out to watch him pass.

Neither did Munson laugh as loud as he had expected. The idea of a tenderfoot putting through the stage line was so very novel, considering that the experienced old hands at Chadwick City had failed, that Munson's citizens shook their heads and postponed their decisions.

"He drove the horses up from the river," Rendell reminded, "and he got them safe to Crumbock, and one failure didn't turn him back. How d'you know but that he'll get the stage line through to Crumbock, too?"

But the buying of the stages was only the first step in a long undertaking. He needed relay stations every eight miles—twelve stations between the towns, and a bigger station and stables at either end of the line. That meant twelve shacks, and two men in each shack, one to handle the work by day and the other to handle it by night. For, day and night, the stages must toil on. The start was to be at 4:00 a.m. The halt at night took place not before 9:00, with an hour's halt at noon for the battered passengers to eat a meal and stretch their cramped limbs. Then, with a new driver, they scurried on again. At night they halted at 9:00 if they were near one of the two sleeping houses that had to be built. And so four stages should be constantly in use, each stage traveling sixteen hours a day.

Nor was this all, for allowance would have to be made for the wastage in horseflesh that would be occurring constantly as the mustangs struggled forward among the rocks and up the terrible slopes of the mountains. Ruined shoulders and spoiled hoofs must be a common occurrence, besides those that wasted under the daily strain. He must have a reserve of stock to meet these contingencies—a reserve of sixty head, at the least. And, the instant that he started operations, he must have a payroll of at least thirty or thirty-five men.

Now, with an overhead of this size looming above him, young Sammy Gregg could understand very well how the Chadwick City line had failed so quickly and so ignominiously. But it also occurred to him that he might be able to buy for a song the timber that they had used in the construction of their own way stations through the mountains. And other thoughts formed rapidly in the brain of Sammy.

In the room of the hotel at Munson that afternoon he wrote the following letter to his old henchman, Gonzalez, at El Paso:

Dear Gonzalez: I am back in Munson, and I want horses again. But this time I want horses that are broke, and that we can take to Munson on ropes. I want three hundred horses. For the purchase, $10 a head, and $10 more a head for the breaking, and $5 extra for bringing them to Munson. Does that sound to you? That will give you a chance to make a little profit on every horse. If everything goes through in good shape, I may be able to increase that price.

As it stands, $7,500 for the herd of three hundred. Write to me that you want the contract and I'll forward $5,000 to you. Get Pedro, if you can, to help with the work, and write back to me at once.

Sammy Gregg

Here Sammy shuddered a little. That amount in the hands of Gonzalez! But upon second thought, he decided that all life here in the West was a gamble, and he would have to go ahead taking chances.

He sealed the letter when a strangely subdued murmur of noises rose from the street. He glanced out the window of his room and saw the tall form and the handsome face of him whom Munson now called The Duke, in other words, Chester Ormonde Furness. He was seated in a buckboard, driving a fine pair of horses, one of which was a great dappled gray that carried, in addition to harness, a saddle cinched around its belly.

There was something covered in the body of the buckboard, and now the wind stirred that covering and revealed two pairs of boots—with the legs of men in them.

CHAPTER EIGHTEEN

Two men, lying side-by-side in the bottom of a buckboard, with only a thin throw of blue calico between their upturned faces and the sun—that terrible, broiling, baking Western sun? No, it did not seem possible.

Furness had stopped his team and the buckboard stood stationary with the sun still baking and broiling upon the calico—and the bodies that lay beneath it. And the horrible conviction entered the mind of Sammy Gregg that living they could not be, since nothing human could have endured that heat without stirring.

Sammy was in the street in ten seconds, and he found himself a member of a crowd that was rapidly being recruited from every corner of the town. There was even old Rendell, who hated activity of any kind, now hurrying out of his store and swinging toward them as fast as he could move his crippled leg. And, old and young, the town drew swiftly together to stare at big Chester Furness as he took the harness off the near horse—the gray—and led it forth in the saddle. Then he climbed into the saddle and sat there with a hand upon his thigh and his calm eyes and his sneering smile fixed upon the crowd.

What might have seemed wonderful to many was that fifty guns did not leap out of the holsters there in Munson that knew Furness so well and that had so many reasons for hating him—that fifty guns did not fly forth to shower lead upon him.

But to Sammy and to the others who were gathered there,

you may be sure that it did not seem strange, while the cold eye of Furness was wandering over their faces, dwelling a little on each one, as though he wished to remember. But, oh, how mightily they hated that handsome fellow. From the tips of his well-polished boots to his whipcord riding trousers and the neat bowtie at his throat, how thoroughly they detested even his neatness, as though that were a vice, also. And indeed, out here in the wilderness of the bare mountains, it seemed almost a vice. And between the rough, unshaven, sweating, hot crowd and that dapper fellow in the saddle, there was a wide ocean. And every wave in that ocean was purest hatred.

And fear, too. I suppose no hatred is perfect without fear thrown in. They feared his scorn, which was as strong as their own rage. And they feared, above all, that faultless, swift, sure hand and the eye as steady as drilled steel—the eye and the hand that would not make mistakes when the time for battle came.

So, in a breathless silence, they watched him. If there had been a dozen sheriffs there, they could not have arrested him, because there were no proved crimes to charge to the account of Chester Ormonde Furness. He was not fool enough to sin recklessly in daylight without a mask drawn over his handsome features. And he had a way of roughening and sharpening that smooth voice of his so that no one could be sure that the ruffian behind the mask was really this dapper Furness. No one could be sure, but they could guess near enough. The whole county could not have delivered testimony enough to have hanged this man, but the whole county did assuredly know one thing, which was that Furness deserved to die with a rope around his neck.

Very strange to Sammy Gregg, newly come from a breath of Eastern life where the law lives in every corner of even the greatest city. Very strange to know that ten days had carried him from Manhattan to Munson.

Furness was making a speech, but still nothing happened in the body of the buckboard, nothing stirred. *Could it be that the men were really dead?* That thought obsessed Sammy and sickened him. And there was something so terrible in the cold eye of Furness that Sammy could well believe he had brought two dead men to the town.

"Gentlemen, neighbors," Furness said, "and I had almost said . . . friends. A pity, too, that I cannot say it. For I am sure that I have done my best to win . . . your respect." He paused and laughed softly in their faces.

A stir of anger worked through the crowd, and terror with the anger. Oh, what a man was this, to play with these fifty human tigers as Chester Furness was playing.

"But though I trust," went on the mocker, "that I may have won your respect, still it seems that you cannot be persuaded to keep at anything but a formal distance. However, you still remain, if not my friends, at least, my neighbors . . . and gentlemen." And he laughed again, filled certainly with an exquisite devil.

Sammy heard an iron-faced man beside him murmuring: "I wish to heaven I had the nerve to try him, but he's got his eye fixed special right on me . . . he knows."

So it seemed to them all, no doubt, as though that omnipresent eye were fixed steadily upon them, each face singled out particularly by The Duke.

"But lately," Furness continued, "it seems that there has been a growing habit among you of sending out people to call upon me . . . to come unannounced and give me a pleasant surprise." He paused, and there was just a little less amusement and a little more cruel edge in his smiling. "The young men of Munson and of Chadwick City have made it a point to drift about through the hills and through the forest hunting for me, to pay their respects. Very kind of them. But it keeps me rather nervous.

117

It keeps me, in short, feeling that I must always have my house in order, seeing that I never know when to expect callers. The result is that I rarely rest, and I really have to keep watchful."

All of those innuendoes were patent enough, and they might have brought a snarl from the crowd, but it was too fascinated with his narrative now to pay much attention even to his insults. Something was coming—something of dreadful moment. They could guess it, and they wondered from what direction the trouble would strike Munson.

"Finally," said The Duke, "when others had failed to find me at home . . . two young gentlemen of Munson decided that they must try their hands and come up to have a look at me. So they came up and in the middle of last night they dropped in upon me. Oh, most unexpectedly. I could only sit up in my blankets and stare at them. And they stood there and stared back at me."

He paused to light a cigarette, while the crowd held its breath. But Sammy, who already guessed the point of the tale, was turning sick with sorrow and with disgust.

"Of course," The Duke went on, "I wanted to make them at home, but they insisted upon doing the honors for me. And they made me sit quietly there by my fire, with one of them on each side of me. We were all very quiet, for a time." He laughed again. And when he stopped laughing, his nostrils were quivering, and his eyes flashed like whips across the faces of the crowd. "They could not think of very much to say, so it seemed, and so they filled in the interval toying with their Colts. As for me, I was so pleased and surprised to have them with me, that you can imagine that I was quite dumb. However, they presently fell into a discussion as to which of them could rightly claim the honor of having found my campfire. After that, they grew quite hot over the point of which of them had the pleasure of first confronting me in my camp.

"You will not believe me when I tell you how irritated they

became. Suddenly they had jumped to their feet. They declared that they had had enough of one another. I, sitting on the ground between them, begged them to lower their voices . . . because the buzzards might be listening." The Duke tilted back his head and laughed, with a sound like the snarl of a wolf buried deep in his throat. "But all I could say was as nothing to them. I have told you already that they had their guns out. Now they jerked them up to the hip. I think young Harper fired twice, and young Blythe fired only once. But, unfortunately, both of them shot too straight." He paused and looked with mock sorrow around him. "To my most stinging grief, I found myself suddenly sitting with a dead man upon either side of me, each shot cleverly through the head. Imagine my confusion and my sorrow."

"And as I sat there through the night with the dead men, it occurred to me that I really owed it to the town of Munson, and my acquaintances there, to let them know just how these poor young men had stumbled into the arms of death, so to speak, in spite of my protests against it And it seemed to me that I should try to find some way in which I could discourage those fine young men of the towns from wandering through the hills trying to catch me unawares. Because I was afraid lest they might, also, quarrel with one another, just as poor young Harper quarreled with poor young Blythe about which of them should take precedence in my camp. And finally it seemed to me that the very best way I could manage the thing would be to carry Harper and Blythe into the town and let their friends see just what they did to themselves. And so, gentlemen, here they are."

He snatched the blue calico sheet away from them and let the staring, horror-stricken people look on the dead faces of the two boys. Their guns were still in their hands, placed there by the devilish forethought of Furness.

"And it is my modest trust," went on Furness, "that the other young men from the towns in this neighborhood will be deterred from following the same example, because I really should not like to waste many more days carting the poor young men back to Munson or to Chadwick City. Gentlemen, I make a present of the buckboard and the bay horse to the town of Munson. Until old Mister Graham happens along . . . as no doubt he will before long . . . to remark that I was forced to borrow it from him. Tell him, then, that the roan horse broke its legs, and so I put it out of its pain and harnessed my own galloper in its place. However, he need not thank me for that. Gentlemen, good day. May we continue to be just as neighborly as ever. But let my next callers announce themselves to save confusion."

Here he was reining his great gray horse backward down the street. No, he dropped the reins, and so perfectly trained was that magnificent stallion that it continued to back gradually down the street, leaving the left hand of Furness free to take off his hat and salute with it the staring crowd, while his right hand still rested jauntily on his thigh, near to the butt of a Colt revolver. He reached the next corner, and a sway of his body caused the well-trained stallion to leap sidewise, like a cat, throwing the master behind cover. And so he was away.

Of course there was a reaching for guns the instant his terrible eye was removed from them, but by the time they reached the corner, the stallion was already out of view behind a hill.

CHAPTER NINETEEN

There was no pursuit of The Duke, for, as Rendell remarked, though everyone knew that Furness had lied rankly and that the bullets that had killed the two adventurous youths had come from his own revolver, yet what way had they of proving what they felt to be the truth? They could only think their thoughts, but so far as a legal case against Furness was concerned—they had not the shadow of a ghost of one. He was not pursued, but allowed to retire into the mountains to work away at his schemes.

"Only," Sammy said to Rendell, "I don't understand how a . . . gentleman like that, could be a robber . . . and a murderer!"

"When I was a kid," Rendell said, "I used to read a little mite. And I remember a book about some of the old gentlemen who used to go around in store clothes that was cut out of cast-iron junk and their idea of a happy little outing in those days was to shy a spear at you and knock you off your horse and then dip six or seven inches of steel dirk through the bars of your helmet and through your eye and into your brain so's you wouldn't feel much pain. A very neat outfit. Well, them ways has got sort of old-fashioned. Gents with them inclinations is discouraged something scandalous most places in the world. But right out here, Sammy Gregg, there is room for some of them to go a-gallivanting around and pick up a little of what they call fun and some spare money, besides. And that's what my idea of Furness is. He's simply bad by nature and by taste, you might say."

Something of that was in the mind of Sammy, also. "But," he said, "how long will it be before the people get together and get rid of him?"

"That always happens, I suppose," Rendell opined.

"I think so."

"In fiction, perhaps, but in actual fact, I don't think so. Some of the worst skunks I ever seen have lived the longest lives, and you can lay to that."

However, there was not much time on the hands of Sammy to indulge in thought about the nature and the ways of Furness. He was too busy with his own affairs in the accomplishment of which, to be sure, Furness appeared as one of the obstacles to the smooth operation of the stage line for which he was planning. But Furness was only one among many obstacles. He and others of his kind, no doubt, would make it a precarious business for any of the miners in the Crumbock lode to entrust their earnings to the stage for transportation. And even passengers, as the Chadwick man had put it, had begun to lack enthusiasm for stage traffic when they were held up two times out of three and their pockets picked.

Yet he trusted that once he got the line in operation, he might be able to swing the deal and keep the stages fairly safe. He refused to cross any bridge until he came to it. And, in the meantime, his hands were full.

He had to employ teamsters, in the first place, to bring the lumber of the station houses of the Chadwick City Company, which he had bought for a song. And when the timber arrived in Munson, he had to send it out to each of the station sites that he had selected for his own route. He had picked those station sites with much care, sometimes making a long distance between points of relay, but always striving, if possible, to give to each station plenty of wood and water and grazing land, which must next be fenced in for the horses.

He had heard from Gonzalez. By the grace of good fortune, that able cavalier had come to Juárez in time to get the letter. Now he was busy gathering mustangs and breaking them, using a hardy crew of men for the work. But it was difficult. To break a horse to the saddle was one thing. To break it to pull a wagon was quite another, most fabulously considered to be an easier task. But the work went forward in spite of all difficulties. The stations of relay were located and built, and the pasture lands fenced in near them, and hardy men were gathered—a ticket agent at either end of the line, and eight skillful, daring men who were willing to risk their lives driving the stages, and twenty men to man the relay stations—and, in addition to all of these matters, a thousand little details that no one but Sammy himself could supervise. He was flying back and forward between Munson and the Crumbock mines nearly every day. He had to keep a string of horses in both towns, and all those nags were worn almost to a shadow.

One pleasant discovery was made almost at the beginning of the affair. The men of Crumbock were disposed to smile at the slender little thin-faced man who declared that he was going to put a stage line through from Crumbock to the outer world, but when word came up from Munson that this same little man was already known there and that he had been as good as his word in at least one other large transaction, Crumbock came instantly out of its smiling humor and began to pat Sammy on the back.

For Crumbock was being stifled—fairly stifled for the lack of proper transportation between its mines and the towns beyond the rough, inner core of the highest mountains. The lode needed manpower for its development, for one thing, and whoever wanted to cross the mountains had to pack up three days' provisions, bought at famine prices in Chadwick City or in Munson, and thence plod wearily on a five- or a seven-day trip to the mines. And men bound for mines do not like to have a week's walk put in at some point on the journey.

But manpower was the least of the troubles at the Crumbock mines. All that was needed for the mines, from ironwork to powder, had to be delayed to the speed of the wagons that crawled wearily across the mountains. A small thing could delay a teamster for a week. A broken axle might stall him indefinitely, and broken axles were common commodities on the road from Munson to Crumbock. So the mines were throttled for the lack of rapid and certain delivery of supplies that were so vitally needed. The slow freight could be handled, after their manner, by the wagons, but when a man needed a set of new drills and needed them in a rush—could he sit twiddling his thumbs while the wagons slowly moiled away to Munson, and there waited for the goods, and then slowly, slowly struggled back to the upper peaks where the lode was? No, for by that time that necessary bit of drilling might be a month out of date.

In short, Crumbock was a place where the necessities of existence were growing more numerous every instant, as the ground was broken deeper and deeper and the mining problem became more abstruse. And there was no artery of supply. There was even no sure way of getting letters through to Munson or to Chadwick City. And a dozen of the larger concerns were each maintaining their own mail service, at enormous expense and uncertainty, dispatching riders into the wilderness.

What wonder then, that a dozen hearts were broken when the Chadwick City line failed them? And what wonder that a great pulse of joy ran through the big camp when it was learned that another line would try the shorter but more difficult passage from Munson to the lode?

Little Sammy Gregg found himself received like a most important personage at the camp. And everyone had time enough to talk business with him.

Then Gonzalez arrived at Munson with the first half of the

horse herd—a hundred and fifty head of fire-eyed mustangs with a far-away look in their eyes and ears that quivered backward and forward to betoken danger. However, they were all broken—after a fashion. Gonzalez solemnly described how he had found a wagon made of iron, with lofty, old-fashioned wheels, and iron spokes, and iron hubs, and, indeed, everything about it except the bed composed of the finest wrought iron. To that indestructible vehicle he had hitched half a dozen mustangs at a time. The harness that he had used was made of heavy chains, very thinly coated with leather. It could not be broken, and the more the mustangs kicked, the more they simply stripped away the leather paddings and exposed themselves to the rusted iron chains that bit through mustang skin and flesh and cut quickly to the bone. Hence certain scabby places on the legs of all his four-legged stock.

But the wagon could not be broken by all the bucking and plunging and kicking—the chain harness had refused to give way—and the iron singletrees had refused to snap. The mustangs might have tied themselves into as many knots as they chose, but when they got through fighting, the driver still sat on the seat above them, long-lashed whip in hand, and with whip and voice he had urged them back toward quiet behavior and good sense. If they tried, finally, to bolt to freedom, the huge brakes of the vehicle dragged the wheels until they had had enough of plowing it through the soft sand. And if they chose to balk, they were whipped until the blood spurted. In this fashion, every horse, as Gonzalez swore, had been harnessed at least four times to the iron wagon and handled with whip and with rein.

"And every team had to pull that wagon two mile, *señor*," Gonzalez informed Sammy. "Oh, yes, these very gentle, now."

Sammy might have his doubt of that. Whatever lessons might have been taught, they seemed to have lapsed back into their native wildness quickly enough on the northward drive to Munson. But at any rate, he accepted the mustangs—he could do nothing else—scattered them in groups along the route at the relay stations, and prepared to make the first trip across the mountains in his stage line, while Gonzalez returned to hurry up the second installment of the horses that were already on the way.

It was an anxious time for Sammy Gregg. He had invested $7,500 in horses alone. He had paid out $1,500 in wages for the building of his relay shacks and sleeping houses. He had spent another $2,500 for harness. It was strong harness, but the price was life's blood from Sammy Gregg. And beyond all that, he had invested $1,000 in the odds and ends of the necessities—such as the coaches themselves.

Before the first coach ran, he had spent close to $13,000, and he had not yet received a single penny in return. Well for Sammy Gregg that he had already been through that Western school of investment.

He had a scant $3,000 in his pocket when he saw the team picked for the first run from Munson into the wilds. And he saw the first return on his labor and his capital, too. Ten men, he estimated, would be in each load, and men were willing to pay $25 a throw to be whirled across those mountains in a single day and a half. $250 for each trip for human passengers alone, to say nothing of what would be paid for the other freight—perhaps another $250. For every journey, then, $500.

As a matter of fact, $650 was paid into the hands of Sammy's Munson ticket agent for the first loaded coach.

Chapter Twenty

So, with the four stages all in operation, Sammy saw himself clearing $700 to $800 at least. Perhaps much, much more. And those were days, be it remembered, when money meant from three to five times what it means to the giddy 1900s.

Oh, Sammy Gregg, those were moments of golden anticipation more thrilling than any reality. Those were the days to build dreams in the millions. Granted that the high prices could not be maintained indefinitely and that he must reduce his rates before a competing line entered—now that he had shown that the trick could be turned—granted all of that, still he would have a sweet harvest. In a fortnight, all his capital would be returned to his pocket and he would have a handsome profit besides.

Such were the stakes for which men gambled in those days.

However, this was the prospect. Now he was to make the trial of the fact. He had ten passengers, and all the luggage and freight that his coach could groan under. And the day for the trial came. Nine men and one woman advanced to enter the coach. And upon the driver's seat sat the gray-headed driver and Sammy. Nine men and one woman, by whom there hung a story told in a letter that Sammy at that moment had in his pocket. It read thus:

Dear Mr. Gregg: I am making reservations in your coach, which leaves Munson on Tuesday, for my daughter, Miss Anne Cosden, who arrives from the East on that day.

She is a headstrong young person who refuses to wait until I can come to Munson to escort her over the mountains in person. She has formed a mad scheme for riding—alone—the trail from Munson to the lode.

I have managed to dissuade her from that by suggesting a compromise. That compromise is your stage line. Forgive me for saying that I look forward to her ride over those back-breaking mountains in an unproved stage line with hardly less apprehension than if she were riding a pony alone through that wilderness.

Nothing but the pressure of the most vastly important business and the interests of my stockholders prevents me from coming to Munson to act as her escort. As it is, I must leave her in your hands, knowing that she will receive the best of treatment from you.

That was the important part of the letter. And Sammy, seeing himself with an only child, a headstrong but none the less precious darling of a millionaire miner's heart put into his hands, had even done his best to select the remaining nine passengers from among the least rough of the applicants.

Then he besought his driver, a bewhiskered buccaneer named Alec, to select from the herd at Munson the gentlest of the lot for the first trip. Alec gave him his oath that he would do so.

"But," Alec said, "when it comes to goin' over a pack of powder and pickin' out the grains that are not gonna explode, it's a sort of a hard job, even with a microscope, Mister Gregg. But I'm gonna go over that lot of broncos with a microscope and see which I can pick out."

So Alec had done his best. For a whole day he had mingled with the Munson herd to pick out the gentlest horses of the lot, and now he was prepared to venture them in the harness where the lives of ten persons or more would be dangled at their flying heels.

The day before the starting time, the only child of Hubert Cosden, miner and millionaire extraordinary, arrived in Munson. And Sammy, introducing himself to this perishable creature for whom her father worried, was struck with dismay.

"Into his hands" the charge had been given. And what a charge. She stood not half an inch shorter than Sammy. And her pompadoured hair and a woman's carriage made her look a great deal larger than he. She had, besides, a certain manner that made Sammy shrink in self-esteem and importance.

But generalizations about Anne Cosden could never give more than the vaguest idea about her. She had lived nineteen years and a few months as the daughter of one of the rich and important men in the country. She weighed a hundred and forty-five solid pounds. Her foot took a woman's size number eight—made large in every dimension. Her hand took a glove equally ample. She had red hair. There are kinds and kinds of red hair. Once upon a time all hair that was red was laughed at. And every red-headed person was hailed as "Brick Top" in youth. Then some genius invented a softer term—auburn. Who says that a rose by any other name would smell as sweet? The sheer influence of a word made a hair color popular, and brown-haired ladies straightway invested in uncertain dyes.

However, the hair of Anne Cosden was not of the kind that could be softened with any pretty name. It was red—plain, unadulterated red. It was flaring, flaming red. Brick red. And it could not be disguised. There were silken tides and misty oceans of it.

Beneath a low, broad brow—the brow of philosophers and prize fighters—was set a pair of eyes to match the hair. Blue eyes, that is to say. For all who have seen Irish red hair will know that Irish blue eyes are needed. No, not Irish blue, for that is dark and rich. But the blue of the eyes of Anne Cosden was pale, and liable to take fire—just as her hair would take fire in the sunlight.

She had a good square chin that would have taken a considerable pounding without complaint. And there was a faint cleft in the center of it. I do not know what a cleft in the chin is supposed to mean. But the cleft in the chin of Anne Cosden meant something ominous.

She was as straight as an arrow. And that is always a little disconcerting in a woman—especially for a small man, like Sammy. When he met her, he tried to make the most of his inches. But he felt that he was just about half a foot short of making any sort of an impression on her.

She had an uncertain voice. That is to say, it was a voice with one of those large, large ranges. And one never knew just what section of her range she would choose to use. She had a gruff tone, for instance, that was almost as deep as the voice of a man. And she had a mellow midway tone in which she could talk and laugh and sing, when she felt so inclined. And she had a higher register as snarling and thin and edgy as the blast of a bugle. And she had, also, a roar—a lion's roar. Or a lioness, if you please.

In fact, as the people of Munson were instantly willing to admit, when they saw the young lady step off the train, she was a "considerable person."

Yet she remained a girl. She was as distinctly feminine as she was distinctly a person. On the side of that leonine head there was set an ear made of the most exquisite pale shell-pink and ivory. Her hand had size enough and there were callouses on the inside from driving and riding lunging thoroughbreds, but still it was a long hand, made with consummate grace. And although she wore a flat-heeled, blunt-nosed shoe, not even a blind man would have taken that for a man's shoe.

The first thing that Anne Cosden did when she got to Munson was to ask for a horse, because she wanted to have a look at the country around, having been, as she said, entombed in a train longer than she had ever been shut off from fresh air before. But when she asked the hotel proprietor where she could get a horse, he rubbed the stubble on his chin and announced that there were no ladies' horses in that section of the country.

"Heavens, man," said Anne Cosden, "I've never ridden a lady's horse in my life. Get me a man's horse. A man-size horse, too."

The proprietor was a fellow with a mean disposition, and though it is most generally understood that no Westerner will take advantage of a lady, you can't count hotel proprietors as typical of the land. He had a big rangy black, wild-caught, at four years of age on the range. And as everybody knows, a horse that has run wild on a Western range for four years is the devil's twin brother, if not the devil himself. However, the proprietor introduced her to the horse and she liked the looks of it so well that she bought it on the spot. And the hotel man charged her $100 which, considering that it had to be broken over again every day of its life, was robbery. Five minutes later Anne Cosden was on the back of the black horse, Charlie.

"I don't care what kind of a saddle," she had said.

Five seconds later, Anne lay on her back in the dust of the corral. And Charlie would have prepared her for her grave, then and there, had she not recovered her wits soon enough to roll under the lowest bar of the fence. She picked herself up in sections, so to speak, and shook some of the dust out of her hair— her hat was reposing in the corral, and Charlie was busy doing to the hat the things he would have liked to do to the mistress thereof.

But, a little later, Anne was in the saddle again. Three times she mounted with some pain. Three times she was deposited in the thick dust, but each time Charlie found the task of shedding her a little harder. The fourth time, while half a dozen men stood by in gaping wonder, Anne Cosden fairly rode the black out of his bad graces and into his good ones. Then she brought him up standing on the curb. She parted her lips and the lion's voice roared forth: "Yank open that gate. I'm going to give this little lamb some air!"

Five hours later she returned to Munson. When she dismounted, it was noticed that she walked with a limp, but so did Charlie.

"I had a bully ride, and it's a great country," Anne Cosden announced. "Did you know that Charlie could jump? Yes, a regular fencer. I'm going to take him home and hunt him this fall. I don't think he'll buck any more."

And he didn't—never again.

Such was the Anne Cosden who Sammy Gregg handed to a place in the stage on this historic day, while the horses were being harnessed in their places.

"I hope," she said, "that there are enough level places for the horses to take a gallop, now and then. This hot air needs to be churned up a little."

A little dried-up man with far-away eyes murmured: "I don't know that they'll wait for the level going . . . exactly."

Chapter Twenty-One

In fact, those horses did not look to be the waiting type as they were produced from the corral. Produced is the word. They were not led forth, neither were they driven. But, since men were plentiful in Munson, the wise old driver distributed three or four men to every horse. And three or four more or less expert wranglers can usually make the worst of horses behave. Also, a half hitch taken in the long upper lip of a mustang is apt to make him mind his manners for the time being. So, pushed, dragged, and beaten into place, the horses were lined up—the six safest horses in the possession of Sammy Gregg.

They looked a little less dangerous than lions. They looked a little less happy than hornets.

The traces were hooked to the chains, and the chains to the singletrees. The horses were straightened out. The leaders took up the slack of the fifth chain. The swing pair leaned into the collar to straighten the tongue of the wagon. Alec gathered the six stout reins in his hands. He loosened the long brake with his foot. He shook out the deadly length of his whip, with which he could cut a horsefly off the hip of a leader without touching the skin of the animal.

"All right," Alec said. "Yank off them blinds." And the blindfolds were removed. "Steady, boys," Alec said gently. "Lean into them collars, pets. Hey, you, Blackie! Git back onto your own feet. Now. . . ." The rest of Alec's language soared from the earth and took wings to fiery regions. For the off-leader saw

133

something about the make-up of the near-leader that he did not like and at once he proceeded, literally, to "climb his frame". He gathered himself and tried to leap on top of his harness mate and bite the top of his neck off at the same time.

The near-leader, objecting, backed up to get out of the way and jammed his rump into the nose of the near swing-horse. And the near swing-horse, being a cannon that shot in one direction only, resented this freedom by kicking the near-wheeler in the nose.

Whereat the near-wheeler jumped over the tongue and bit the shoulder of the off-wheeler, who planted his heels in the body of the coach and then tried to jump through his collar. Which disturbed the off-swing, which, like a jack rabbit, turned end for end in his harness to find out what the trouble was all about.

And that was only the beginning of the affair.

Little Sammy Gregg, seeing six horses and his hopes of a fortune going to wrack, uttered a shout that was almost a scream.

A stern voice behind him rumbled: "Keep quiet, little man. You'll scare the horses."

He turned his head and had a vague glimpse of Anne Cosden. The face of the millionaire's daughter was a study in contempt. But Sammy, at that instant, did not care. He was merely thinking that he had paid $1,300 for the privilege of seeing six mustangs kick a daydream into atoms and make a frontier town dissolve in laughter.

However, they did not laugh themselves to helplessness. Before the six mustangs had smashed each other to a pulp, a crowd of staggering, shouting wranglers leaped at their heads. There was a wild uproar. Presently six horses lay on the ground with their heads pinned down under the weight of men.

In the tremulous silence that followed, Sammy announced in

a voice that fitted in with the pause: "I'm afraid we can't make the start today, gentlemen."

"Nonsense," the strong voice of Anne Cosden declared. "The fun is barely starting, and none of us would miss the ride for a thousand dollars."

Two young men, who were about to slide over the back of the coach and drop to safe *terra firma*, heard that calm announcement and sneaked back into their places, where they sat quivering, hoping that no one had seen them. And the rest of the passengers began to lift their heads from their bristling coat collars and look about as though wondering how they could still be intact.

Sammy was silenced, but his dismay was not the less.

It was Alec who spoke. "The lady wants to go on with the party," he said. "Lemme get down and see how many patches we'll have to make."

There were not so very many, after all. One singletree, tough hickory though it was, had been twisted neatly in two. And there were some broken straps about the harness, here and there. However, the omnipresent baling wire repaired those breakages, and presently the horses were dragged to their feet. The broken singletree was replaced.

"Hold hard," Alec cautioned. "I'm going to see if I can't scare these boys into a little run."

So, when the blindfolds were removed, he whirled his whip, cracked the long lash, scourged each of the six, apparently, with one and the same movement of the lash, and uttered a ferocious scream. The six mustangs swung of one accord, curled like a snake, caught the coach with an abrupt cross pull, and yanked it flat upon its side.

Sammy Gregg, being the lightest missile, sailed the farthest. He found himself pausing for an instant astraddle of the back of the off-leader. But from that point of vantage he was presently

135

bucked into space again and landed once more—this time in a group of bystanders. When his senses came back to him, he saw the fat man in whose stomach his head had been buried, sitting with a stricken look where he had fallen. The rest of the crowd was busy righting the team and the coach. And the leader in the good work was Anne Cosden.

Munson had wrecked the second hat that she had ventured to wear there. It sat now—or a fragment of it sat—atilt on one side of her head, and half of her bright red hair had slipped out and tumbled down her back. But she held the refractory off-leader securely by the nose, twisting his upper lip until the agony made him tame.

"The third go will bring us luck, boys!" Anne Cosden sang out. "Drag out the baggage and heave the old wagon up on her legs once more. There's enough of you to do it!"

There was not a member of the party—not even Alec—who would not have relinquished all thoughts of the trip for that day, at the least. But men cannot let women see the white feather in their hats.

Sammy Gregg, shaken from his fall and weak-kneed with terror, set doggedly about doing his share. And as he struggled with the head of the near-leader he heard her singing out encouragingly: "Get him by the nose . . . and twist!"

The near-leader was pacified at last.

"That was a bad fall you got," Anne Cosden said good-naturedly. "I thought you'd never stop sailing."

"Where were you, to watch?"

"Sailing, too," Anne replied, grinning. "But I happened to land in a thick spot of dust, so I'm all right . . . seems to have shaken you up a bit, though."

"I'm not hurt," said Sammy, who believed in the truth. "But I'm scared . . . almost to death. And so are the rest of 'em . . . except that you've shamed them out of it."

She looked at him in amazement. It was the first time in her life that she had heard a man admit fear. And for that reason, I suppose, she suddenly liked Sammy.

"You're the owner of this mess, aren't you?" she asked.

"Yes. I put up for it."

"Cheer up," Anne said sympathetically. "A rainy morning makes a good fox hunt. And we'll be in at the kill in Crumbock, after all. There . . . they've got the coach up."

Thirty pairs of willing, heaving, struggling arms had managed that trick, and the stage, stripped of baggage, was bolstered up—then rocked suddenly into an erect position. Minus a little paint, it was otherwise unharmed. For those wise Yankee brains and hands that planned and built the wagon had made it like a ship that is meant to travel through stormy seas. Not a spoke of a single wheel had been sprained. Not a single board had been broken. She was as sound as when the first attempt had been made to start the coach.

Once more the baggage was piled in. The wan and silent passengers, each with a covert eye upon this slave-driving girl, climbed to their places. The blindfolds were snapped from the six heads, and once more Alec rose to his task. A little streak of crimson was dashed like war paint upon one cheek. He was covered with dust, but covered with courage, also. And the terrible lash of his whip cut a thin, deep gash in the hip of the boisterous off-leader.

That told the tale. With a wild snort—half grunt and half neigh—that was a true stampede signal, the off-leader hit his collar with a weight that made the fifth chain groan, and the rest of the clan, true to their breed, answered the stampede signal by stretching their heads forth and striving to squeeze through their collars.

In another instant the coach was shooting down the street of Munson. The dust cloud rose high behind it. It swung out of sight, cutting the first corner on two wheels, and the dust cloud, still rising, spread broad, moth-like wings behind and still soared dimmer and dimmer above the roofs of Munson.

"There'll be eleven dead men and one dead woman before that trip is finished," Rendell opined.

"No," said another. "She'll get to Crumbock if she has to make it riding bareback on that devil of an off-leader." Which was the general opinion in Munson.

The first mile of that journey was enough to turn hair white, even on the head of a hero. Six flying, straining, wild horses whirled the stage over what was called a road in that part of the country. There were rocks like great teeth ready to spike the stage as it passed. And there were ruts eager to break wheels, and hummocks guaranteed to overturn the wagon. But still Alec managed to shave the edge of these dangers one after another until the first steep grade was reached.

Then there was a different story. For behind the heels of the wild horses there were two tons of weight, living and dead. A trifle on the level, but a very great deal to whip up a sharp gradient. So the six slowed abruptly from a gallop to a trot, and from a trot to a walk. And then they would willingly have stopped altogether, but the whip in the hands of Alec was a sword of fire, and when they tried to jump out of the way, their collars were hands of steel. So the stage lurched heavily on its way.

CHAPTER TWENTY-TWO

The six wild horses that had been harnessed to the stage at Munson were only the pick of the whole lot. There were other sets to be hitched to the stage before it was rolled into the dirty streets of Crumbock. And the other sets were a sketchy lot—the first that came to hand at any of the stations of relay along the way.

Needless to say, the stage on its first run was not on time. They averaged exactly one hour of time to make each change of horses. And, when the change was made, there was a fearful rushing through the hills. But still the stage rolled on its way, and no matter what else happened, it was not again overturned.

At two relay points from Munson they came to the rougher region of mountains, and there, at the second relay from Munson, Sammy Gregg had arranged an escort of honor, so to speak. Because the progress of this first stage through the mountains was apt to be a dangerous affair.

The outlaw who first stuck up the new stage was apt to be remembered long, and for that very reason there was apt to be a good deal of crowding for the post. In the stage itself there were means of defense. In the first place, there was hardly a passenger, outside of Sammy, who did not carry a gun, and most of them were supposed to know how to use their weapons—while old Alec on the driver's seat had a sawed-off shotgun hanging in a leather noose by his leg. It was a monstrous old brute of a weapon, fit to have served as an elephant gun, and in its two enormous barrels there was poured a fair double handful of slugs of various sizes.

"From toothpicks to marbles," Alec was fond of saying, "this here old gun don't much care what it shoots."

Of course such a weapon was of no more use than a hand sling at any distance. But at short range, it was accurate enough. No great degree of accuracy, indeed, can be demanded of a hose. And like a hose was that historic weapon of Alec's. Its great sluicing discharge had been of proved usefulness, also. Three times in his career the stages that Alec drove had been stopped by desperadoes, and it was the glorious record of Alec that he had beaten off every attack. Three dead men had been left behind him, filled with sundry queer fragments that had been belched from the muzzles of his mighty weapon.

"It'll cover the whole width of the road," Alec would say "and sweep a whole company clean away. I'd walk up to a regiment of tigers with this here gun and sass 'em back right in their own language, boss."

That was not all. There were many valuables in the cargo aboard that stage, and the temptation to stop it was apt to prove too much for the gentlemen of the road. So, at the second relay, Sammy had hired two men of wide repute for their skill with shooting irons of all kinds.

Lester and Andrew Gunn were men who had stayed within the limits of the law for only one good reason—which was that the law had never happened to be looking very hard their way during certain interesting moments in their lives. Ten years before they were on the way to making quite a reputation for themselves and decorating the noose of a lynching party's rope, someday, when a certain famous sheriff took the trouble to read them a lecture on the law, its ways and means. They took that lecture so much to heart, that they had decided upon the spot to follow his good advice, and, from that time forth, they became strict adherents to the party of peace. Because, as some cruelly said, they already had had their fun.

But they could shoot just as straight as ever, and at various times, always side-by-side in every pinch, they had demonstrated their willingness to support the nearest sheriff as deputies. Such men were sure to be known and dreaded. And so, by reputation, they had become known to Sammy Gregg.

You may be sure that he did not hire them because he liked them. There was not a man in the mountains, for that matter, who would have owned himself a friend to the Gunn brothers. Their narrow, swarthy faces and little animal-like black eyes warned all beholders that they were brutes of the lowest type— without nerves or consciences to trouble them. They looked, in short, exactly what they were—hired gunfighters.

Even the steady composure of Anne Cosden was shaken not a little when she was told that this dismal couple was to act as guards to the stage. But they jogged on ahead of the coach and most of the time they did not spoil the view with their presence. They were always just around the next curve of the trail that the freighters had carved deep, even in the rocks. A very efficient couple, no doubt, and their services for this single day had cost Sammy Gregg $50, heart-felt.

"For one day?" he had cried at them in surprise.

"You never can tell," Lester Gunn had answered. "It might be our last day. And a gent's last day is worth something extra . . . for funeral expenses, you might say."

That grim joke settled the question. "If someone tackles them . . . we hear the trouble and can get ready," Sammy explained to Miss Cosden, "and if they tackle us first, the Gunn brothers will hear the racket and they can come back to us. You see, it works both ways."

Miss Cosden looked him fairly in the eye. "Yes," she said, "if all the men on the stage are willing to fight."

Sammy turned a bright crimson. But his eye did not flinch from hers. "I'm no hero," he said. "And I don't know anything about guns. But the other men on the stage have weapons and they can use them well enough."

She shrugged her shoulders. "I don't know," Anne Cosden said, "but I've heard that a rifle has a very quieting effect . . . if the man behind it has the drop. However, we won't have any trouble. The old days of road agents are done with. This is modern life."

It is usually that way. All evil belongs to the dark days of the past. The present lies in a white sunlight of innocence and freedom from wrong.

The afternoon wore out. The sun was no longer an intolerable lump of white fire. It was a dazzling golden ball dropping little by little toward the blue tops of the western peaks. A little more, and the evening was coming on them. Have you seen the evening come over the mountains, ever? It is a thing to see and never to forget. For in the mountains, the evening seems to come in two ways. First, it is cropping out of the sky. Secondly, it is rising out of the deep valleys like a dark, cool mist.

Every time the stage dipped into a hollow the world seemed already more than half lost to the night, and every time it rocked up onto a high point, the world seemed saved to a beautiful part of the day, still. So they wavered up and down the trail, between darkness and light.

It was as the stage mounted to the top of one of these many knolls that Andrew Gunn was heard to cry out in a sharp, snarling voice, and then there was a loud, rapid blur of shots. Just an instant of gunfire, you understand—a single second packed with the crackle of musketry. And then a dizzying silence.

"Jiminy!" Old Alec grinned as his hand relaxed from the reins that he had begun to draw taut, and as he lowered again the terrible muzzle of the sawed-off shotgun that he had jerked up at the first alarm. "I thought for just a minute that it was . . . but I suppose the boys just seen a rabbit or something like. . . ."

And just then Sammy, looking half worried ahead of the nodding ears of the leaders of the stage, saw a beautiful big gray horse covered with a mottling of large dapples step into view around that corner of the road where the Gunn brothers had disappeared. And next he saw big Chester Ormonde Furness.

There was no mask upon Furness this time. Perhaps he had decided that he and his horse and his ways were becoming so well known that it was useless to try the masking game any more. Perhaps he was tired of it. Perhaps, and this is indeed the most likely of all, he simply wanted a new thrill, and therefore he was letting himself be identified with that sort of a crime that hangs the criminal when he is caught. The old way was so safe, so dull, that it would not serve any longer.

But, most significant detail of all—and the first detail for everyone on that stagecoach to see—there was a beautiful, long-barreled repeating rifle cuddled into the hollow of the shoulder of Furness and his head was leaned a little to one side, as though he were whispering loving words to the breech of his gun. He was steady as a veritable rock. There was not a glimmer of waving light as the barrel of that gun steadied upon the top of the stagecoach.

Those practiced eyes that beheld this tableau understood the meaning of that steadiness. Instantly there was a forest of arms upon the top of the vehicle—a stiff-standing forest raised just as high as possible above the heads of the travelers, and the arms of Sammy Gregg were almost the first up.

Even old Alec knew that he had been beaten at last, and he did not more than half raise the shotgun that was his pride. Instead, he let the muzzle sink by degrees while he moaned: "Oh, my Lord, if I'd only taken the first think more serious . . . if I'd only played that first hunch . . . the first hunch always bein' the only good one when it comes to guns."

The last part of this remark was torn from his lips by the explosion of a revolver just behind his head. For there was one person in the stage who had not thrust up hands at the summons. And now there was one revolver leveled at big, handsome Chester Furness. Not a big black Colt .45. This was a more refined .32-caliber pistol with a pearl pair of handles and a beautifully burnished octagonal barrel.

"One of them kind that pricks you pretty bad, but mostly never does no killing," as a Westerner would have expressed it. Whereas a blunt-nosed .45, if it does not kill the victim, will probably knock him quite flat like the blow of a fist.

Now, however, this little .32 was thrust out and twice it exploded. And the broad-brimmed hat leaped from the head of Furness and exposed his fine features to the light of the late day. She had shot the sombrero fairly from its place.

Then one of Gregg's hands descended, brutally hard, and the thin, hard edge of his palm struck her wrist and turned all the nerves in her hand dead, and made the six-shooter and its four unfired bullets drop into the dust.

"You idiot!" the girl cried to him. "How did you dare . . . ?"

She did not complete the sentence. For just then big Furness spoke, and the sound of his voice made all other things seem unimportant.

"Madame," he said, "I thought you were about to do a murder, but I'm glad that it is not to be on your conscience. Thank you, Sammy."

CHAPTER TWENTY-THREE

Cool? Yes, it was very cool, and he looked fully as calm as his words, and about ten times handsomer and bigger and stronger and more deadly than anything that had ever come across the path of anyone in that stage—including Miss Anne Cosden among the rest.

His gun, you see, had not wavered for an instant. And yet neither of her bullets had missed him. Her second shot, obviously, had torn the hat from his head. And now it was seen that her first slug had touched his cheek, which, when you come down to it, is not half bad practice for a girl doing snap shooting from the wavering top of a big, lumbering stage.

One could not tell how badly he was hurt. Just scratched, perhaps. But there was a visible stream of crimson working its way down the side of his face. It was a staggering thing to her. It was even more staggering to the rest of the men on the coach, for they all had heard of this man and most of them had seen him. There had been talk about him, rather naturally, during this very journey toward the hills. By a common assent, he was put down as the cruelest, coldest-hearted devil that ever threw a leg over a saddle west of the Mississippi. Which is another way of saying that a worse man was never born, for other men could commit crimes and live unplagued by any conscience, but it required a perfect uniqueness to revel in his work and dare to appear in a town, as the big fellow had done, and expose two of his latest victims to the public gaze, together with a sneering story of his own manufacture.

However, here he was now, allowing a woman to nick his head with one bullet and knock his hat off with another, without making a movement to fire back at her. And I think, for all the boasted chivalry in the West—and certainly there is plenty of it there—there is no record of a man laying down his life so that a girl may have the convenience of his head as a target for her practice.

Yes, it took the breath from every man on the stage, and it took the breath of Anne Cosden's own fierce self, the moment she heard him speak. I suppose it made it a little more poignant to her—the fact that he spoke in a pure grammar with the voice of a cultivated man. He was one of her own class. A villain, beyond the slightest shadow of a doubt, he was nevertheless a gentleman and a hero as well. He had just demonstrated that fact twice over.

Anne Cosden sank into her place, and she was trembling. Almost for the first time in her life she was trembling. And it was fear, too, that made her tremble—not the thought that she had almost taken this man's life. Indeed, I think there was a hot wish in her heart that she *had* killed him. Because now he had filled her with a chilly dread unlike anything she had ever dreamed of before. And she leaned a little forward, gaping at him in a most unromantic and ungraceful way—and the beauty of that fine face and head of his sank upon her eyes and upon her heart—and his smile—and the dark shining of his eyes as he looked up to her—and the quiet music of his voice. . . .

Yes, she wished that one of those bullets had gone a little lower, or a little more to one side. Poor Anne Cosden.

Then, from beyond the curve of the road, for the first time, she and the rest heard a low-pitched, stifled groaning. Not one voice, but two—the sick, weak, bubbling groaning of a very badly wounded man.

Have you ever heard that sound? It will make a hospital ward turn pea-green in an instant; it makes even a doctor need a drink. And it drained the very last thought of resistance—if they had any in the first place—out of the systems of the men in that stage.

They obeyed in the most perfectly regular fashion, doing as he directed them to do. They climbed down to the road and stood there in the gathering chill of the evening, listening.

He said to the girl as she got to the ground. "Will you run to take a look at those two poor fellows? I don't think they're as badly hit as they sound."

She gave him a nod. And as she went by, he trailed his glance quietly over her—and her eyes went wide under the touch of his, and how far he looked into her heart she dared not guess. But she ran down the road, and there she found her hands filled with work—gruesome work enough, at that.

Furness carried his rifle carelessly tucked under one arm. And yet it was held as lightly and as firmly and as surely, it seemed, as though he had gripped it in both strong hands. Also, his right forefinger was curled constantly about the trigger, and everyone in the group knew perfectly well that that finger was not there for nothing.

He lined up the passengers with their faces to the side of the road. Then he went behind them and frisked their pockets. A neat little haul even for a Furness. Not so much as he would have taken, you would think, from a crowd coming back from the mines. But, as a matter of fact, there were no fewer than three professional gamblers in that shipment, and from them alone, on their way to work the rich gold diggings in their own peculiar fashion, he took more than $14,000 in cash. There was that much more taken from the rest of the group. And now he paused behind Sammy Gregg.

"I suppose," he said, "that you have a pretty considerable

wad of money in your pocket, for a payroll, and what not. But I really don't see how I can take from a man who brings me so many excellent customers. It would hardly be considered good etiquette, on the road. Do you think?" And he laughed, did Furness, and swung onto his gray horse with a movement so swift that even if they had had eyes in the backs of their heads, they would hardly have been able to seize the right moment to whirl and shoot. Also, their guns had been thrown in the middle of the road by his foresight.

He backed his gray stallion up the road. How beautiful and proudly disdainful that glorious creature seemed as he pranced in that fashion, backward, obeying the will of his master, but not his hand. "After I am around the corner," he advised the party, "it will be safe for you to move, but not before, if you please. And remember, my friends, that this is a rifle that I carry under my arm . . . not a revolver, you know. So . . . if you want to hunt me up . . . don't tread too close upon my heels, because you might have your toes barked."

And then, there he was at the corner, and around it in a flash with the big horse. He paused beside the girl. And she was a changed sight.

She was dabbled with crimson from head to foot, and she was quite white with the sight of so much of it. But she stuck to her work. Good work, too. It pays those who hunt and ride to understand first aid, and Anne Cosden had learned her lesson well. She was making every touch count, and every touch was dragging those two wretches farther and farther from the shadow of death. Yes, there was Andrew already bandaged. The deadly running of the crimson had been stopped. But still his eyes were closed and his pale forehead was puckered as it had been when he felt the strength of his life leaking swiftly out from him—ebbing away in great pulses. And now Lester Gunn was being saved.

Furness stooped from the saddle above her. And he saw her shrink and shudder beneath the sense of his nearness. He undid with the deft tips of his fingers a clasp that secured a delicate little gold chain around her neck. There was only a little ornamental locket at the end of it. And she, with both her hands employed, merely said without raising her head: "It's worth nothing in money. I'll pay you to leave that with me, Mister Furness."

"I have to have it," he said. "I don't know just what it may mean to you, but I'm certain that it can't mean so much to you as it does to me."

Only that—and then the stinging dust spurned into a cloud before her face as the stallion's hoofs bit strongly at the road and shot him away at full speed from that standing start. Away down the road, swiftly, swiftly. And, from the corner, a crackling of guns to pursue him. She paid no heed to those guns. She did not even look up to see the result, for she knew he was safe. No man such as those in that stage could touch the life of this hero of the mountains, for she felt that he controlled his own destiny as surely as though it lay in the palm of his hand.

They left the Gunn brothers there by the roadside. Two men volunteered to stay with them as nurses. Bedding was placed for them, and provisions, and the promise given that more help would be rushed back from the next relay station, only three miles away. And so the stage rolled on.

No one did very much talking. Alec, because, with an aching heart, he was thinking of younger days, when his hands would not have been so slow in yanking up that sawed-off shotgun to fire. And the other men were silent because some of them had lost much money. All of them, too, were a little depressed, just as chickens, which fill a yard will cackle sharply when they see the topping hawk, and then are all hushed and still, and waiting for a long time after the sliding shadow has passed away.

But Anne Cosden, sitting with bowed head, paid no heed even now to the terrible red stains on her clothes. But she rubbed slowly, patiently a red mark upon her wrist. It was where the edge of the palm of little Sammy Gregg had struck her.

He, sitting beside her, could not help noticing. And he said softly, at last: "I'm sorry. I needn't have hit you so hard, I suppose."

She raised blank eyes to him. It was as though he were miles away and she were staring to find a trace of him and his meaning. "Oh," said Anne Cosden, "I wasn't thinking of that."

What was she thinking of? Sammy Gregg was not a fool, and now he had something unusual working in his heart and head to stimulate him, so that he guessed well enough what it was. For there was everything about big Furness to make him a woman's hero, thought Sammy. Size, courage, and that wonderful beauty of face, and above all the strangeness of soul in which he was wrapped. What, in contrast, was there in such a man as Sammy himself, and his wretched inches, and his starved body, and his unheroic soul?

She need not have said any more, for Sammy was already perfectly convinced. But how was she, being what she was, apt to guess that this small creature was following the windings of her soul? So she said aloud, but more to herself than to him: "No, I'm glad that you thought quickly enough to strike my hand down. Otherwise . . . I . . . I might have . . . killed him. Think of it!"

Was not Sammy thinking?

CHAPTER TWENTY-FOUR

If anyone could have said to Sammy Gregg that there could have come into his life, on that day, a thing greater than the stage line, he would have laughed them to scorn. But before they reached Crumbock on the next day—close to midnight— Sammy had been forced to confess to his heart of hearts that he loved that big, noisy, stalwart Anne Cosden more than he loved any other thing in the world. More, even, than he cared for the stage line and its success.

Of course, it was a wretched confession to make, because he knew he had never a chance of winning her. He was ashamed of himself for being so absurd as to desire her, and he hoped, in his shrinking heart of hearts, that no one would ever guess at his secret. He had a miserable sense of guilt, when he saw big Hubert Cosden meet his daughter when the stage arrived under the big lanterns that illumined Sammy's Crumbock terminal. What if she should tell her father something of the things that had happened during the ride—no, not the ridiculous maneuvers at the start, but what had gone on inside her spirit when she sat on the top of the coach and looked down to the handsome face of big Chester Ormonde Furness?

However, there was some spark of joy for him. And that was the furor that Crumbock raised over him and his stage. To be sure, it was just half a day late, and it had been robbed on the way. But those, they assured him, were unlucky incidents that might happen to anyone.

Sammy stayed in Crumbock for a while. He told himself, miserably, that it was because he wanted to work up the business at that most important end of the line—as though business *needed* any working up. But, in reality, he knew that it was because he wanted to be close to Anne Cosden.

In a week, the four coaches were working steadily, and all the three hundred horses were being worked in turn. Aye, and a hurry call was sent to Gonzalez for more. And the dollars began to flow steadily into the pockets of Sammy, where they were needed so much.

In the first seven days, he cleared $6,000—which gave some idea of how badly that stage line was needed at Crumbock. And during that first week nothing went wrong. There was not a single hold-up. There was not so much as a broken axle. And even the terrible mustangs from the Southland, once they had had a single turn at the work, became a smaller nuisance. Their deviltry was exhausted by their work, just as it should have been.

On the eighth day there was the first sign of impending trouble. The northbound stage rolled into Crumbock bearing two extra passengers, in the form of the bodies of two would-be stage robbers.

It was old Alec and his sawed-off shotgun, again. The old fellow was so proud of himself and his gun that he couldn't help telling over and over again how it happened.

"I seen a winkin' and a quiverin' of the leaves in a couple of bushes on a bank, over the road. I says to myself . . . 'There ain't wind enough to make that stir. Them there ain't no tremblin' aspens nor poplar, nor nothin'.' And then I looked right close, and sort of inside the shadow of the greenery, I could see the outline of a pair of gents waitin' there. And I sort of slipped my hand down on the old gun and got her ready, you might say. Sort of done it automatic. And just then the bushes was busted open and a couple of yaps jumped out with their guns at the ready. And they was yellin' . . . 'Stick up yuhr hands . . . *pronto!*' Well, sir, I just swiveled the old cannon around and pulled both the triggers. Kick? Well, sir, I sure enough thought that my old arm was tore off at the shoulder. But them two rascals on the bank, they was tore right off at the foot, you can believe me, and they was throwed away into the scrap heap forever. They was sluiced right out of this here life and neither one of them didn't feel a thing. It was plumb merciful, that was. I'd like to die that way myself. They was just killed in about ten places, each of 'em. And when I meet up with Mister Chester Furness the next time, you can lay to it that he's gonna remember the day for a long time."

Poor Alec.

On the very next day he insisted on driving the stage back again, instead of taking his lay-off. "You got to have one man," Alec said, "that's able to bring these here stages through all safe. And I reckon that I'm just about that man."

Poor Alec.

He got just three miles outside of Crumbock—hardly over the first rising range to the south, when a familiar form on a glorious dappled stallion rode out before the coach, a rifle at the ready. Alec reached for the mighty cannon, but as his hand fell on it, a bullet tore through his shoulder.

And Furness lined up the passengers beside the road once more. He even paused to give kind words to Alec. "But after all," Furness said in conclusion, "you're a little too old to be playing a hand in this game."

But the loss of Alec was only one thing. In that stage there was the first shipment of gold that had been entrusted to the new line. Fifty pounds of dust, or more than $16,000 in value. And it was lost with the rest of the plunder. How much was taken from the belts of the men no one could more than guess, for each one put a pretty high estimate on his losses.

However, it was a pretty bad loss to the miners, and it hit the reputation of the stage line pretty hard. One robbery was to be expected. It gave expectation and spice to a ride over the line, one might say, but two robberies, and a third attempted, all within the space of eight days, was a little too much. There was a lot of disagreeable talk in Crumbock, and Sammy knew from afar that the same sort of talk was going the rounds in Munson.

Yet the patronage of the line did not fall off. Men still bought tickets, but they bought them with doubtful frowns, and the doubtful frowns were still worn all the way to the end of the trail.

On the tenth day three worthies attempted to stop the southbound coach. They were armed with rifles, and they got the drop. But it happened that that stage was crammed with a dozen young men who had *not* filled their pockets with gold at Crumbock. They had lost their money, but they had not lost their desire for adventure. And when they saw the morning sun turning the barrels of those three rifles to diamonds, and when they heard the three youths in the road singing out, the men in the stage simply reached for their own guns.

Four of them were badly wounded, but the three in the road were shot down, also. Two were killed. Another was taken to the next relay station, where he recuperated, and then escaped. But it was felt that this adventure might discourage further attempts upon the line.

No, for the next day—the eleventh since the line was put in operation—the rider on the gray stallion appeared in the road and took the southbound coach almost exactly at the spot where the three desperadoes had appeared before. It was plain that he was saying to the world: *What three cannot do when they don't know how is ridiculously simple, if one simply understands how to go about the thing.*

For his part, he understood, and since the shooting of the two Gunn brothers and the bullet through the arm of famous Alec, resistance to the marauder was unpopular. He had taken three stages, now, and the men in Crumbock said: "He's got enough to retire on, unless he's in this game for fun."

However that might be, they were not willing to take the chance any more. Could they be blamed? There had been five attempts at robbery within eleven days. Three of them had succeeded, and, in one of the failures, four of the passengers in the coach had been wounded as they had fought off the robbers.

The Western mind was made up with Western suddenness and Western thoroughness. The stage line to Munson was unsafe, and instantly no one would take a passage on it, except men who had not a penny to their names. They went gladly enough.

Sammy, in despair, waited for three days and then announced the excursion rates, cutting the fare fairly in two. But still no one was willing to ride, and the receipts had fallen away to zero.

"There ain't nothin' wrong with the fare, Gregg," said one old-timer. "It's the weather that you furnish along the road that makes us hold back. You give us too much scenery."

And the climax came when two reporters hurried out from the East solely for the pleasure of riding on this already celebrated line. By the time they got to Munson, they found that the hold-ups had become even more frequent than they had hoped. And they went over the line slowly, taking many snapshots. Oh, what labels for their pictures. "Dead Man's Curve"—where Andrew and Lester Gunn were shot down by the famous desperado, Chester Furness, *et cetera*. Those were only samples.

They took pictures of everyone, beginning with Sammy Gregg, and finishing up with the Gunn brothers, who were now sullenly convalescent. And then they published an account of the Munson-Crumbock trail that made little boys sit up late at night, staring at the blackness of the windows and wishing that they could grow up to be desperadoes, too.

All this publicity might have been good to attract tourists if it had been just a little less recent. But battlefields are the popular spots for tourists—not battles.

Sammy found that his stages were wandering slowly over the mountains—empty—and a payroll of forty men a day was rapidly consuming the cash in his pocket.

Oh, a desperate time for Sammy, when good common sense was telling him that it was high time for him to surrender this losing venture, and when the gambling instinct assured him that, if he would hold on just a little longer, the luck was certain to turn.

He grew hollow-eyed, nervous. The days were long nightmares to him. And so dull had grown the wits of Sammy that, when he encountered a certain young man on the long, winding street of Crumbock, he did not recognize that face, though it had played a most important part in the life of Sammy, you may be sure, and the stranger had to walk up to him and slap him twice upon the shoulder before Sammy rubbed his eyes and looked up from his daydream of misery.

He saw a handsome youth before him, a slender, willowy figure of a man with soft, lazy brown eyes, and a cigarette, rolled Mexican style, dangling from his finger.

"Jeremy Major," Sammy said.

"You look sick," Jeremy said. "I'm coming to see you tonight. Start thinking for me. I'm terribly bored."

CHAPTER TWENTY-FIVE

Jeremy Major walked on down the street—for he seemed to be busy following a tall man in a white sombrero—and Sammy turned to stare hungrily after him. In all the world, there was only one Jeremy. He was a unique without a duplicate anywhere. And the world could wag on a thousand years and still there would be no second Jeremy to puzzle it. And yet, physically, Sammy could never understand him.

Inch for inch, there was no vital difference of height between the two of them, and, pound for pound, there was no great advantage on the side of Jeremy Major. Still he was as physically superior to Sammy as a hundred-and-forty-pound leopard is superior to a hundred-and-forty-pound dog. The dog might hurt a man by chewing his leg badly. But the leopard would tear his throat open with one terrible stroke of its paw and then carry him away—silently, softly, out of a room filled with other men.

Well, Jeremy Major was like that. Not that Sammy put him down as a mere murderer, but the possibilities of Jeremy were so infinite that Sammy's imagination ran amok on them, for Sammy himself had seen enough strange feats performed by the slender youth. Sammy himself could never forget those various settings in which he had seen young Jeremy Major as the central figure. Gambler extraordinary, tramp and loafer *par excellence,* gunfighter, horse trainer, and, above all, unconscionable idler and pleasure-seeker. Such was the Jeremy Major that Sammy knew.

What he was doing now, Sammy could not guess, unless it were that he had designs of inducing the tall man in the broad hat to enter a game of cards with him. But what advantage was it to the spendthrift to make money, when he cast it away again, like rain water falling back to the sea from which it came?

But Jeremy was bored. It meant a great deal to Sammy to learn that. Jeremy wanted action and entertainment. And when the leopard begins to thrust forth its claws to try their edge, it is time for house dogs to hunt their kennels with all speed. If Jeremy took his exercise in Crumbock, great would be the noise thereof, beyond a doubt.

And Sammy, with a somewhat malicious grin, cast his eye over the town. It lay sidelong by one edge of Crumbock Creek, which had given its name to the town and to the mining in that gulch. The creek wound, and so did the town. It was rarely more than one house deep, and it stretched for two miles along the creek. In the daytime it was a fairly quiet street, except for the creaking freight wagons and the cursing teamsters as they lurched in or out of the town. In the night, it was a hot slice of hell frying on earth. There was no other name for it. Though Sammy, who sought his bed early at night, had seen little of the carryings-on in the evening.

But it was the world in which the gambler, Jeremy Major, could be expected to move altogether. And if Jeremy were sincerely bored with life, it was in that little night world at Crumbock that he would hunt for relaxation. Sammy instinctively sighed and shook his head; he was very glad that it was not his duty to keep that young man in order.

For that matter, who was there in the world who could manage Jeremy? What man had force enough of hand and brain?

A red-faced boy came tugging at his arm. "Hey, ain't you

Sam Gregg?"

"Yes."

"Well, you must be pretty near deaf. I been yelling at you as hard as I could for a whole block. Mister Cosden, back yonder, he wants to talk to you."

Sammy went back and found the rich Hubert Cosden sitting sideways in a buckboard, dangling his feet over the side of the seat. He had two sweating buckskins harnessed to the light wagon, and when a buckskin sweats, as everyone knows, it is a sign that there has been some hard work behind the heels of those horses. A mass of dust and dried mud covered the buckboard, the driver, and the horses. He was talking eagerly but wearily with the Crumbock representative of a big powder company. But there was no use in wasting words on the powder man. He had taken the lip of every miner in camp and his only reply was: "If I can't get the powder here, I can't get the powder. I can't work miracles, gentlemen. I ain't here to do it. You fix up your stage line, and I'll get in the powder fast enough."

So here they parted, and Hubert Cosden began with Sammy by apologizing for sending for him. However, there was on the mind of the millionaire a weight so heavy that he had to get it off at once. "And what do you know about this man Furness?" asked Cosden.

"I know about as much as most people do," Sammy replied. "I arrived from the East on the same train that brought him. I saw him bullied by the first and last crowd that will ever try that trick on him. I saw him shoot the first man he killed in Munson. And I had a herd of two hundred broncos swiped by him, and I had him sass me to my face about the mustangs. I've seen him right from the start, so far as this part of the country knows him. What do you want to know about him?"

"You're an intelligent man, Gregg. You wouldn't let personal injuries prejudice you too much. Now, personally I know nothing about this fellow at all. I want to ask your opinion. Do you think that there's a shadow of a reason to hope that he might ever go straight?"

There was something about the urgent tone in which this was asked that made Sammy suspect that Cosden wished him to say yes. And so he answered: "He's not a boy, and he wasn't a boy when he started in at Munson."

"Nobody likes a man without some spirit," Cosden said. "And nobody likes a man who won't fight."

Sammy smiled.

"Well?" Cosden asked sharply.

"Nothing. Except that I think you're answering your own questions, Mister Cosden. Nobody wants a coward . . . but nobody really wants a thief and a murderer."

"Murder?" Cosden answered. "Isn't that a very strong word to use? Has it ever been proved that Furness has ever taken a human life unless in self-defense?"

"I don't suppose it has," Sammy said. "But you see . . . the trouble is that he's had to defend himself so often." Cosden was gloomily silent, and Sammy drove home the point. "You'd think," he continued, "that once a man got the reputation that this Furness has, he'd have no trouble. People would dodge him like fire or poison. But that doesn't seem to be the way of it. Poor Furness is being hounded all the time by bullies and gunfighters, and he has to keep on killing people in self-defense . . . guards of stages, for instance, that he's about to hold up."

Cosden, turning very red, raised his hand. "That's enough," he said. "I suppose I understand the rest of what you have to say, and I suppose I have to agree with it. And yet . . . confound it . . . one cannot help hoping that these strong young men . . . there's a lack of strong men in this world of ours, Gregg!"

Sammy Gregg blinked and nodded.

"Although," qualified burly Cosden in haste, "there are

several kinds of strength . . . physical, mental, and all that, I am very well aware."

But Sammy smiled, as one who would say: *I am not proud, even when you step on my corns.*

"Well," Cosden said, "the idea just hopped into my head. But you're right, I suppose. Yes, of course you're right. The fellow is a . . . rascal." A mild name for the deeds of Furness, to be sure.

"That's all right," Sammy said good-naturedly as he turned away. "I don't blame you for wanting to know about him." He could have bitten out his tongue the instant he had said that, and so he turned away hastily, hoping that what he had said in parting would not be noticed.

He got two strides away, and then a ringing voice blasted after him: "Gregg!" He whirled around as though he had been shot. His face was burning, and so was the face of Cosden. Mutually they read the thoughts of one another and grew redder still.

"Gregg," Cosden said more gently, "I've got to know what you mean by that."

"Why," Sammy lied gallantly, "nothing, of course. But everybody in the town is interested in the man who's held up three stages."

Cosden shook his head. "Well done, Sammy," he said, "but it won't do. No, you had a particular thought in mind when you said that. Confess what it was."

"Why," Sammy said, "there's no law against guessing, is there?"

"I suppose not. But what is your guess?"

"Miss Cosden. . . ."

"Good Lord!"

"Only a guess . . . and it's legal to take a guess, Mister Cosden."

"Does the whole town know?" Cosden gasped miserably.

"Nobody dreams of it," Sammy assured.

"But you. . . ."

"I was sitting in the seat beside her, when the stage was stopped by. . . ."

"Well . . . I suppose you did your guessing then?"

"Yes."

"You are a good guesser, Gregg," the older man said gloomily. "And at that rate, you ought to make a success on the street. You could read the minds of the stocks. You guessed, but you said nothing to me."

"Mister Cosden, you wouldn't have believed me. And it was none of my business . . . to guess out loud."

The other nodded. "The first I knew of it was last night. The scoundrel sneaked down to the town and I actually found him as big as life in my house talking to my girl. I came in and took them unawares. He was as cool as the devil. I half think that he *is* the devil. And, of course, there's no nerves in Anne. I had a fine talk with them, you may be sure. And, for all I know, Anne may be riding away over the edge of the world with him at this moment . . . curse me for a talking idiot . . . why am I telling you all of this?"

"I could guess," Sammy said, very white and sick of face.

"There's nothing to be done," Cosden said gravely. "All I can do is to wait . . . and pray that she will have good sense and do nothing rash. But if I oppose her . . . ah, Gregg, if only we could find a way of killing him off to save her."

"He has a habit of defending himself," Sammy said.

"I know that. But surely there must be in the world some man or men able to fight fire with fire."

And then the great thought struck Sammy.

CHAPTER TWENTY-SIX

One hunts for opposites as antidotes—the fat to counteract the acid—the boxer to beat the slugger—the bird to kill the serpent. And so Sammy, thinking of the big shoulders and the heavy body of handsome Chester Furness, naturally and instinctively turned his mind toward the opposite of so much brute force and what he thought of was the slender, supple body of young Jeremy Major.

Not that one thought of Jeremy Major as being young, any more than one thinks of a statue of a youth as being young. It may date from the 5th Century B.C. And so with Jeremy—he simply was—he existed—as fire exists, without an age.

And, thinking of him, it seemed to Sammy that he had the solution. And suddenly he began to chuckle.

"Has it turned into a laughing matter?" Cosden asked bitterly. "Is it worth no more serious thought than this?"

"I was only wondering what would happen when they meet," Sammy said.

"Who?" asked Cosden.

"Did you ever see an old cat tackle a dog in earnest?" Sammy asked rather dreamily.

Cosden gaped; he felt that the youth was possibly taking leave of his good wits.

"Well," went on Sammy, "he's like that. Only bigger. And not a house cat. No, because he's wild from the heart out."

"Who? Who under heaven!" Cosden cried. "Who is wild, and

what difference does it make to me?"

"The man who will beat big Furness for you, I think," Sammy answered.

Cosden showed signs of interest at once. "Tell me about him," he said. "Is he another one of these men who have to defend themselves often?"

"Oh, no," Sammy said. "It doesn't happen very often. He'll duck out of the way of trouble, you see, the way a jack rabbit will double away from a dog. Trouble doesn't get him into a corner very often, but when it does. . . ." He paused significantly.

"Some honest, honorable fellow?" Cosden asked.

"A crooked gambler," Sammy replied, "when he meets other crooked ones. A loafer who never did a lick of work in his life. A good-for-nothing tramp king and spendthrift. That's all you can say for him, logically."

"Very well," said Cosden. "If it's matching one of that kind against the big fellow, I suppose I may call it fighting fire with fire. It doesn't make much difference which of them goes down. The world will be benefited by it."

"Oh," Sammy said, "there's no doubt about who'll go down. No doubt about that at all."

"Is this friend of yours such a terrible fighter?"

"He's terrible enough. I never saw him fight. But I know about him. The only trouble will be about getting him to take the job."

"If that is all," Cosden said, "then we can stop worrying. Money is no object to me in a matter like this. If it will bring my girl over the rocks safely, I'll spend it like water. You yourself, Gregg, hire him and promise him anything you like. If he wants an advance . . . that sort of a man usually does . . . tell him to name his own figure."

Sammy shook his head. "Money will never turn the trick," he assured. "Never in the world. Money isn't what you want. He's had as much money in his hands as you've had, I suppose. Millions must have drifted through him at the gaming tables. But it's dirt to him. It's water to him. He's thrown it away. Given it away. No, money will never tempt him."

"The devil take him. This fellow seems to be a freak. What *will* bring him, then?"

"Partly because he's getting bored."

"He won't do a killing for money, but he might do it for pleasure?"

"Exactly."

"A pleasant man." Cosden shuddered.

"But I think," Sammy said, "that the only way to go about it is for you to hunt him out and tell him the truth."

"The truth . . . Gregg, are you quite mad? The truth to such a fellow?"

"It would be safer with him than with me or you," Sammy said.

Cosden threw up his hands. "I give it up," he announced. "Everything that you say about this fellow is at outs with everything else you say. He seems to me made up of nothing but opposites."

"That," Sammy said, "is exactly what he is."

So it was that Hubert Cosden, the millionaire, went down the street with Sammy and found the goal of his search in a gaming room, sitting idly on a bench at the side of the room. And a big, bearded fellow beside him was pouring forth a tale of hard luck.

"Look here," Cosden heard the youth break in upon the miner, "what would it cost you to tackle that job again . . . with the right sort of help?"

"Here's millions lyin' idle, goin' to waste, because there ain't nothin' legitimate to put 'em into. But fifteen hundred would stake me. But can I get anybody to give my idea a try . . . ?"

"Here," slender Jeremy Major said, "is the fifteen hundred and a little extra. So long. Run along. I don't want your thanks. Never mind the contract. Your word suits me. I don't want a witness . . . good bye." And so he fairly pushed the man away and the prospector ran, red-eyed and joyous, into the street.

"And he's not a fool?" Cosden asked Sammy.

"It looks that way, but he's not. Here, I'll introduce you."

Men did not take long to get down to even the most important business, in those days in the West. Cosden found himself taking a hand no larger and just as soft as the hand of his daughter Anne. He found himself looking down into dark, melancholy brown eyes. And then he was walking forth in the street with Jeremy Major at his side. Gregg had gone off and left them to their own devices.

It was a very hard story to tell, but then the need behind it was very great, and Cosden brought out the tale haltingly, stiffly. When he finished, Jeremy Major made a brief resume.

"This fellow, Furness, you think needs killing, and I'm to do the job. Partly for any sum I want to name and partly as a sort of a public benefaction."

That summed it up, neatly enough, and Cosden smiled and nodded.

"Well," Jeremy said, "I'm not a public benefactor. And I never was. And, in the next place, I am not so sure that your daughter is worth all this fuss. I don't want to hurt your feelings. But I might as well tell you right now, to begin with, that the only person I'd tackle big Furness for is the lady herself."

It was rather bold talk—much bolder, at least, than Cosden was accustomed to hearing. But there was really nothing for him to do except to bear it as best he might.

"I suppose," he said patiently, "that the thing for me to do is to take you home and introduce you to my daughter?"

"It won't do at all," replied this calmly self-assured Jeremy

Major. "She's a rough sort, and hard to know. Of course I've seen her. Everybody has seen her riding that black horse that she brought on from Munson. But one doesn't feel like tackling Furness for the sake of a girl that seems to care about nothing in the world except the highest fence that she can jump her horse over. Suppose you get short of help in your house . . . and suppose you give me a job . . . something sort of easy, if you don't mind. Because it kills me to work."

Cosden smiled grimly at the thought of the gunfighter trembling over the prospect of work. And yet, in spite of himself, he could not help wondering if Sammy Gregg had not been covertly amusing himself in presenting this fellow to him as a destroyer of men.

"You can do what you like," he said. "Pick out any kind of job around the house that you want to. My cook quit this morning, and my daughter is doing the cooking and the rest of the work. Which is plenty, because we have to feed eight men."

Major writhed at the thought. "Eight men." He sighed. "And this sort of weather." He glanced deprecatingly up at the blazing sun. "Well," he continued, "I'll tell you how it is . . . work doesn't agree with me, somehow. I have bad nerves, d'you see? And work interferes with them a surprising lot."

"Name what you please," Cosden said. "Or, if you want, I'll bring you up there as a visitor . . . or a driller waiting for a. . . ."

"Could you do that?" Major said, brightening. "But, no, I should be working. Working, so that I'll have a chance to talk to her. I'll tell you . . . washing dishes is about my speed . . . if you have a good airy kitchen with plenty of windows and doors to it. Or chopping . . . the kindling wood, maybe. I wouldn't mind that sort of work."

"Young man," Cosden returned, "will you tell me how you ever managed to get along as a boy, or were there no chores around your house?"

"There were chores," Major answered, with a pained sigh of recollection. "And there was a stepmother who had a special talent for getting those chores done by her stepsons. But somehow, after she had tried me out on the jobs for a long time, she came to decide that maybe it was better for someone else to do the work . . . because I was so clumsy that I was always breaking something. After a while, there wasn't much work for me to do, and I was raised easy. But it took a lot of thinking, always, to get out of that work."

"Well," Cosden said grimly, "if you had been around my father's house, you would have done your chores or taken some mighty tall lickings in the place of them."

"As a matter of fact, I was never licked, after I got to be boy size," Jeremy said.

"Never licked!" Cosden cried. "Well, that explains it. I'd as soon try to persuade a mule with pleasant talk as to try to persuade a boy."

"I suppose," Jeremy said, but there was an odd little smile in the corners of his lips, and Cosden thought he saw a flickering yellow light glint into the eyes of the young fellow, and out again. He could not be quite sure about it, but it gave Cosden a distinct pang of uneasiness. And, filled with all manner of odd thoughts, he took Jeremy Major up the hill to introduce him to Anne Cosden.

CHAPTER TWENTY-SEVEN

The best that could be said about that combination was, briefly, that it did not work. When Cosden came wearily home from the mine that night, and eight weary, dirty, hungry men with him, and when he slumped through the door of the shack, he found his daughter with a face white and pinched with anger.

"And what's wrong with you, Anne?" her father asked.

"I thought I had seen men of all kinds," Anne said in a wild explosion. "I thought I had seen the most worthless types in the world. But this precious good-for-nothing that you found for me is the worst yet. A helper? He's not even a shadow of an excuse for a man. And . . . why, Dad, he can't even chop kindling wood straight or without going to sleep over it. I'm sure he hasn't slept a wink for a month. And . . . or. . . ." She groaned through set teeth to express the greatness of her disgust. "I'm not going to quit on the job, Dad," she added hastily. "I don't mind cooking for hungry men. But I hate having that creature around. And impertinent, too. When I told him that I'd pay him off and he could quit, he told me that he would take orders from nobody but the man who hired him, when it came to stopping his job."

There was a growl of rage from one of the men—a big, two-handed fighting man, with a shock of hair as red as Anne Cosden's and a chin of wood and a nose that was obviously a pliable button of India rubber. "Let me go out and handle him," said the big fellow. "You're a tired man, Cosden. Let me go and take care of him."

Cosden weakly gave way to temptation, because, be it understood, he did not really believe that Sammy Gregg had told him the truth about this strangely lazy lad. And though there was that about the youth that gave him an odd, eerie feeling, still, he was not quite sure. And he was rather glad to have his warrior from the mine try out Jeremy Major.

So tall Dick Harrison paused in the door of the kitchen and scowled into the interior. "A bum," he said, speaking his thoughts with unnecessary loudness. "A plain, good-for-nothing tramp."

The others crowded as close to the door as they could, and they saw the slender, shiftless-looking fellow at the sink glance hastily around over a hunched shoulder as in fear. And then the work of washing the pans was resumed with a sudden flurry of noise and a splashing of greasy dishwater. Yet the work did not seem to get forward any faster.

Dick Harrison strode into the kitchen. "Look here, bo," he roared, "I hear you've been talking back to the lady?"

"Mister," the shrinking form of Jeremy Major said, "I'm doing no harm."

"You . . . rat," Harrison said, nodding with the conviction of his emotion. "Just . . . plain . . . worthless . . . rat."

"Dick!" Anne Cosden cried. "You won't be too rough with him. He's not very big, after all. And he really didn't say much back to me."

"Oh, I'll be gentle, I will!" Harrison snarled. And he reached out a brawny hand and fixed it upon the shoulder of the new kitchen helper. "You get out where I can have a look at you," he said. And he dragged Jeremy lightly forth from the kitchen and out into the light of the dying day. Oh, how fresh and how bright was the evening, and from up and down the street of the town there was a subdued rattling of contented voices of hungry men, back from their labor on the lode above them, and ready to eat as only laborers know how.

"Dick Harrison!" cried the girl in a fresh alarm. "You won't hurt him, really?"

"Don't you worry about him," Harrison said over his shoulder. "I know how to handle this kind, if I don't know anything else. You leave him to me."

"Leave Dick to look after him," said others among those who stood about. "He won't give him any more than is good for his troubles, you can bet. That's just an ordinary, greasy, lowdown hobo."

"Now," Harrison said, "I hear that you wouldn't be fired today."

"I was hired by a man," Major said, giving the effect of dangling bodily from the thick, suspended arm of Harrison. "And I thought I ought to be fired by a man, too."

"Well," Harrison said, "you were hired by a man, and now it *is* a man who fires you." He added—"Get out!"—and he swung his heavy hand through the air.

It just missed the head of Major as that young worthy ducked toward safety. The hand of Harrison carved the air only, while Major, having slipped oddly from the grip of the other, stood at a little distance saying humbly: "I'm sure I don't wish any trouble, you know. But I have to wait to be fired by Mister Cosden."

"You have to wait?" Harrison shouted, more than a little flustered because that swinging, open hand of his had not cuffed the cheek of the tramp. "Then wait and take this."

He ought not to have done it, considering the superiority of his size and the thickness of his athletic shoulders, and the length of his heavy, muscular arms. Certainly he should not have struck with all his might at an opponent so much smaller. But Harrison was a hot-tempered man, and now his anger quite got the best of him. Besides, he was of the school that strikes first and thinks afterward. He struck with the precision, too, of a trained boxer. No lumbering, roundabout, club-like blow, but a snapping punch from the shoulder with half the back muscles rippling into it.

One looked to see that terrible plunging fist dash right through the meager body of little Jeremy Major. But, no, by some lucky chance he seemed to have blundered out of the way of the blow. Or was it entirely by chance?

"Won't somebody please take him away before there's any trouble?" Major called.

"Dick Harrison!" cried Anne Cosden, who saw that the matter had gone too far and that Harrison's wild temper was apt to do the smaller man an injury. "Dick Harrison, that's enough. Don't you dare to touch him again."

As well have called to the stormy wind. Harrison, with a snarl of growing fury, rushed wildly in. There was something terribly brutal in the charge of that big body upon the smaller man, when the mere weight of his hand seemed so amply sufficient to put an end to the fight, if fight it could be called.

And then the oddest thing happened. For it seemed that Jeremy Major, as he huddled away from the other, with his hands raised timidly before his face in a most unmilitary posture—it seemed that Major, as Harrison rushed in, stumbled, and stumbled forward, and he seemed to reach out his left hand to stop himself, clutching at the empty air as a man will do. Except that this time, by the veriest accident, of course, the knuckles of that flying left fist clicked just upon the ridge of Harrison's jaw bone. And his rush stopped.

Indeed, he was brought up standing, as the saying is, and rocked back upon his heels. And from the spectators, who indeed were seeing stranger sights than they had ever dreamed of seeing, there broke a groan of wonder. From Harrison came a roar of bewildered fury.

Jeremy Major had leaped back an astonishing distance. He seemed to have grown, suddenly, two or three inches in height. He filled his clothes more sleekly. And he was poised on his toes with the lightness—well, with the lightness of nothing human, you may be sure.

"Will you take that clumsy fool away from me before I do him any harm?" Major said in a peculiar voice. "Will you take him away before I have to . . . ?"

It was Cosden, whose brain was a vital second or two faster than the brains of the men, who heard and understood at once. And he uttered a yell to Harrison and tried to break out to get at the fighters. It was too late. He could only paw and strain to break away through the jam at the doorway, while, before his eyes, happened one of the oddest things he had ever witnessed in the length of a very full and active life.

As Harrison leaped in again—warily, now, as a trained fighter who realizes that he has an enemy worthy of his steel—Major went to meet him. You could not say that Major exactly leaped as Harrison did. But he slithered low over the ground, and one was simply conscious that he had left one place and had appeared again at another.

Somehow, he managed to straighten up just under and inside the arms of big Harrison, and the result was worth traveling long miles to see. For truly it was as though a shell had exploded in front of big Harrison. He made a clumsy effort to strike at his smaller foeman with both hands, but the fists of Major had sunk into the midsection of Harrison's anatomy. He tried to stagger in and close with this elusive fellow. But his efforts were only too successful. Major met him in mid-air. They swirled into a tangle of twisting, writhing bodies, and then Harrison collapsed.

It was all so quick that no one could see exactly what had

happened. Only the results were visible. And the most important result was the picture of Harrison lying prostrate upon the ground with his eyes wide and staring, as the eyes of a dead man, and his face swollen—either with effort or from being nearly throttled.

It wasn't a pleasant thing to see. They went to pick him up, and it was odd to see them go in to him like children advancing toward the edge of a fire, so carefully did they keep their eyes fixed upon the form of Major in the background.

He made no effort to persecute his fallen enemy, however. He seemed to be shrinking away into the distance, as though ashamed of what he had done.

They raised Harrison. He himself half recovered from his swoon at the same instant and put out a hand to help himself up, but the arm that he extended crumbled under the strain and he uttered a wild scream of pain. And everyone nearby could hear the gritting of the broken ends of the arm bone. At some time in that brief and terrible struggle, Jeremy Major had snapped the arm of his enemy like a pipe stem.

I suppose everyone there had seen a good deal of rough-and-tumble fighting. Even the girl had seen her share, for Anne Cosden loved boxing almost well enough to try her own turn at the gloves. However, there was no jubilant shout from the spectators, no shout such as usually goes up when the smaller man of a pair wins a fight. And the reason was that this was different from ordinary fighting.

There were not many outward signs of a fist fight on the body of big Harrison. His face, as has been said, was swollen and discolored a little and his jaw was marked with a purple patch near the point. But, on the whole, he looked rather like one who has collapsed from a great shock rather than one who has been beaten with fists to insensibility.

And the same touch of horror that was in his eyes was in the eyes of the others as they raised him to his feet. He saw Major, then, and uttered a groan. Then he was led, staggering, into the house.

The men were busy with him. Only Anne Cosden remained behind in the yard of the house with Major, and now she turned and looked at him with a frown.

"Well," she said at last, "I see that you've been playing a part, all day long. I suppose you've simply been hungry for the trouble to start so that you could show us what you could do."

And he replied quietly: "Do you think I really wanted that fight?"

When she looked back on the affair, she had to admit that he certainly had not pushed himself forward in the fray. And yet she could not help a feeling that his lazy, shrinking indolence had been all an assumed mask. No one, with this devilish, compacted energy within, could have been utterly nonchalant at a moment when battle was in the offing. And then, too, there had been a destructiveness about his fight. It was not like a mere encounter of fists. Usually in those struggles there is a vast deal of swinging and smashing and puffing and heaving. But here there had been hardly more than a brush—one tangle— one thrust—and there lay Harrison, swollen of face, crushed, perhaps broken in spirit forever, and here was this slender youth untouched.

In the older days, no doubt, this matter would have been put down to a little use of black magic, and though there were few girls more level-headed than Anne Cosden, yet even Anne had a slight sense of weird awe.

"Well," Anne said, "and what do you want to do now?"

"Stay here, ma'am, and go right on working," Major replied.

"Working?" echoed Anne. "We'll keep you, though. Out of curiosity, if nothing else. But will you please tell me where you learned to fight like that?"

"Why, yes," Major said. "I used a lot of patience, you know. I had to admit, when I was younger, that I was a good deal weaker than most boys of my age. And so I had to make a good deal of myself if I were going to hold up my end with the other boys. I had to do everything in the best way, or else I couldn't do it at all."

"*Humph!*" Anne Cosden said. "All very probable, I'm sure. And the same sort of patience, I presume, taught you how to work so fast, with so little effort. Young man, are you trying to make a fool out of me?"

"No," Major answered blandly.

And he and the young lady stared at each other—she with a bright-eyed challenge in her eyes, and he calmly defying her and smiling inwardly, so it seemed.

In the meantime, Hubert Cosden had busied himself with Dick Harrison, and that stout young man gradually came back toward consciousness with a brain still reeling. He wanted to know where he was, and if the fight was over. And when he was assured that it was, he shamelessly thanked the Lord for it. After they had poured a dram or two of hot brandy down his throat, he recovered a bit more and gave them his own impressions of the battle.

"It was like hitting a bunch of feathers and . . . finding that they were carved out of rock," he explained. "I thought my fist could hardly be kept from going clean through him. But when he got his hands on me . . . I thought I'd fallen under the feet of a thousand buffaloes stampeding."

And so young Harrison talked on, without shame, not as one who details a defeat, but as one interested in the portrayal of some inhuman phenomenon.

Hubert Cosden felt that there was a heavy moral responsibility on his hands for what young Major had done. And he gave his men a little talk in which he told them that it was possible that Jeremy Major would be on hand for some time, and, in that case, he hoped that they would make it a point not to indulge in any more quarrels with him. Cosden discovered that he need not have troubled himself about this matter. His young men were not at all inclined to experiment after Harrison had opened their eyes.

CHAPTER TWENTY-EIGHT

Early the next morning in the canvas-walled, floorless place that was known as The Hotel, young Sammy Gregg was wakened by the capable hand of Hubert Cosden upon his shoulder.

"Gregg," said the miner, "tell me at once just what you know about this fellow Major . . . this Jeremy Major."

It took Sammy hardly ten minutes to tell how he had first seen an unsuccessful young beggar blowing improvised music with a flute in Munson, and how he had dropped $10 into the hat of the stranger, or how he had seen the same figure grown brilliant and playing with huge sums in a gambling den in Texas not very many days later, or how he had encountered him later in a tramp jungle, and how Jeremy Major and his horse had driven a herd of wild mustangs through the mountains to Crumbock.

Cosden listened to these details with a hungry interest, but still he continued to shake his head, as though he did not find in what he heard the sort of answers that were satisfying to him.

"It seems to be out of the frying pan and into the fire, Gregg," said Cosden. "There is something about this Western air that affects the head of my girl. I've never known her to pay any attention to men, except to laugh at them. But now . . . confound it, Gregg, she seems to be fascinated by young Jeremy Major. She watches him . . . the way a bird is said to watch a snake."

"He's done something, then?" Sammy said.

"Oh, curse him, yes. A most uncanny, grisly thing . . .

178

smashed up the strongest, most athletic man I have. A trained boxer, too. Broke him up in the most amazingly easy style. A weird style, too."

Sammy Gregg, nodding and with wide eyes, did not interrupt. For he knew that a man in this frame of mind could not keep from talking.

"And the young scoundrel seems to be enchanting my daughter," Cosden went on. "So that I don't know which to dread the most . . . the influence of big, handsome Furness, who may be a rascal, but who seems to be a gentleman . . . or the influence of young Jeremy Major, who seems to be a wild, lazy, mysterious good-for-nothing. And, between you and me, what I really wish is that I could get my girl safely out of these mountains and away to the farther side of the world.

"Do you understand? It's a dangerous business, using fire to fight fire, or poison to fight poison. My one hope is that the business will be over soon, and if they don't mutually brain one another, I shall be disappointed. Jeremy Major is coming to see you. He has told me that he is willing to do whatever he can to handle Furness for me. And he thinks that he needs you and me both to arrange the matter. His idea is an odd one. And yet there is something a little attractive about it, too. What he wants to do is to throw out a sort of general challenge to big Furness. He says that Furness is not holding up stages merely to get the money out of them, but also because he is rather amused by the exciting work. Confound his heart.

"Now, then, what this fellow Major wants to do is to have me entrust a good fat shipment of gold to the stage. You yourself, Gregg, will go along to deliver the shipment and to check up on all that happens. There will be a driver, and there will be young Major. Or, if a driver doesn't want to handle the risky job, Major himself says he will drive the coach and fight it, also.

"You understand the scheme? Everything is to be published

far and wide. Jeremy Major is going to attempt to push a stage, carrying a good many thousands in gold, straight through the mountains to Munson. And the hope is that Furness will take it into his head to meet Major and dispute the way with him . . . partly for the sake of the money and partly for the sake of maintaining himself as ruler of the roost."

This was the origin of that odd plan that Jeremy Major had conceived, and that he also desired to execute. And Sammy, listening to the scheme, found a good deal that he could object to. But he also saw two great advantages for himself for which he would willingly have sacrificed himself a thousand times over. One advantage was that he would, in this fashion, be rid of Furness. Another was that if Major traveled on that stage line to defend it, it would discourage not only Furness, but perhaps all other prospective thieves who had sundry villainous intents in mind.

He announced on the spot his willingness to direct the whole affair and travel in the danger stage himself for that purpose. Also, he would provide, if he could, a driver and a good team to make the first relay run.

There would be no trouble about the provision of horses. For the Texas mustangs, which had lost so much flesh during the first few days of the operation of the line, were now waxing fat again. And their spirits were rising with their flesh. For poor Sammy had been forced to reduce the number of stages until now only one was making the trip. It came from Munson to Crumbock. And at Crumbock it was relieved by another vehicle that started back under the same driver.

But the patronage of the line had fallen off so hugely that even the running of one coach was not worthwhile. It was never a third filled. And that third consisted of penniless adventurers. For the coach from Munson to Crumbock and back had become known throughout the range as the danger line, or the danger stage—a name to which it had lived up only too well.

But now, with the mines booming more strongly than ever, with the pressure of business coming closer and closer to the boiling point, the one rapid and effective means of communication between Munson and Crumbock was practically abandoned by miners and travelers.

Sammy had to admit that they were right. All he objected to was that they made a joke of his line. Yes, even the men who were on his payroll were inclined to smile at the prospects of the stage. All of them were looking forward to a necessary change of work before long, and all of them were loafing on a job that no longer required their industry. And Sammy, remarking the fact that the rats were leaving the sinking ship, felt every day more convinced that his doom was surely creeping upon him.

Furness, of course, was the main rock upon which he was splitting. All the other ruffians who had infested the highway across the mountains had not been as dangerous to life and property as that single man. And now there was a last hope, that Jeremy Major might meet and crush the famous rider of the gray horse.

Sammy himself saw the stage looked to, and every nut in her tightened and the wheels greased. He saw the six best horses he had prepared for the work. Then he set about finding a driver for the team.

This, however, was a different matter. The news had purposely been sent far abroad that the stage, on the 14th of the month, was to start out for Munson with $15,000 in raw gold aboard her. And it was perfectly well understood why that information had been cast out. It was that a hook might be baited for Chester Ormonde Furness. And there was a very generally expressed opinion that Furness would not only be snagged by the hook, but that he would straightway swim off with hook, line, sinker, and fishers, also.

Nobody, in short, wished to take the job. Old Alec, with his crippled arm, wrote in to sympathize with his old boss upon the cowardice of his successors on the driver's seat. But Alec himself had been rendered not available by the very enemy who now they had specially singled out.

If there were any doubt as to what might become of the news that had been sent out in the general direction of the mountains that sheltered Furness, it was removed when a neatly written and quite surprising letter was received by Sammy in the following language:

Dear Mr. Gregg: It is so long since I have seen anything but frightened tramps in your stages that I am delighted to hear that you have changed your policy and that you have now made yourself responsible for a shipment of gold.

I am so interested that I must convey to you my intention of taking special charge of the gold at the earliest opportunity.

Believe me to be most faithfully yours, and in gratitude for many favors consigned by you in the past,

Chester Ormonde Furness

Over this letter young Sammy Gregg pondered with a gray face. He was fairly well convinced that, no matter how formidably slender Major might be, Furness was unbeatable. And therefore he carried the letter to Cosden with a gloomy silence.

However, Cosden was indomitable. "I have seen this man handle his hands. If he can use a gun half as well, he will be fairly invincible. Don't talk to me about failure. He cannot fail. The gold goes by that stage, and, if you cannot persuade another man or young Major himself to drive, I'll drive the infernal wagon myself."

There was no need of that. Jeremy Major willingly took upon

himself to manage the team, and upon the appointed morning, with the June sun just turning the sky to rose and gold, Major stepped into the street and passed through the dense crowd that had gathered to see the danger coach start. Six men held the dancing, furious horses, all high strung from their long stay in the pasture. But when Major mounted the seat where Sammy was already waiting for him and picked up the reins, it was noted that under his hand and voice the team became suddenly quiet. A moment more and the brake was eased with a screech, and the big wagon lurched away down the street.

CHAPTER TWENTY-NINE

There was a final thrill for the crowd of spectators after the coach had rolled down the street and while they were still standing shoulder to shoulder, watching the pair on the high-pitched seat rock with every inequality of the road.

Someone called out: "Look here! Look at this stray! Hey, boys, who owns that horse?"

There was such a note of wild excitement in this call that every head jerked around and presently they were aware of a tall, black stallion hoofing it down the street in strange guise. For he was fully saddled—most beautifully saddled, in fact. And upon the horn of the saddle there was tied a bridle that was one mass of burnished metalwork. But the head itself of the horse was free, and, as he trotted along, he tossed his crest high and glanced disdainfully from side to side upon the people in the street. For he was of a royal dignity, this king of kings among horses.

There was not a white hair on him. He was as black as tar from head to foot. Yes, and the hoofs themselves were as black as though they had been newly stained. And he shone, too, as though he had been newly burnished, so that one could speak of the brightness of his glimmering flanks, but hardly of their color. Yes, the very hoofs flashed as though they had just been waxed and polished. And yet one knew after an instant of attention, that Nature was the groom in this case.

Again, another sang out in quick warning: "Mind yourselves,

boys! I know that horse. It's Jeremy Major's horse. And he's a nacheral killer. Mind yourselves!"

They minded themselves quickly enough. They scattered to either side, and, through the lane thus formed, the big fellow skipped with a wonderful lightness. There is a gait that exceeds in beauty either the racing step or the swinging canter or the high or daisy-cutting trot, and that is the walking pace of a truly fine horse. For, as he walks, his actions are not too swift for the human eye to follow the play of light upon his shoulders and the exquisite cushioning flexibility of the supple fetlock joints. And what these knowers of horseflesh saw as the big black walked past stirred their hearts. One did not need to know horses. A child would have understood that here was the speed of the wind.

Presently he broke into a gallop, swept out from the town, and away after the stage and up the hill, following his master.

"Look," Anne Cosden said to her father. "He can let his horse run free behind him. What in the world does he do to animals?"

So thought the rest of Crumbock, and a deep-throated murmur ran up and down the street.

But the black was away in his stride, which did not alter until he had put himself ahead of the swinging trot of the stagecoach that Jeremy Major was driving over the mountain way. And, still in the lead, he idled along, keeping himself just beyond the leaders, pausing now and again to crop a tempting bunch of grass, and then brushing on.

"If Furness should get away . . . ," Major said, and finished by pointing to the stallion.

Out from Crumbock there was a three-mile slope to climb, and after that for a distance the trail wound along the crest of a ridge. They had covered a good mile of this easier going when Major called softly and suddenly to the horses and at the same time shot the long handle of the brake forward. There was a screech of the brake pads against the heavy iron tires. The coach slowed to a walking pace, with the traces of the team slack, and then for the first time Sammy Gregg saw a reason for the halt.

Through the trees at the next bend appeared the body of a great dappled gray horse with a tall rider in the saddle—Furness, with his rifle at the ready—Furness with the rifle butt against his shoulder.

It cracked. A sound as of a whirring hornet darted into the ears of Sammy, and Major was out of the seat and lunging down—with a bullet through body or head.

No, for he had landed astride of the near-wheeler, and then flicked off again onto the ground, and while he was still in the air a bit of steel gleamed in his hand. It spoke as the feet of the owner touched the deep dust. Sammy saw the rifle slip from the grip of Furness—saw it hang from the fingers of one hand—and then the Winchester dropped while Furness clutched at one arm with his other hand.

At the same time, he swung the gray about with a sway of his body and a twist of his knees—and the forest closed instantly behind him. Through the silence that fell with a sudden weight as the jangling noise of the coach stopped, Sammy could hear the horse of the fugitive crashing through the underbrush.

Was this the end of the battle toward which he and the other people of the mountains had looked forward with so much eagerness and dread? No, for here was Major catching the black stallion, Clancy, and leaping with a cat-like lightness into the saddle. Another instant and the black was sweeping down the road, his head a little turned and his mouth opened to receive the bit of the bridle that his master leaned forward along his neck to fit between his teeth. In an instant the bridle was in place, and Major had twitched the stallion from the road into the brush.

There was one more glimpse for Sammy. He could look from his high seat far down the hillside to a clearing among the trees, and an instant later he saw the gray horse dart across the opening, dodge through a thick hedge of bushes, and pass on out of sight.

An instant later the black flashed into view, with Major pitched forward like a jockey on the neck of the stallion. There was no dodging for Clancy. He rose like a steeplechaser at the hedge and cleared it with an arrow-like leap. Then he, too, was lost in the forest beyond.

There was no doubt in his mind about which horse would win the race. The gray was a grand runner and a good mountain horse, used to this work. But he might as well have been matched against a hawk as against the black. But as for the battle that would ensue when the two met—that was a different matter. For it was the left arm of big Chester Furness that had been wounded and his right—his revolver hand—would be as accurate as ever. It seemed to Sammy that the power of Furness and the terrible speed of Major would make a resistless force and an immovable object meeting somewhere yonder in the wilds.

But he still had many thousands of dollars' worth of gold in the stage. There was no guard to help him. A gun was useless in his hands. And the management of the coach team was a very sufficient mystery to him. At the first open space he turned the stage and its six horses laboriously around and started back for Crumbock.

What difference did it make whether or not the stage was pushed through to its destination? He and everyone else understood perfectly that what was of importance was not the traveling of the stage, but the defeat of Chester Furness, if that could be arranged.

But when his team was seen cresting the slope above Crumbock, that busy town suspended all work and flocked in a noisy mass to learn the news.

Was the gold gone?

Had they seen Furness?

Where was Jeremy Major? Dead on the road and his horse stolen by the outlaw?

All they got for an answer was that the great pair had clashed, and that the first round of the battle had been a victory for Major, and that the last seen of the outlaw, he was riding away for life, with the black stallion in swift pursuit.

That was the story he told over again to Hubert Cosden, when the miner came to ask hasty questions—and receive back the gold that had been for the baiting of the trap.

"And Miss Cosden?" asked Sammy timidly.

"She has set her teeth and will not show a thing," Cosden replied. "But . . . come up to the house tonight. I want to talk to you and get all the details over again. Now I'm busy. But I want to hear everything, and you can wager that Anne wants to hear it, too."

So that eventful morning ended, and the roar of the mining town began again, and the mere thought of what had happened seemed to be lost.

Not lost to Sammy, however, as he sat in his office, which had once been so thronged with business, and which was now so empty of all interest. Only the sign was outside the window: *Munson-Crumbock, through stages. The only fast, regular, and safe means of transport.*

Some wit had underlined in red chalk the word, safe, and Sammy had not the heart to erase the line.

All was a jumble of confusion, now, in the mind of Sammy— Anne Cosden, big, sunny, cheerful, strong of hand and mind, and wild Jeremy Major, and handsome Chester Furness with his record of dead men behind him, and the dying stage line. Out of all those wrecks, what could be salvaged by Sammy?

CHAPTER THIRTY

At least he had the night to wait for, the talk with Cosden, and perhaps a glimpse of Anne. But, oh, how slowly the day waned, and how many hundreds of times he looked wistfully and vainly toward the dark forests of the southern hills, hoping against hope, still, that the rider of the black horse might emerge, unscathed and triumphant. Or perhaps was Cosden right? Would it be better for everyone if both of those warriors fought until the two lay dead in the woods, with only the owls to watch them fight and die?

The evening came at last. Sammy saw the men from the mine come for supper to the Cosden house. He waited nervously until they left, and then he climbed the slope and presented himself at the door. Cosden took him in. The rattle of pans in the kitchen died away, and big Anne Cosden came swinging in and sat down on the arm of a chair improvised from a packing case and some supple bent boughs.

"I'm mostly interested in just one thing," Anne Cosden said. "When they fought . . . is the story true that Chester Furness turned and rode away?"

"With a bullet through his left arm," Sammy said honestly. "I saw the red stain."

"Then," Anne Cosden said with a firm conviction, "they are both dead."

There was a sharp exclamation from her father. "What makes you think that, Anne?"

"If Furness couldn't beat him in the first fight, he could never beat him after once turning his back. And he could never escape. Nothing that lives could escape from that black horse, with a cat like Jeremy Major in the saddle. And . . . I'm going back to work. I don't want to hear any more about it."

She was as good as her word. She returned to the kitchen and left her father staring gloomily back at the door.

"I don't know," he said to Sammy Gregg. "I can't tell. Sometimes I think that she doesn't care a whack about either of them. But I'm not sure. She beats me." The last was whispered, and his eyes fixed upon the outer door of the cabin and grew wide with staring.

Sammy turned with a start, and he saw over his shoulder the slender form of Jeremy Major standing in the doorway. Beyond, there was the stamp of an impatient horse. Clancy—standing dimly in the night. Then Major came in and slumped into a chair.

"It was mighty hot this afternoon, wasn't it?" Major said. "I lay up on the edge of the woods for a long time waiting for it to cool off. There was a pair of gray squirrels that couldn't agree which owned the tree I was lying under. They kept paying visits to each other. And finally they clinched. They made the fur fly, I can tell you. Finally they tumbled off their branch. I thought they'd drop eighty feet to the ground and break themselves to a pulp. But they didn't. Did you ever see a squirrel dive for the ground? The fellows hadn't fallen twenty feet when they shook themselves apart, and spread out their tails and flattened their bodies, and fluffed out their tails behind them. Those big tails were like balloons, holding them back when they fell. Oh, they dropped with a clunk, of course, but they weren't hurt. They scampered up the trunk of the same. . . ."

"Wait a minute," Cosden broke in.

"Well?" Major said blandly.

191

"Do you think we give a continental damn about the pair of gray squirrels in their infernal pine tree?"

"Ah," Major said a little sadly, "I suppose you don't."

"Then tell us what we want to know, in the name of heaven. What happened between you and big Furness?"

"Why," Major said, "we met each other, after a while, and we had quite a talk. We came to a sort of an agreement."

"Go on, Major!"

"And he gave me a note to take back to you here. Let me see. I hope I haven't got it all rumpled up. Here you are."

It was a single sheet of paper, folded twice, and pinned with a sliver of wood. And it was addressed to Anne Cosden. Her father took it with a scowl and carried it silently out to the kitchen. And by the sudden whitening of her face, he knew that she recognized the handwriting.

She opened it eagerly, swept through it with a glance, and then ripped it across and threw it on the floor.

"What in the world," asked Cosden, "has Furness got to say to you?"

"The man is a coward!" she cried in bitterest scorn. "What do I care what he has to say? Read it, if you wish."

He picked up the pieces of torn paper humbly enough and read it over slowly, to himself. "Does he call you by your first name, girl?"

The letter read:

Dear Anne: I have just finished a long talk with Jeremy Major. I have to admit to you that he is a most convincing talker. And, after listening to him, I have decided that I must give up this foolish amusement of keeping the stage from running.

Also, I think it is rather dangerous for me to linger near Crumbock. So I suppose this little letter must serve to say good bye to you.

A thousand regrets that we have not had an opportunity to come to know each other better.

Chester Ormonde Furness

"And there we are," murmured Cosden to Sammy and Major. "The end of that chapter. What the devil will the next chapter turn up? But I think you understand, Mister Major, that I am eternally grateful to you . . . because it was Gregg's stage, but it was my money."

But that was not the end of the stage.

The next morning there was a change at the Crumbock office of the Crumbock-Munson stage line. Men were waiting. And the gold shipment of Cosden, doubled in size, was joined by two other shipments, hardly smaller. It was a jammed, packed stage that finally crawled up the slope, and dipped into the woods beyond.

And three days later word came whirling back to Crumbock that the trip had been made in perfect safety and in excellent time. And business thrived, and rates climbed. And Sammy Gregg saw the swift hundreds pouring into his hands every day and mounting to thousands each week.

"If you'll stay on as regular guard," he said to Jeremy Major, "I'll pay you a hundred a week . . . with nothing to do except to trail the crooks, if they ever try to hold-up the stages again."

"It's sort of a hard life," Major sighed, "cooking chuck for oneself. . . ."

"I'll hire you a cook," Sammy said, "above your wages. And a servant, if you want, to take care of your horse and your guns for you."

Jeremy Major sighed and stared up at the pale blue sky, where the sun was burning. "Matter of fact," he said, "I've made up my mind that I'd better be traveling south. You see, I have a touch of rheumatism up in these northern countries."

So Sammy attempted no longer to persuade.

Major was gone. And after his departure, Anne Cosden had suddenly taken the stage for Munson, bound East. And suddenly all that was left for Sammy was to sit quietly wherever he pleased and watch the gold flood flow steadily into his coffers. He had won, but the glory was small in his eyes. For Sammy had been growing since he first left Brooklyn, and now he had reached a certain pitch of mind where money alone could not satisfy him.

There we leave him, not calmly submitting, but swallowing his despair. For the one thing he wanted was Anne Cosden, and, were she East or West, he felt that she was beyond his dreams. There was only one bitter satisfaction, that through his engineering he had put her beyond the dreams of handsome Chester Furness as well.

CHAPTER THIRTY-ONE

To understand the extent to which the mountains were shocked, one must consider what Hobo Durfee was, before the tragedy happened to him. His nickname of Hobo had been honestly earned. He had been nothing hut a tramp, a lazy, good-for-nothing scamp who wandered about the country inventing new methods for avoiding labor in any form.

This continued more than halfway through his life, but, when he was forty years old, Hobo Durfee suddenly contracted what might be called the industry fever. Some said it was due to the fact that he had loaned a friend $1 and that the man paid him back $2 the next month. At any rate, Hobo Durfee never forgot. He laid the thought of that dollar of interest away in his memory, embalmed in myrrh and spikenard. And that started his interest in accumulating money.

He began to put away every bit of it that he could lay his hands on. But he did not really have the courage to be a stirring thief. So presently he learned that his love of money was greater than hatred of work, and he began to work steadily, earnestly. He accumulated more and more money. In five years he had a shade over $1,000 in a bank, and then the bank failed. Durfee got his money out, because he was one of the first to call with a check when an evil rumor got abroad. But he never forgot how close he came to losing his money on that day, and thereafter nothing in the world could persuade him to trust his money in hands other than his own. It was known that all his wages were turned into gold, and that all of that gold was hidden away in some secluded place on his own land. For he had a little shack of his own and a patch of ground down in the river bottom. It was just as much as he was able to cultivate by himself. And on it he raised, during a part of the year, vegetables for the market in Munson, which was fairly near his place. No one else, in that region of timber and mines, had ever so much as thought of raising vegetables, and therefore his labor brought him quite a rich reward.

Besides, he was working on his land only a part of the year, and the rest of the time—even now that he was fifty-five years old—he approved himself a good cowhand in every sense of the term by his work on the cattle ranches. It was estimated that Hobo Durfee, in the last years of his life, must have laid up between $5,000 and $10,000 in gold, all hidden some place on his little estate.

Of course that brought the crooks in a swarm, and for years they almost literally plowed the ground of the Durfee Ranch to get at his treasure every time he left his house. They never found it. Old Durfee was too foxy to leave his precious money without having it so securely tucked away that not even an eagle's eye could have located it. So, after a time, the crooks left off trying and Durfee was in peace. A pretty well-deserved peace, too, as everyone agreed.

The old man liked to talk to people about the money he had saved and about the good old foolish, happy, sunny days in trampdom. He liked to talk so well that he kept open house and would entertain anyone who came by with food and chatter.

Well, in the West they appreciate hospitality. In a country where men know desert travel and the heart-stopping joy of coming in sight of a human habitation with smoke curling out of it, they put a high rating upon sincerely hospitable folks. And such a value was placed upon Hobo Durfee.

He grew a lot of strawberries in the spring of the year, and, as they came ripe, he used to gather them and stew them into a delicious jam. That Durfee jam became famous for more than a hundred miles around. And literally hundreds and hundreds had taken a trip scores of miles out of their way in order to come at Hobo Durfee, sit by his stove, eat his pone and delicious strawberry jam, drink his coffee, and then go their way.

He was very happy when he was talking about the good old days when he never used to turn a hand at work. He had never stopped hating work. He had simply come to love money more. And when he began to turn to the subject of how he learned to labor and to save, the boys used to sit around and laugh at him a good deal. But he was willing to be laughed at. It was part of the game, and he liked company so well and liked an audience so well, that he was very willing to have them laugh at him.

It would have done you good to see the red-brown face of that old chap with a grizzled fringe of whiskers more or less long, for he was not like most misers. The point was, some said, that the knowledge that he had a quantity of gold hidden away kept him bubbling over with so much happiness that he just wanted others to hear about it. And so the door of his shack was never closed.

You must know all this to understand how old Hobo Durfee jumped up, one night, and laughed and nodded to some horsemen who had stopped outside of his shack and then had crowded into the doorway. There had been no other callers there on this day, and Hobo Durfee was warmed clear down to his boots when he saw so many forms of men outside his door.

He called out: "Come on in, boys! I've just finished up making some of the most sizzling good jam that you ever seen. And I'm just after finished mixing up some pone and shoving the pans in the oven. And outside of that, I've got about five minutes to start the coffee. Which there ain't never been no better coffee than I make, and there ain't gonna never be none better never made."

Then a voice outside the door said: "Tell the old fool that we ain't come to eat his chuck tonight. And tell him it's something else we want."

Then the leading two men crowded in through the doorway and old Hobo Durfee saw that there was a mask on the face of each. A real hundred percent mask made of black coat lining turned into a sack and pulled down over the head with just a couple of big holes left for the eyes to look through and for air to come in. I suppose it was right then that Hobo guessed what was coming.

He saw that he didn't have a chance. His gun was clear across on the far side of the room. And I suppose there was no particular desire in Hobo to get the gun, at that. All he wanted to do was to make people happy. And besides, what could they get in his house except jam and pone and coffee—which he offered them just as freely without any sign of a mask or a gun?

"Well, boys," he said, "you're mighty welcome to anything that you can see around here. Just look around and help yourselves. But I guess that you ain't gonna see nothing much worth carrying away . . . unless it's some of my cans of jam . . . or maybe the new saddle blanket."

"Leave off the guff, will you, Hobo, you old fool?" one of the men barked. "We ain't gonna do any of the looking tonight. You can do the looking for us."

You can wager that poor old Hobo Durfee was hard hit by that. But he blinked at them for a time and tried to smile around the well-chewed stem of his corncob pipe. "All right, boys," he said, "I guess that I know how to take a joke."

"Joke?" another fellow said, squeezing his way into the house. "You chuck out the coin, old bo, or you're gonna find that this here is the hottest joke that you ever laid hold of in your life.

And don't you forget it."

It took the smile from the lips of Hobo Durfee and he stood rather weakly, looking from one black mask to another.

"Show him what we mean," one said tersely.

It was done in an instant. They seized upon Durfee, who made no resistance to such numbers, and they stripped off his boots. They then opened the firebox of the stove and carried him up to it until the heat burned his socks and he uttered a yell of pain and terror. They took him away from the fire at once.

"All right, Durfee," they told him. "You show us where the money is or you see what you get."

When poor old Durfee saw that they actually meant what they said, he was silent and stared at them. He simply could not believe. No matter what the first part of his life had been, the past fifteen years had been so flooded by kindliness that I suppose it was impossible for the ex-hobo to understand that this brutality was really intended—or that there were creatures in the world capable of it.

At any rate, he maintained that silence until they caught hold of him and actually thrust him up to the firebox so close that his socks caught fire. He screamed in earnest this time and they brought him away and demanded with a snarl if he were ready to give them what they wanted. But he was not ready. And they pushed him up to the blazing wood until his feet. . . .

But Munson saw those feet afterward, and it is better to leave that part until later.

According to the approved story, Durfee fainted after one of the applications of the torture. But they threw a half bucket of cold water in his face and waited for him to come to. Then they began again, and he stood the fiendish cruelty until the fire had actually. . . . But this is unspeakable.

All that one can say is that when he finally surrendered he

was too far gone to walk. He was too far gone to creep. He had to be stimulated with whiskey, and after he had half a pint of that under his belt, he was able to whisper to them and they carried him with them out of the house and they brought him to the old shed where he kept his horse.

It had once been a house. The shed was built up around the last standing parts of the chimney and a portion of the north wall. Inside that chimney, which no one knew about, by reaching down half an arm's length and removing a few loose bricks, they found an aperture, and inside that aperture they found the treasure of Durfee.

There were nothing but $20 gold pieces. And there were three hundred and eighty-seven of these, which made exactly $7,740 that they looted from him.

There were six of them altogether.

No, just at the end a big man came galloping up, and when he found what they had been doing, he cursed them and said that he was through with them forever. But they pointed out that the business was done and that he might as well share in the profits and forget about it.

Which he did.

So that the total was only just a shade above $1,100 per thief, and for that small sum they sold their souls, certainly, into the deepest part of purgatory.

CHAPTER THIRTY-TWO

They left old Durfee lying in the horse shed, and that was what saved his life and brought danger to the gang. Because he managed to drag himself onto the bare back of his horse and he rode on into Munson. Or, rather, the horse took him there, for when Jack Lorrain found him in the night, Durfee had slid unconscious from the back of the old gelding and lay in the street before his hoofs, and the horse stood above his master with his head dropped wearily, looking uncannily as though he were grieving for the thing that had been done.

Jack Lorrain, as he said afterward, thought that it was some drunk who had taken too much liquor and he was about to go on past, when something about the patience of the old horse standing there over its master and waiting for him to rise touched the heart of Jack. And he decided that a man who was worth the trouble of a horse, in this fashion, must be worth the trouble of another man, also.

So he went to the quiet form that lay in the dust and seized him by the shoulder, and the body was just as limp as drunkenness to his touch. Jack Lorrain was again on the verge of passing on, but he decided to take a look at the drunk so that the boys could laugh about the thing the next day. He scratched a match, accordingly, but what the light of that match showed him kept him speechless until the flame pricked the tips of his fingers sharply. And then a roar broke from the lips of Jack—a roar that rang and reëchoed through Munson and brought men tumbling out of houses all around. And when Lorrain had gathered quite a crowd, he lit another match and showed them what he had found.

They picked up Hobo Durfee with a womanish tenderness and they carried him into what had once been Mortimer's saloon, famous for iniquity until big Chester Furness, the first day he came to town, shot Mortimer and treated the boys over the bar, leaving gold on the bar to pay for the drinks. Gold for a dead man.

The saloon was somewhat less celebrated now, but truly it was hardly less wicked, and what transpired inside of its walls would have filled many a chapter in a wild history every day. It was filled with carousal even at that moment, but the procession silenced them suddenly and completely.

They gathered with drawn faces and looked at the frightful thing before them. And all at once everyone became as busy as they were silent. Some dozen mounted horses and rushed away in varying directions to find Dr. Stanley Morgan. And some heated water and brought it. And one youngster, newly in from the East, offered a flask of fine old brandy, such as had not been seen in rough Munson town for many a day.

Others cut the clothes from the body of Hobo Durfee. Others washed him. Others prepared his bed in the back room of the saloon—piling it thick and soft with blankets, and clearing all the rubbish from the chamber and all the dirt from the floor.

Here the doctor arrived, just as Durfee began to groan his way back to consciousness, and by the doctor's care the feet were thoroughly dressed before consciousness fully returned to Hobo. All agreed that it was a mercy that his sleep had lasted until that dressing was completed.

The boys of Munson wanted to know what would become of Durfee, and they were assured that he would never walk again without the aid of a pair of crutches. It was a sentence almost worse than death, and they quietly interchanged glances. Morgan was not much of a doctor. He would hardly have dared to set up for anything more than a veterinary in any other part of the world. But his opinion about such a matter as those feet was not to be doubted.

In the meantime Durfee had regained consciousness completely. But the doctor had put enough opiates on his feet to keep him from torment. He was merely weakly drowsy, and kept turning his head slowly from side to side and staring at the faces around him in terror and in horror that would gradually melt away as Jack Lorrain or some other, sitting by his bed, patted his hand and would say: "Buck up, old-timer. You're all right now. We're gonna take care of you. Steady along, old buck. There ain't nothin' to be skeered of, Hobo. Nobody but your friends here."

So Durfee would manage a faint, incredulous smile, and then shake his head and frown while he closed his eyes and seemed to be trying to think back to the confusion of troubles that had closed around him.

After a time they tried to press him for a little information. But he could only say: "Seems like I had a sort of a falling out with some of the boys . . . I dunno about what. I disremember exactly what the argument was all about. They was het up considerable, though."

That was all he could say, and the doctor decided that it would be wise not to press him too much that evening.

Half a dozen volunteers decided to sit up and take turns watching Durfee through the night and another half dozen mounted horses and rushed furiously out to the little Durfee shack in the bottom land.

They descended into the damp, cool air of the river side. They came to the cabin and found all neat and orderly there, with the lamp burning steadily on the table. Only there was a faint cloud of bluish smoke hanging in the corners of the room, and, when they opened the doors of the oven, they found four big pans of pone burned to a crisp.

Then, with lanterns, they went over the ground outside and very quickly they decided that someone had been there before them. A party totally indifferent to the condition of Hobo's garden. For his choicest patches of ground had been trodden and torn by random tramplings of hoofs. Being experts at this business, they very readily decided that seven horses had been there.

"What were seven riders doing here," they asked one another, "interrupting old Durfee while he was baking his pone?"

Jack Lorrain, who was one of the party, said solemnly: "Boys, I hate to think it . . . I ain't gonna really think it till I'm cornered . . . but I got a hateful sort of a lingering suspicion that them burned feet of poor old Hobo's ain't no accident. It was done to him on purpose by them gents that rode in here over his garden."

No one answered Jack, because it was a little too horrible for them to speak about. For though there has always been plenty of brutality in the West, following the frontier, yet it has been brutality of the man-to-man type. The Indians were never able to establish any precedents with all of their efforts. However, the searchers did not discover the plundered cavity in the chimney in the horse shed.

They returned to spread a vague rumor of horror through the town of Munson. In the morning, people had come from a distance to learn the facts as soon as old Durfee was able to relate them, and, among others, there were some celebrities recently come down from Crumbock. They came with the others to the saloon, and with whispers in the front room they were told about the condition of the sufferer in the back room. They were Hubert Cosden and little Sammy Gregg, who had pushed through the celebrated stage line from Munson to Crumbock, nearly a year before. People said that Sammy was himself worth more than a quarter of a million, now, what with the stage line and little investments here and there among the mines, made at the advice of his friend, Cosden.

With them came big Anne Cosden riding a strapping black horse on which she had kept pace from Crumbock with the stage, doing the hundred miles in a day and a half—a hundred miles of terrible ups and downs in thirty-six hours. One might have thought that she was tired out, after such a performance, but she was not. Or at least, she seemed to forget about it when she saw a sick man.

In ten seconds she was in charge of the room and Hobo Durfee in it. And before the first minute had elapsed, she had a bucket of hot soap suds and was giving that floor the first scrubbing of its short but eventful life. She washed it until it dried white. And then she washed the walls. And when she was ended with that, she sent little Sammy Gregg forth to get wildflowers, and these she distributed around the room in any receptacles that she could get out of the saloon.

About half an hour after these changes had been made—with the windows of the room opened, and the doors opened, also, so that a refreshing wind could pass through—old Durfee opened his eyes and said in a tremulous voice: "Dog-gone me if spring ain't come ag'in." And then he saw the girl and flushed. He was not used to be tended upon by ladies.

"Of course it's spring," Anne Cosden said, sitting down beside his bed. "It was just about a year ago in the spring, too, that I came by your house and you asked me in to have pone and strawberry jam."

"Ah," Hobo Durfee said, abashed. "I disremembered for a minute. But I guess that you're Miss Cosden, and. . . ." A wave of pain struck him. He stiffened and fought out the battle.

"Lord, man," Anne Cosden said, "groan . . . that'll let some of the corked-up pain out of you. When I was a youngster, I used to take pride in not making any noise when I was hurt. I was always spilling off a horse, you know, and breaking a collar bone, or something like that. But after a while I found that it did a lot of good just to lie back and shout when something hurt me."

Old Durfee chuckled. He had forgotten his pain. And little Sammy Gregg, noiseless as a shadow in a corner of the room, worshiped big Anne Cosden.

She flashed a glance at him and moved her lips in a whisper that the sick man could not hear, but which said plainly to Sammy Gregg: "Will you please get rid of that goose look?"

Then suddenly old Durfee was saying: "I'm beginning to remember. It sort of begins to work back into my mind. . . . I see 'em standing there outside the door of my cabin. And . . . oh, my Lord, they got all my money! They got fifteen years that I can't never live no more and they put them years of my life in their pockets."

Anne Cosden, with a consolatory murmur, put her hand on the hot forehead of Durfee, and at the same time a slight nod brought Sammy Gregg instantly to her side.

"You know shorthand, Sammy. Now he's about to talk . . . and you get every word down."

"Paper . . . ," Sammy said helplessly.

"Darn it," Anne Cosden said, "write on the floor, if you can't do any better."

206

CHAPTER THIRTY-THREE

This was the fashion in which old Durfee told his story, slowly, stretching his tale over more than an hour, for often the horror of the thing that had happened would rush back upon his mind and stop his speech. But always Anne Cosden, sitting beside him, soothing him, letting him groan when he would, letting him speak when he could, sympathetic, gentle, filled with intuitions of the right manner of persuading him to talk, drew the story forth in every detail. While in the corner, unheeded by the sick man, little Sammy writhed and listened and writhed again, and, while his teeth were set, his rapid pencil took down the words of the sufferer.

He had a little memorandum book that served him. Presently the memorandum book was filled—with the questions of the girl, and the responses of the sick man. And then he took out old letters and scrawled upon the backs of the sheets and on the outside and on the inside of envelopes, the utterances of Hobo Durfee that were to bring death to so many men.

One might not have realized, looking in upon this scene, that Justice was no longer a blind goddess but was opening her eyes and beginning to prepare to strike, while that rapid, cunning pencil made the swift signs that could be reinterpreted as speech.

The thing was ended. Old Durfee lay exhausted, but happy at last now that the tale had been told. For, just as the girl had told him, some of the pain seemed to pass into the groans and the words with which he had expressed himself.

Then Anne Cosden, stifled with anger and grief, with tears in her eyes and with her square chin thrust forward, nodded jerkily to little Sammy, saying as clearly as words: "Now go out and let the world hear what we have heard."

So Sammy went softly out and faced the dense crowd that waited, in a deadly silence, in the outer room of the saloon. Not a word had been spoken out there. Not a drink had been tasted. But every man had a pair of revolvers belted around his hips and most of them leaned upon rifles, and in the street each man had left his fastest and strongest horse.

At the nod of Sammy, and, seeing the paper in his hand, they followed him forth from the saloon. They gathered again in the street around him. But he was not tall enough to let all their eyes find his face, and therefore stalwart Hubert Cosden caught him up and perched the little man upon one of his broad shoulders.

From this position, Sammy read forth his account, giving each of the questions of the girl, and each of the answers of poor Durfee. And there was not a whisper from that crowd. But every crook in it—and there were many of them there—felt like an honest man when he thought of the horror of it all.

They came to the end of the document. Sammy reading off of an envelope, crowded with charactery.

"Miss Cosden: Did you recognize any of their voices?
Durfee: One of them I thought I did. I ain't quite sure.
Miss Cosden: Who was that?
Durfee: It was him that come the last. It was the seventh man.
Miss Cosden: And who did he seem to you to be?
Durfee: I disremember. A name come into my mind at the time, but it's slipped out again.
Miss Cosden: Don't try too hard to remember. It may pop

back into your mind again. What sort of a man was he? Tall or short?

Durfee: *Oh, he was considerable of a tallish sort of a gent.*

Miss Cosden: *Young or old?*

Durfee: *Sort of betwixt and between.*

Miss Cosden: *And what did he say?*

Durfee: *First I thought that he was gonna take my money away from them.*

Miss Cosden: *Did you think that one man could take the money away from six?*

Durfee: *I dunno. He was sort of a leader with them.*

Miss Cosden: *What did he say to them?*

Durfee: *He cussed them out considerable and said that what they had done was an outrage, you see. That was when I begun hoping.*

Miss Cosden: *And then?*

Durfee: *One of them up and said that now that they had turned the trick and got the money that so many others had tried to get and failed, that the chief might as well take his share.*

Miss Cosden: *But did he take it?*

Durfee: *Yes. I heard them counting the money out and I heard it go crashing and jingling into his wallet, I guess. I turned my head, and I seen him take it and I squinted hard to make out his face.*

Miss Cosden: *Didn't he have on a mask?*

Durfee: *No, there was no mask on him. But there was a sort of blackness running around in front of his eyes and I couldn't make him out clear.*

Miss Cosden: *Was there anything else about him that struck you?*

Durfee: *Nothing but his horse.*

Miss Cosden: *What sort of a horse was it? Or could you see it in the night?*

Durfee: I couldn't've seen it if it had been any other color. But it was a gray horse and mighty big and upstanding, sort of. It looked like a fine horse. I could tell that much. A horse that could carry a big man, too.

Miss Cosden: I think you're tired, now.

Durfee: I'm sort of hankering for a little sleep."

Sammy Gregg lowered the envelope. "That's the end of it, boys," he said. "There wasn't any more, after that. He quieted down. And I came out to you. But I wonder if any of you think the same thing about the gray horse that I'm thinking?"

There was an instant of scowling silence that showed that a good many had a thought but that they were unwilling to speak it. Then Jack Lorrain broke out: "I'll tell you what I thought about . . . a gent that used to play a lone hand, but they say that he's been mixing up with some of the other crooks, lately, and letting them do part of his work for him. The rest of you know who I mean. He's a big man . . . and he'd be the leader of the gang, and he rides a gray horse that's about as well known in these parts as the rider is known. I mean, Chester Furness."

And there was a sullen roar of assent.

Then another in the rear of the crowd shouted: "Then let's go and hunt him up!"

There was another shout. And a movement toward horses was stopped by the thunder of Hubert Cosden: "You'll never get him that way!"

They paused, itching for action.

Cosden went on: "I've seen gatherings like this before. A hundred well-armed and well-mounted men all set on getting some scoundrel . . . though we've never had scoundrels quite as black as these seven. But it always ends up the same way. We get hot under the collar. We jump onto our horses. We ride like sixty through the mountains with no particular end in mind. And, the next day, about half the boys have tired their horses . . . there's no real clue before them . . . and most of them troop off back to town and to work. The rest stay on a few days longer, perhaps. They hear a couple of rumors . . . ride to hunt them down . . . find nothing . . . and then they go home and say that it's the business of the law to handle these affairs, after all. But there is no law here. If we had a sheriff, we wouldn't have affairs like this one of Durfee. There is no law except such law as we make with our own hands. And I say that the time has come for us to adopt new tactics. Do any of you agree with me?"

They agreed. A good deal of their flare of enthusiasm vanished as he mentioned so many hard-faced facts.

"But what do you suggest, Mister Cosden?"

"I suggest that we have one man to direct all of us. Better to have one head, even if it's a poor one, than to have fifty heads all wanting to do different things."

Anne Cosden came out to tell them to make less noise, for her charge was now asleep. But she remained to listen to the most exciting part of the scene that followed.

Big Rendell, the storekeeper, walking with a frightful limp because of his battered hip, uttered his advice in a roar that had to be heard: "Gents," he said, "I know the man to plan the work for you. He ain't a fighting man. But he's a man with brains. He can't throw a rope, or handle a knife, or shoot with a gun. But he's got a head on his shoulders. I mean him that brung the first big herd of ponies from Texas, which was something we all said couldn't be done. I mean him that pushed through the Munson-Crumbock stage, after everybody else had tried it and failed. I mean my friend, Sam Gregg. He's the man for you!"

Anne Cosden could not help smiling as she looked at the five feet and eight inches of which Sammy Gregg was composed— and the thin face, which the sun could never entirely turn brown—and the nervous, eager body with which he had been furnished by nature and never improved by exercise. Sammy Gregg seemed immensely embarrassed and shook his head, and Anne Cosden waited for this crowd of proved men—killers, many of them, rough frontiersmen nearly all of them—to burst into a roar of laughter at the jest.

But to her bewilderment, they did not laugh. They did not seem to take it as a joke, at all. And she was more amazed than ever when she saw them nodding gravely to themselves, and muttering.

Jack Lorrain said: "That's what I call good sense, Rendell. There's enough of us to shoot the guns and ride the horses. We need a gent to sit back with a good head on his shoulders and tell us what is the next best trick for us to take. Here's Sam Gregg that has done what nobody else could do. I say, let's have Gregg to tell us what is what. He's our general, I guess. And we'll keep him off of the firing line, if we can. He'll be headquarters for us. What you say, Sammy? Will you take the job of doing our thinking for us?"

Sammy Gregg was most reluctant. There were twenty better men than he among them, he declared. And then he saw the astonished, almost thunderstruck face of big Anne Cosden, and his own color grew hotter still.

"But," Sammy said, "I've sat in the shack of old Hobo Durfee. And I've had his pone and strawberry jam, the same as most of the rest of you. And if you want me to take charge, I'll do it. And do my best to bring in the whole seven of 'em, dead or alive . . . but mostly big Chester Furness with a rope around his neck. He's been my bad luck ever since I came here. We landed on the same day. And my first job was to try to bring up a herd of horses from Texas. And you all know how that herd was stolen by Furness. Then I tried to open a stage line, and it was the robberies of Furness that nearly ruined me. Now it's my turn to try to get him, and I'm going to do my best. If you want me for the job, say so, and I'll take half an hour to think it over, and then tell you what looks best to me."

There was no doubt about the heartiness of the response. It was a true, old-fashioned, Anglo-Saxon throated cheer.

Anne Cosden fairly staggered back into the room where her patient was stirring fretfully in his sleep. For to Anne, little Sammy had never seemed more than an imitation man before this day.

Chapter Thirty-Four

They gave Sammy Gregg what he wanted—time to think out a plan—and he went off by himself and sat down on a stump behind the hotel and embraced his skinny knees with his thin hands and pondered his problem, and watched a pair of busy hens foraging among the seeds that the grass had dropped, under the surveillance of a lordly rooster with a red-helmeted head and a cuirass of curious greens and crimsons and rich purples.

Sammy, watching this kingly fowl, thought to himself that there were men like it. There was Chester Furness, for instance, filling the eye utterly—big, handsome, stately, sure of himself. But he, Sammy Gregg, was surely none of these.

A shadow whipped across the yard. The hens ran together in a huddle, squawking. Even the big rooster cowered, and spread his wings, and stretched out his neck foolishly to scan the sky above him. There was a hawk sliding through the sky above them, already away, and tilting out of sight behind the head of the nearest tree. There were men like that hawk, too—swifter than others, armed by Nature more than other men, keen, alert. And that strange fellow, Jeremy Major, was one of these.

Or was Jeremy Major a type? Was he not rather unique?

At least Sammy knew that he was neither rooster nor hawk. He was simply plain, common, or garden humanity. He was just the average height—or was he a little under it? And he was just the average weight, or was he a trifle lighter? And he had no strength of body or no skill of hand, and he had no strange talents, like Jeremy Major and other men. He had only common sense.

Perhaps, indeed, he differed in one respect from most people. He could give himself wholly to a task that he had at hand. He could pour brain and soul into his labors with a perfectly focused intensity. Other men, by the very wealth of their powers, were apt to give only a quarter of their strength and a tithe of their time and attention. So he had struggled up a little beyond the mass of men. At least, his bank account was considered fatter than theirs.

Yonder lay poor Durfee, a ruined man because of the treasure of some $7,000 that he had put away. But Sammy Gregg, still far under thirty, was master of a competent fortune. Not that he prided himself upon what he had done. No, for he took it all very humbly. It merely showed him that the constant use of even the smallest means may eventually carry one to the top of the mountain. And now, most astonishing, most shocking to all that he had ever expected of himself, he was appointed to construct the plan of a manhunt. Seven human lives were the goal of his endeavors—he who could not ride a bucking horse, or shoot a gun, or read a hundred feet of the plainest trail. But those rough-handed fellows who could do all of these things— they themselves had chosen him.

It was only for a moment that he contemplated the strangeness of his work and his place in that work. Then he lost all thought of self, and his mind was rapt in the contemplation of the problem. It was more than an hour before he called together the leaders among the men—the well-known figures who were familiar to cowpunchers and miners alike.

More than one of them, no doubt, envied him his eminent position on this day and would be willing to scoff at his schemes. He must win their trust and confidence first of all. So he stood with them at the corner of the street and laid his plan bare.

It was more complicated than they liked, he could see that, but the longer he talked the more willing they seemed to agree with him. In the first place, he decided that the seven, having drawn together, would never content themselves with one such act as the robbery of poor old Durfee.

Furness was not the sort of a man to assemble forces merely because there was a handful of money like this in the offing. His own gains in the trade of highway robbery must now be mounting to the scores and scores of thousands. And if he called together seven men, it was never for the sake of robbing a helpless old fellow like Durfee.

For, as Sammy pointed out to them, Furness was a fellow who lived as a road agent partly for the money but mostly, he had no doubt, as a means of amusing himself. No, it was plain that he had appointed to his followers some rendezvous near the house of Durfee. He himself had been late, and, while they waited for him, they had started out to make a little money on the side. And the horrible torture of Durfee had followed.

But originally they must have been summoned to effect a raid of major importance. No such blow had been struck within the last few days. Therefore it was plain that the work for the band had not yet been accomplished. It was still to do, and they could trust to Furness that the blow would most surely fall. If the countryside were roused against him, so much the greater reason would there seem to him to push his scheme through, no matter what it might be.

With this in mind, what Sammy Gregg proposed was that they learn, as soon as possible, how many of the men who were assembled in Munson on this day could be relied upon to campaign for a matter of a week, at the least. There were now more than a hundred under arms. But perhaps more than two thirds of these could not leave their work for a long manhunt.

Better find out the permanent men for the posse at once.

For now, Hubert Cosden would enter the stage and make the journey back to Crumbock as fast as possible. There he would spread the alarm in the same fashion and gather as many permanent men as he could.

"Now," Sammy said to his new henchmen, "there's half a dozen places where Furness's riders are apt to strike. They might tackle Munson. They might try Crumbock. They might land at Chadwick City, or Little Orleans, or Buxton Crossing. Or they might even ride as far as Old Shawnee. Look at the map." He sketched in the dust with his forefinger as he talked. "Here are the mountains in a lump . . . an armful a hundred and fifty miles across. Crumbock is fairly close to the center of it. Munson is off here to the edge. The other towns are out on the plains beyond. Very well. No matter where they rob, Furness and his men always head for the heart of the mountains. That is their hole-in-the-wall country. They hide there as soon as they can after they've made a raid.

"Now, what I plan to do is not to try to herd them away from all the towns, but cut off the line of their retreat. We ought to get thirty or forty men out of Munson, and the same number out of Crumbock. Then split those men into two sections each. That'll give you four posses of between fifteen to twenty men each. Then post each of the four in the mountains, in a square. Every side of that square will be about seventy or eighty miles long. We'll put men here and here and here." He jabbed out the places on his rudely sketched map.

"Now we'll make no more noise about this thing than we have to, but we'll at once send riders from Munson to go to each of the towns where big Furness is most apt to strike. In the towns they'll not speak a word or give any warning that we think that Furness is going to raid. Because, so far as we know for sure, he may not raid. But we'll have our men there, as messengers. Now, the instant a raid is carried out, the messenger in the town that is raided will ride . . . not on the trail of the raiders . . . but straight into the mountains until he comes to that section of the posse that is located nearest to his own town. When the word is brought in, in that fashion, the party that is warned will give the messenger a fresh horse and send him on to warn the other nearest sections of our posse. In the meantime, it will have fixed in its own mind the most likely routes along which the seven are apt to hit into the mountains from the nearest town. In a way, you can say that we'll have Furness and his men running right into our hands. Fifteen or twenty men, who know what to expect, ought to be able to handle at least the seven men in that gang. The advantage of surprise will be all on our side."

Perhaps it was a little complicated. Perhaps, also, it was a little more selfish than a real sheriff's posse would have dared to be. But the need was urgent. And the scheme appealed most strongly to the imaginations of the men to whom Gregg talked.

There was one chief danger. They needed three full days in order to set their trap. And if the raid occurred before the trap was set, most of their preparations would be wasted. So the first thing was speed in those preparations.

All was arranged with perfect harmony. In another hour, Cosden was whirling away toward Crumbock to gather what good men he could in the mining camp. Jack Lorrain and others were weeding out the volunteers of Munson. They got thirty-four men who declared their willingness to remain at least a week on the job. Besides, they were furnished with five messengers who were to scatter to the points of danger exposed to the attack of Furness—namely to the five towns.

When that was arranged, the Munson volunteers were split into two sections and marched at once out of the town. They only delayed long enough to load up with plenty of bacon and flour and salt at Rendell's store. And then they were off.

Anne Cosden waved farewell to them from the front door of the saloon, as cheerfully as though they were off on a picnic, and she herself left behind among old friends. She had her own work, which was to care for old Durfee in his pain, with the meager assistance of Dr. Stanley Morgan.

But the rearmost rider of the second party that started for the upper mountains was beckoned to by her. It was Sammy Gregg, who rode over before her and removed his hat obediently.

"Sammy," she said, "I hope that you're only riding out of town with the boys to see them off. You're not going with them."

"Why," Sammy responded, "after starting a thing like this, I couldn't stay behind."

"Will you tell me," Anne Cosden said impatiently, "why you should put yourself in the way of bullets when you don't know the first thing about how to shoot back?"

"Oh, no," Sammy said, "I don't expect that I'll be of any real use when the bullets begin to fly. But I thought that I could be handy around the camp."

"Are you a camp cook?" Anne Cosden asked sternly.

"I can wash the pans, at least," Sammy replied, and he rode on with a grin.

"Young man," Anne Cosden called out, "don't be silly and try to be a hero!"

CHAPTER THIRTY-FIVE

At the head of that party from Munson of which young Sammy Gregg was himself a member, there rode that tall and long-mustached viking, Cumnor. It was he who had abandoned all such industries as mining and lumbering and even cow herding for the reason, as he said, that they were the sign of a new country, and what he wanted to be in was a country that was permanent in its occupations and in the returns that it yielded to good law-abiding citizens. Therefore, he had established himself, after a time as a rancher, in the smaller field as farmer. It was said that he and poor old Hobo Durfee were the only real farmers in that part of the world, and now that Durfee was unlikely ever again to till a field, or afford to have one tilled for him, Cumnor stood alone in that branch of work.

He was proud of this lonely eminence, and he was fond of saying that the rest of the members of the community were no better than mere temporary interlopers, whereas he was the forerunner of the men who would make the country rich and great. The time would come, as Cumnor was fond of saying, when those mountains would be terraced high up their sides and thriving farms would throng in every valley.

For that reason he had not hesitated to establish himself in a district where there was a good deal more scenery than there was soil. There were great crops of rocks, and the faster they were removed, the faster they grew. But the good nature and the optimism of Cumnor were as long as his yellow mustaches.

It was said that he was losing money hand over hand every year, and that often he did not receive back from the soil the seed that he had sowed upon it. But his courage was never daunted, and he was fond of saying, when he was asked how he was doing: "Well, sir, I fenced in a new quarter-section last month."

Indeed his expenses for fencing ran very high, especially as the cow owners grew more numerous and their men developed wicked habits of cutting any wire fence lines that happened to be in the way of their cow drives. However, Cumnor would not down.

"I'm building for the future," he would vow. "My grandsons will be thanking me for the work that I've done around here."

"But why, Cumnor," Sammy asked upon a day, "do you want to fence in that big round-headed knoll over yonder? It will cost you a lot to drill post holes in that rock."

"It's worth the money," vowed Cumnor. "Because right yonder is the spot that overlooks all the rest of the land, and my grandson or my great-grandson will thank me for having included in the estate the right site for the mansion."

Of course there was no arguing with a man like that. And people merely stood by and shook their heads and waited for him to go broke, which was the direction in which he was headed as fast as he could go. But, as some pointed out, although he knew no more about farming than to order all sorts of new and unneeded implements from Rendell's store, he was on the other hand an expert cowman of long standing. His talents were simply diverted into the wrong channel. Most pitiful of all, there was no way of getting rid of his grain, unless he could find a mill to grind it to flour, when it would sell readily enough. But this merely inspired him to build great, capacious granaries, in which he stored each year's product.

"Look at the way the population of the country is growing," Cumnor used to say. "I guess that there is your sure sign that prices for wheat and barley is gonna stay right up there in the clouds for a long time."

And if some of the stored grain began to rot in the winter damps, he was merely inspired to reinforce the foundation of his barns. "You got to pay for experience," Cumnor would say.

Perhaps it would have been hard to tell whether big Cumnor was more amusing or pathetic as the owner and operator of a farm, but at the head of a trailing party, he was a dignified and important person. His school was the badlands of the Great Plains, and there he had been trained up in the terrible discipline of the Indian wars. And he remained rather a grim fellow, whenever he was put with his back to a wall, as young Sammy Gregg could testify strongly enough. But that was long ago, and they were now firm friends.

It was a beautiful sight to see Cumnor lay his course through the mountains to the spot that had been designated as his location. He had been given the post of honor at the angle that was nearest to the two towns of Chadwick City and Little Orleans. The warning messengers from either of those towns would find the party of big Cumnor first. And now the farmer guided his band swiftly among the growing peaks.

He did not need a compass to tell him the way. That was a trail that he had never traveled before, but any old plainsman has learned to stock his brain with all manner of landmarks and signs, and when he comes out of the plains, where it is difficult enough to find any sort of a mark, it is simple enough when he finds himself among the mountains. For they are not to him what they are to the uninitiated—simply great forms, monotonous as waves in the sea. Rather, they are so many faces, each with individual features.

And the general landmarks were so well fixed in the mind of Cumnor that now he led the party on with a perfect surety, never pausing to make his reckoning at any point along the journey. They crossed the first range of heights before noon of the starting day. Then they swung down into a rough, narrow valley that extended between that range and the next just off to the north.

A narrow, rising wisp of smoke attracted the sure eye of Cumnor at this point. On the trail, the trail leader is as absolute as the captain of a ship at sea.

"Ride over, two of you, and see who's at that campfire. Burton and Si Manning, go along, will you?"

"Campfire?" echoed Si Manning. "I dunno that I see any smoke."

"Look yonder ag'in' that rank of big pine trees, will you. There you'll see it, right under that big strike of yaller porphyry."

Any stone that does not fit in with a definitely known class of rocks is put into the category of porphyry by the amateur geologist, like the self-taught prospector. But toward that yellow strike of rock, Si Manning and Burton, his companion, looked, and after a moment they saw what looked like a tiny little blue-white cloud under the rock. It was so dim that it was lost to sight the instant it had nothing but the blue of the sky behind it.

And Si Manning winked aside to his companion, as much as to say: "The old boy is pretty much of a mountaineer at that."

Then they started on their detour, crossing the valley rapidly, while the main body held on toward the summit beyond. They dipped out of view among the rocks at the bottom of the valley, and then they were lost to the following eyes.

For a full hour they were gone, though Big Cumnor had held back the pace of the main body to a slowly dragging walk. And finally he halted his men and turned to look back down the trail with an oath.

"Damn them no-account Paiutes," Cumnor sighed. "Are they taking a damned *siesta*, maybe? Or do we have to go back and see what's happened to them?"

But, just as that moment, the whole party heard the crack of a gun in the distance, and then a rapid chattering of bullets. They looked, and behold there came two riders—their own men—Si Manning and Burton, riding for dear life, leaning well over the necks of their horses and firing back from time to time at the trees out of which they had issued a moment before. And the sharp, metallic clangor of a rifle echoed back to them from the trees.

Some of the party would have scattered back toward the point of danger, had not Cumnor stopped them. "This here little game is their own making," Cumnor said. "Now they got their wits addled and they're pretty well scared. We'll hear a wild yarn when they come in. But when I send out gents to scout for me, I expect them to be able to take care of themselves . . . and us. It's what I got a right to expect. The scouts is the eyes and the ears and the hands of the main body. Look at 'em come lickety-split!"

Even when they dashed their foaming horses up to the others, Si Manning and Burton did not seem at ease, and, in response to a volley of questions, Manning would only shake his head for a moment and, panting, point to Burton.

As for Burton, he looked as though he had been kicked in the face by a heavily shod horse. It was Manning, however, who told the story, little by little, a rather confused narrative, but the chief points of it were made out clearly enough.

They had crossed the ravine, as the main party saw, and the pair had then proceeded more carefully, attempting, if possible, to steal upon the hidden campfire unobserved. They had got well within the edge of the trees when they were met by a good-natured hail from the glade just before them, and then accordingly gave over their attempt to stalk and, feeling very foolish, had advanced into a small clearing among the trees. They had expected to find a number of people there, some one of whom they felt must have given warning to the rest of the approach of strangers, but, when they came in, they found—at that moment at least—that the camp was occupied by one person only.

This was a slender youth, handsome, dark brown of eye, very genial and lazy of gesture and of voice. He had greeted them kindly and without surprise and invited them, if they chose, to have supper with him, only stipulating that they should pluck their own supper, a task that was too much for his single pair of hands. He illustrated by pointing to a heap of dead birds. Some few of these were of a fair size, but the rest were mere little puffs of feathers.

They thanked him but told him that they had to push on. And yet, as Si Manning said, it was a most tempting spectacle that they had before them—the stranger taking up one by one the birds that he had plucked and cleaned and spitting them on a long, clean stick. Apparently he had selected the cream of the kill for his first ration. And now, as he turned the birds above the blaze, the fragrance of the roasting meat was almost too much for the always-raging appetites of two true mountaineers. The other, turning the spit with care, kept glancing in dismay at the heap of slaughtered birds.

"A mighty shame to have them all go to waste," he said. "I didn't realize that I had snagged so many of them. And there they are . . . poor little beggars . . . and all for nothing but fun, you might say. I wish you strangers could stay a while and eat up the batch for me."

"Why," Si Manning said, "d'you mean to say that you're only gonna be able to eat the few that you got on that stick there over the fire? Ain't you got no more room than that in your stomach for such game?"

"Matter of fact," said the youth, "I suppose that I could eat two or three helpings like this. There isn't much to 'em, you

see. But when it comes to sitting and pulling out the feathers
. . . why, that's quite a job. I'd rather go about half hungry than
stay here drilling away at work like that for another half hour."

They could see that he meant what he said.

At this point a great black stallion, which had apparently
been approaching through the brush, but with all of the uncanny
silence of a stalking moose, appeared within the clearing and, at
the voice of the man, walked straight up to him, just as a dog
would have done. It was the grandest-looking horse that Si
Manning had ever seen.

"Ah," the stranger said, "you've found water, have you,
Clancy, you old scamp? Well, you can lead me to it, after a
while. Now go back and find the best grass around. You may
have weak pickings tomorrow."

The stallion, exactly as though he had understood the spoken
words, had turned and started across the clearing, when Burton
intercepted him. The beauty of the wonderful animal had been
too much for him, and he had stepped forward with his hand
outstretched.

"Be careful," warned the stranger. "That horse is dangerous."

"Dangerous nonsense," Burton said. "I've known horses all
my life and I can tell the bad actors by the look in their eyes.
This here horse ain't no more'n a pet."

As he spoke, he went close to the big black, which had
paused, with pricking ears. But now the ears flattened like magic
and the stallion flung himself suddenly at Burton.

The master cried out sharply—and in time. The head of
Clancy was thrown up as though he felt a strong hand wrench-
ing on a curb bit. But the impact of his lunging shoulder had
struck Burton and knocked him flat. Altogether, it was a very
uncanny affair.

But Burton had leaped to his feet in a wild tantrum. He had
been made a fool of a little too thoroughly to suit a man of his

humor. "Damn you and your tricks!" he had shouted at the stranger. "Here's a trick that's worth a dozen of them all!" And he took a hearty swing with his big fist at the head of the owner of Clancy.

The latter had been seated, but in some manner he had floated up to his feet and away from the blow. And the next instant he had struck Burton a staggering blow that had sent the latter reeling across the clearing. After him went the stranger, with a leap like a panther's. And there was such a devil in his face, Si Manning vowed, that it still curdled his blood to think of it. He caught Burton at once and struck him to the ground with a blow that fairly crushed that unlucky mountaineer. He was by this time too frightened to feel the effects of the blow. He simply rolled to his feet with a yell and leaped into the saddle on his horse. Si Manning had followed the example.

"There was something about that kid," Si Manning said. "I dunno what it might've been, but after I had had one look at his face, I forgot all about having a pair of Colts on the hip. All I wanted was to get distance between him and me. I didn't remember a gun until I was in the saddle and he was shooting after us."

"Burton must've been right part ways," declared big Cumnor, who, like the rest had listened in amazement to this weird tale. "But why wasn't he able to drill you boys good and proper?"

"Gimme another look and you'll see what he could've done if he'd wanted to." He snatched off his hat and held it before them. At least five bullets had flicked through the high crown of the hat, tearing it to ribbons, but so sharp was their razor-edged flight, that the hat had not been torn from his head.

"And how far was he missing you?" Cumnor asked Burton.

"The devil was shooting for my ear, I guess," Burton drawled. "I heard his bullets come singing past my ear about a quarter of an inch away. He give me a regular breeze along the side of my face, you might say, but, somehow, that breeze never blew me cool all the way across to you." He added: "I say, let's go back and clean up that gent. He's aching and spoiling for trouble. He's queer . . . that's what he is. And he's tricky. He's loaded with tricks. Besides, what right has he got doing his tricks with a man-killing stallion like that? Is it nacheral? Is it anything that you or me could do?"

"Tell me, Si," Cumnor began. "Did this fellow really start any of the trouble with you boys?"

"He done nothing but give it a mighty thorough finishing," Si Manning admitted. "And if the gang rides in to mess him up . . . well, you'll all ride in without me. I'll stay behind to do the burying."

Chapter Thirty-Six

When such a man as Si Manning admitted with this frankness that he did not care to engage an enemy even with fifteen proved men at his back, it was enough to underline his expression of opinion, and the entire posse was thoroughly impressed.

"But," Cumnor said, "who the devil is this fellow?"

"If none of you know," broke in Sammy Gregg, "I can tell you quick enough. It's the same man who brought the herd from Mexico for me and kept them together in spite of stampedes and thieves and everything else. It's the same man, too, who cleared the stage line of big Furness so thoroughly that although you notice that he is raising a good deal of devil in other quarters, he has never touched one of my coaches, ever since. Some of you may not have been on the inside news, but I was there and I knew all about it. This young chap simply frightened Furness away. And if you want to clean up the whole Furness gang, there's only one sure way of doing it. And that's to get Jeremy Major . . . for that's his name . . . to work with you."

Cumnor gasped at this flood of information, and Sammy filled in the interval with more news: "Because there's no trail so dim that he cannot find it, and no horse so fast that his horse can't catch it, and no fighter so great that he cannot beat him."

Here Burton looked distinctly uncomfortable.

"We'll camp about three miles farther along," Cumnor announced. "And in the morning you can go back, if you want, and try to persuade your friend to make one of us. But I got an idea that you ain't gonna have no luck. Ride along, boys."

Sammy did not argue that, if he waited until morning, there would probably be no chance to find Jeremy Major. He had come to know that there are many subjects about which it is foolish and useless to argue with a Westerner. So he held his peace and rode on in the troop.

The next morning, early, he was on the road—on the road before the sun was more than a dim brightness to the east. But even though he started so early, when he reached the spot where young Jeremy Major had camped the night before, he found that it was deserted.

He looked vaguely about him for a trail, but not with any hope. He had a suspicion that the trails that Jeremy Major left behind him were of a kind that would quickly puzzle even the wisest trailer in Cumnor's outfit. Where had Jeremy Major gone and when? No one could tell. The first whim that stirred him would be the one that controlled him. Too lazy to pluck more than enough of the birds he had shot the day before to keep himself from starvation, yet, if the fancy entered his head, he might mount his horse at daybreak and be away, or he might have thrown himself upon black Clancy in the dark middle of the night and darted like one pursued through the upper mountains.

So Sammy made not the slightest effort to pursue the man, more than he would have made to pursue any phantom. He merely turned his horse from the black embers of Jeremy's cold campfire, and rode slowly back to Cumnor's band. And to Cumnor he made his brief report.

"Why," Cumnor said, "maybe it's as good. I dunno that a gent like him would work in with the rest of us. He's a lot more likely to play his own hand, and a lone hand at that. We'll get along and I believe much better without him."

The rest of that day they labored slowly along through the mountains with the yellow flannel shirt and the rigidly squared shoulders of Cumnor in the lead. That evening they camped on the spot that had been chosen for them by Sammy Gregg before the start. They were now at one of the four corners of the square that the scattered posse sketched across the surface of the mountains. And from that time forth they need do nothing except wait from day to day for news of the raiders.

So two lazy days in the camp passed away—comfortable days of rest for the men with Cumnor, but days of torture for Sammy, for he was not one of those who are plentifully entertained by the sights and the sounds of the great outdoors. If someone cared to sit down and talk to him about the nature of the stones or about the trees and their peculiarities, their ages and their uses, he was glad enough. And there were many men who could make a most fascinating tale out of the sign on the trails that crossed the mountains. However, if left to his own devices, Sammy could only sit and twiddle his thumbs.

Left to himself in the dreary silences of the camp, he could only wonder if any success would ever attend this complicated scheme of his, or would it be another of the failures that had always attended every effort to bring back Chester Ormonde Furness to the hands of the law?

It was on the fourth evening that the news came. They had started the campfire to cook the evening meal. Cumnor himself, left free from camp duties as the leader of the expedition, was walking across a hill to the east of the fire, when they saw him pause and then wave his hand and shout. A moment more and they heard the rapid drumming of hoofs. And after that, a horseman loomed suddenly beside Cumnor—a man who talked with many violent gestures.

It seemed that Cumnor refused to listen. He turned and led the way to the fire, the rider still rattling forth news as he went.

But when they came in to the scene of cookery, Cumnor said: "There ain't gonna be anything gained by saving five minutes here and now for the sake of confusing everybody. A gent always fights better and rides better on a full stomach, and without no hunger or curiosity eating away in him. Now what I claim is best is for you to set down here and roll yourself a smoke and tell us what news you bring in from Chadwick City. Take it easy. We got lots of time to listen and you got lots of time to talk."

The other dismounted obediently and stretched. "All right," he said. "You're the boss. I can't turn around and catch the whole seven of 'em with my bare hands. But sure as fate, they're comin' right at you now, boys . . . makin' a beeline straight for where your camp is."

"All right," Cumnor said. "The straighter they come, the easier it's gonna be for us to get our hands on 'em. Now you talk and tell your yarn. Ain't any of you boys got any coffee ready? Are you gonna make a gent talk with his throat all caked up with dust?"

Coffee was brought in a great tin cup that held more than half a pint. The cigarette was rolled.

"All right, Cumnor," said the messenger. "If it comes to takin' time and sippin' coffee and smokin', I reckon that I can do about as good as any of you. I'll yarn it for you as much as you want. You go back to the time that I was sent off to Chadwick City. I didn't think much of this here scheme. Askin' the pardon of Gregg, who I see now for the first time. However, I didn't think much of the idea of sendin' about a hundred gents off into the hills to set there and wait around and try to hatch an egg with Chester Furness inside of it. Y'understand?

"But I didn't care much if I wasted a few days lazyin' around Chadwick City, where I know some of the boys pretty good. I put up with a friend of mine, Hank Treecomer. Maybe some of you know him, too? Well, I laid around at Hank's place every

day, swappin' lies with Hank, when he was around, and lazyin'
pretty much in general. But along about when night comes, I
sort of set up and opened my ears and my eyes, gettin' ready in
case something should happen along that I had ought to know.

"Well, things went along like that until this mornin', along
about ten, when the day begins to get sort of hot and sleepy.
Jest when I was takin' a nap for myself in the hammock in the
back yard of Hank's place, I hear a terrible loud bang, like the
slammin' of a door with all bolts let go.

" 'Somebody is leavin' home mighty fast,' I says to myself.
'And maybe they's a couple of flatirons follerin' him.' Right
then I heard a half dozen more bangs. There wasn't no mis-
takin' 'em this time. When a door slams, it don't cough, if you
gents can foller what I mean. And these here noises had a sort
of a cough to 'em. Right on the hind end of that, I hears a yell
. . . a sort of a long yell that died out weak toward the end, like
somebody was terrible sick. 'There's a dead man or a scared
woman, one of the two,' I says to myself. So I rolls out of that
there hammock and I come around to the front of the house,
but, before I got there, there was a roarin' and a smashin' of
rifles and revolvers about enough to deafen you. And everybody
in that there town had turned loose and was yellin' and hol-
lerin' and tellin' everybody else to get 'em quick.

"Well, when I got around to the front of the house, all that I
seen was a cloud of dust wingin' up from the street and a lot of
men gallopin' away in the dust like shadders inside of a fog. Just
then one of them horses went down . . . slam! And a puff of
dust went up, like somebody had dumped loose a whole sack of
flour. And there was a gent that was down, sprawled flat on the
ground. He got up, staggerin', and I seen that there was only a
sort of an empty hole where his head had ought to be. And then
I seen that he had a black hood pulled down over his head. Sort
of ghostly-lookin', he was. And about a hundred gents started in

yellin' and pot-shottin' at that poor beggar. But just then the tail end of that dust cloud was kicked out and through the hole there came a gent that all of you boys would be pretty glad to see dead. He didn't have no mask on. Like as if he would say that he didn't care about how many bad things he done, nor who knowed about 'em. He comes sashayin' back with a Colt in each hand, turnin' em off pretty loose and liberal. And if I seen one man duck for cover, I seen about a dozen. And the shootin' at our end of the line got sort of scarce. And I seen this big gent on the big gray gallopin' horse . . . that was Furness, as I s'pose that you've guessed a while back . . . I see this here Furness rush up to the gent that had lost his horse. He was a pretty good-size man . . . as big as me, anyway. But Furness just leaned out plumb easy and picks him up with one arm and throws him like a sack over the pommel of his saddle and goes smashin' off down the street, turnin' in the saddle and loosin' off behind him a gun that was shootin' so straight that nobody cared to step out and take no chances with it. You might say that was a sort of a thriller. And it sure took all of my breath away from me."

CHAPTER THIRTY-SEVEN

At this point the narrator paused, not as one who requires much urging before he will tell his story, but rather as one who wishes to close his eyes and taste again, in reminiscence, the strangeness of the thing that has passed.

"It was Furness and his crew," murmured big Cumnor. "What a roaring scoundrel that gent is . . . and what a man. You could take him and spread him out and there would be enough of him to carve out half a dozen little ordinary gents, like you and me, boys."

All, apparently, were willing to concur with this view of the gentlemanly outlaw.

"But when it comes to roasting the feet of poor old helpless men to make them give up the money that's been worked for?" suggested Sammy Gregg.

"He didn't do any of the roasting," Cumnor put in.

"He took his share of the coin, which was just as bad as helping at the torture of poor Durfee."

"Aye, and he'll roast in purgatory for it," Cumnor muttered. "All right, old son, you go on with your yarn. I suppose Furness just about cleaned up the town, before he got out if it?"

"He didn't bother nothin' but the bank," said the messenger. "What he done was just to ride right up to the door of the bank and get off his horse and walk in. Seems that about a dozen gents seen him go down the street, just joggin' his horse along, free and easy. And every man says to himself that it sure must be old Chester Furness and his gray galloper. And then everybody says to himself that it *couldn't* be Furness, because not him nor nobody else in the world would have the nerve to come ridin' into the town in the middle of the mornin' like that, all alone, and take the chance of bein' blowed to bits."

"Alone?" Cumnor broke in, surprised.

"Wait a minute," the messenger said. "That part is comin' next. Because when Furness gets off his horse and walks into the bank, the cashier is busy with some accounts and bendin' down low over the list that he was addin'."

" 'I beg your pardon,' says Furness, 'but may I cash this order here?' You see there was two or three women standin' there in the bank room, that minute, and they didn't catch on that there was anything gone wrong. 'All right, in a minute,' says the cashier, and goes right on doin' his addin', and not lookin' up, and big Chester Furness goes right on standin' there, hummin' a tune to himself mighty calm, and tappin' free and easy on the edge of the counter with his fingers. 'All right,' says the cashier after a minute. 'Now let me see your check.' And this is what he read . . . *Please pay to bearer and charge to my account all the cash that is in the bank.* And it was signed S.S. Colt.

" 'S.S. Colt?' says the cashier. 'I've never heard of him. Who the devil may he be?' 'If you have never met him,' says Furness, 'pray let me have the pleasure of presenting to you Mister Six-Shooting Colt.' And he lays the barrel of a long gat on the edge of the counter under the cashier's window bars. The cashier was pretty much staggered, as you or me might have been. He looks up again into the face of the hold-up artist and he says in a whisper . . . 'Furness.' 'Thank you,' says Furness. 'I'm glad you know me. Then I can hope that I shall have to do you no harm.'

"Well, that cashier didn't wait. He just walked right over to the safe and he opened it right away quick, the same as you or me would have done, with that Colt starin' us in the eye, all the time. But all the time, that gent was thinkin'. And he says to himself that there is about a cool quarter of a million in banknotes in that safe, and that it is a devil of a shame if the bank has got to be ruined because one crook like Furness has took a fancy to that cash. Now he reaches inside the safe and he unlocks the inside drawers all fast and steady, and he reaches into the first drawer with both hands, as though he was gonna bring out a whole double handful of packages of banknotes. But instead of that, what he had his grips on was the handles of a mighty snug little gun. Because he was a game sucker, this here cashier, y'understand? And he knew how to handle a gun, and he was a sure enough a fightin' fool when he had a chance.

"Then he draws back from the safe and turns quick and tries to get in a pot shot at big Furness, but there wasn't no time for that. He couldn't even get turned halfway around. Because Furness was watchin' all of the time, d'you understand? And he seen something change in the face of the cashier, I guess. But anyway, he planted a big Forty-Five-caliber slug of Army lead right in the shoulder of the cashier and knocked him flat. Like that . . . d'you see?

"Of course, there was the devil to pay right quick. And there come gents runnin' from every which way. But Furness didn't even turn around to see who was headed for him. He just grabbed hold of the steel bars that was over the cashier's window and heaved himself up by them and he sings out as he climbs . . . 'Guard my back, boys!'

"The boys was right there for the job. It seems that a number of gents had showed up at the doors of the bank while Furness was standin' there, chinnin' with the cashier, and the minute that Furness sung out, these six gents stepped inside of the bank, and from under the edges of their sombreros they yanked down black hoods that covered their heads front and back. And they outs with their guns . . . one in each hand . . . and they had the drop on everybody in that bank so bloomin' bad that it would've made you sick to see it, I guess. And they kept things covered.

"Then some gents that was supposed to be right in there savin' the bank . . . them bein' the hired guards . . . they started firin' pretty free and plenty in through two of the windows and the six boys peppers them right back. And in the meantime, there was big Furness just swingin' himself over the tops of the steel spikes and dropping down on the floor inside. Once he was there, it was mighty easy to scoop the stuff out of the safe and throw it in bundles over the top of the bars, and his boys on the outside scooped up the stuff and dropped it into a sack.

"After that, they scattered for the street, big Furness heavin' himself over the bars again in fine style and singin' out to the cashier . . . 'You're a nervy kid. If the bank doesn't take care of you, you can depend upon it that I shall take care of you.' And dog-gone me if I don't think he meant what he said.

"And then they go swarmin' down the street, raisin' a dust that made shootin' after 'em pretty much like guessin' in the dark. But there's one funny part of this here game that you gents had ought to notice . . . that there was enough lead spilled around to make up a regular battle. But there was only three wounded . . . all on the side of the town and countin' the cashier as the first of the three. And on the side of the outlaws there was just a horse killed, the way I told you, and there was no other harm done. Which is something that I wouldn't've believed if I hadn't been there myself and seen.

"Matter of fact, I dumped a couple of revolver loads of shots after them rascals myself, but I'm free to say that the sight of that there big Furness sort of shook up my nerve, and, though I did some shootin', it was just the same as though somebody had hold of my elbow and was shakin' it a little all of the time. Y'understand? I was plain scared, and so was most of the rest of that town, and so would you boys've been if you'd been with me there. And maybe so you'll be if you ever do have the bad luck to fall in with big Furness and his gang. Which I'm hopin' that you don't. For your own sakes, I'm hopin' that you don't."

"Go on," said Cumnor. "Then you come riding right on to us?"

"I only waited about ten minutes in town to get all the news and find out how many thugs there had been along, and, when I found out what I wanted to know, I just slithered out of Chadwick City as fast as I could come and hit the beeline for your camp . . . or where I thought your camp was . . . which was about a mile north of this here. I did some pretty steady pluggin' along, because the pinto horse, yonder, is sure a good fast stepper and he don't wear out much easier than iron. I rode along for about five hours. It was right along in the afternoon, and then I pulled up to give the horse a mouthful of water and rinse him off a little and loosen the cinches and let him have a couple of free breaths. And while I was waterin' him at a little creek that I come across, I heard some horses down the road, and through the branches of the trees I seen seven riders come slatin' down the road.

"Well, you can say for yourselves how mighty sick I was. I seen that there wasn't any chance for me to scatter out, because I was in easy range of a rifle, and there wasn't no doubt about what them rapscallions would do if they seen a gent tryin' to ride away from them. Besides, the horse ain't been foaled in these mountains that could ever keep up with that gray galloper of big Furness. He would've rode up and put me in his pocket, and then they would've took me apart to see what made me tick.

"So I waited there in the shadow of them trees, mostly hopin' that I wouldn't be bothered . . . but mostly guessin' that I would. Dog-gone my heart, though, if they didn't come right up to the edge of the creek. I thought they was gonna cross over, and then I would've been a goner. But they just rode into the water and begun to let their horses have a mouthful or two.

"I slid out of the saddle and shoved my hand into the mouth of the pinto horse, yonder, so's he wouldn't let out no neigh. And while I stood there, the wind parted the leaves, some right in front of my face, so that I could look out and spot every one of them gents, as clear as day. And they sure could've looked right through the leaves and seen me and my horse because the leaves wasn't much thicker than enough to make a sort of a veil. Y'understand? It was a mighty naked feelin'. And every minute I expected to hear a gun and feel a bullet come smashin' right through me, by way of sayin' that they had spotted me.

"I dunno what kept them from it, neither . . . unless it was that I was so dog-gone' close and that they didn't expect to see me. If they'd had any idea that there might've been a gent within ten miles of them, they'd've spotted me that quick and I would've been dead before I knowed it, you might say. But somehow, a gent's eyes is made so that they're apt to see nothin' except what they expect to see. Know what I mean when I say that? You walk right on top of a deer and don't know it till it throws up its tail and runs for it. But you never do that when you're huntin' for it.

"Well, there I stood, as I was sayin'. And them not twenty yards away from me, and them laughin' and me sweatin' blood, you bet."

"What were they talkin' about?" asked one of the posse.

"You'd think they would talk pretty serious. Well, they didn't. I knowed five out of the six gents that was with Furness. There was Goodall and Sloan, and that good-for-nothin' gent, Thompson, all from Crumbock. And there was Lewis and little Reimer . . . you know him? . . . right out of Chadwick City, where they'd just been tryin' to murder the gents so scandalous. What did they talk about? Why, they talked foolish. 'Have you got a chaw of that nacheral leaf?' says Thompson to Lewis. 'I have,' says Lewis, 'and what's more, I'm gonna keep it.' 'Aw,' says Thompson, 'don't be so dog-gone' unfriendly.' 'I ain't unfriendly . . . I'm just usin' sense,' says Lewis. 'I'm kind of tired of bein' the goat for you and your chewin'. I'm glad that you got enough money now to buy your own chewin' for a week or two.' 'I'll tell you what,' says Thompson. 'I would pay twenty dollars for the half of what you got left of that plug.' 'D'you mean that?' says Lewis. 'I cross my heart to die.' 'All right, and that's a bargain and here you are.'

"He pulls out a plug of tobacco, and dog-gone me if there was much more of it left than the size of half of your thumb . . . and the boys all let out a whoop and a holler and Lewis cut the plug of tobacco in two and Thompson, he had to pay twenty dollars for his half. He put it right smack into his mouth . . . the whole thing. And it wasn't more'n a good-size chew, at that. 'How does it taste, Thompson?' says one of them. 'It tastes right smart like there was more gold to it than there was tobacco,' says Thompson, and everybody haw-hawed.

"That was the way they talked, like nothin' in particular until one of their horses begins to nicker. My pinto horse, here, he starts in quiverin' and shakin', he wanted so mighty hard to nicker back. 'Looks like that horse of yours has smelled something nigh here,' says one of the boys. 'Naw,' says another, 'the dog-gone' old fool, he don't smell nothin' nor he don't see nothin'. He's jest blame ignorant, that horse is.'

"Well, sir, there I was, listenin' and sweatin' mighty bad. But there wasn't any lookin' behind the leaves of the trees along that creek, and in another minute the whole seven of them was ridin' down the road ag'in, as sassy as you please. I just waited until they was over the hump of the next hill, and then I up and rode here for the camp as fast as the pinto could leg it along.

And you take my word for it, that unless they camped mighty early . . . which they ain't no ways likely to do, they ain't more'n three or four miles away from you right now. For they was headed right along this here trail."

CHAPTER THIRTY-EIGHT

Counting the messenger, there were now nineteen men in the party. And though Sammy Gregg was considered hardly of much force as a fighting man, his counsel on the way might be worth as much as any of them.

Cumnor, however, gave all of the directions for the hunt. He decided to start moving at once, and he selected from his party seven men on the best horses who were to ride well ahead of the main group. They were to scatter out, each man a full hundred yards from his nearest neighbor on either hand. In this fashion they would sweep with their eyes an expanse of about half a mile, searching that ground thoroughly. The moment any one of these advance men found any traces of the quarry, he was to turn about and ride at full speed to carry the tidings to those who were in the rear.

There was only one difficulty with the plan, and that was that, if they searched at night and covered on a half mile swathe across the mountains, they might miss the outlaws altogether if these had turned aside ever so little from the main trail. Whereas, if they waited for the daylight, they would have ten times greater chances of spotting the outlaws.

But against that chance there was to be posted the great probability that Furness would keep his men riding in short stages all through that night so as to reach the inaccessible fastnesses of the upper mountains in the first long and quite tiresome march from Chadwick City.

There was at least one aid to the searchers. There was a clear half moon that had arisen while the sun was still filling the west with crimson. Now, as the day died, there followed a short time when neither sun nor moon seemed strong enough to do more than confuse the eyes. It was at this time that the search began. But with every moment, as the west darkened and the moon rose higher, it was more and more possible to see to advantage wherever the mountainside was at all clear. Where the forest hung in clouds along the slope, to be sure, nothing could be made out that stirred inside of its shadow.

But they pushed west at a brisk pace, with the advance riders as a rule just beyond sight of the main body, or only occasionally seen as moving blurs in the distance. But still the moon brightened and brightened, or their eyes began to grow more accustomed to the light and to their work. Confidence increased, and the very manner in which they held their guns had altered.

They had not continued a single hour, however, and there was still a faint, faint rim of light to the west, when a rider slid out to them from the front with hurriedly gasped tidings.

"I seen the whole gang of 'em . . . all ridin' in single file. I could've drilled Furness clean as a whistle. Boys, we're gonna snag the whole lot of 'em . . . come on with me."

Sammy Gregg felt his blood turn cold and rush back upon his heart—which was like ice in turn. And it seemed as though Cumnor must have known what was passing through the mind of the tenderfoot, for his first word was for him: "You've shown sand enough in sticking with us this far. The gun work ain't your work, Gregg. You keep back, will you, and tend the horses? Because we're gonna go ahead, here, on foot."

"Let someone else mind the horses, or else turn them loose. I've come too far to miss the fun, Cumnor," Sammy said. "I have that much coming to me."

"Then keep along with me, kid. And try to do what I do.

Which'll be only common sense, and nothing rash, I can promise you. Get off your horses, boys, and throw them reins. And if there's any of you that have horses so poor trained that they won't stand when the reins are thrown, let 'em stay behind with their horses. Because we got to have men with free hands. Now strike away, partner, and we'll trail you. Mind you, boys, not a word spoke on the trail. Not even in a whisper. If there's any talking that must be done, I'll leave it to myself to do it. Y'understand? I don't have to tell you to remember to shoot low when you see 'em. Remember that everybody that gets excited shoots too high. There was nothing ever killed by a shot that was too high, but there's been plenty hurt by bullets that come ricocheting off the ground. That's all I got to say. But run silent on this trail."

Then they started off, striking at once into a long-swinging trot that began to cut into Sammy Gregg's wind in bad fashion. However, he stuck manfully to his work, keeping his place just behind big Cumnor. They traveled not more than a half mile in this fashion when the leader threw his arm up to stop the others and dropped instantly upon his face.

The rest followed that example and they learned the reason for it instantly. Out of the moon haze before them they heard the steady jingling of horsemen—the clicking of hoofs upon the rocks, the rattle of bits and curbs and chains and spurs, and then the occasional grunting of a laboring, weary horse.

The posse began to crawl softly forward toward the crest of the hummock that separated them from the view of the riders in the hollow beyond.

Then: "What's that moving over yonder?" called a clear voice.

To Sammy, it sounded very like the voice of big Furness, and the chill returned upon his blood, even though it had been so heated by the run up the slope.

"Nothing moving."

"Use your eyes, you fool . . . and back there to the right . . . they're on top of us! Cut for the trees, boys!"

A gun rang from the hollow. And there was a hoarse, distant shout. Plainly one of the unlucky forward scouts of the posse had been sighted by chance and dropped by a long-range shot. But there was vengeance coming behind the men of Furness at last. To the top of the hill lunged the followers of Cumnor, and they had before them a clear, short-range view of seven riders plunging toward the trees that were just beside them. The dozen rifles steadied for a brief instant on their targets. They crashed. And three of the seven horses that reached the woods were riderless.

Four were gone, however. Aye, and as the line of riflemen surged forward, they were encountered by a spiteful crackling of guns among the rocks on this side of the wood. One of the fallen men was either stunned or had gone to his long account. But two of them were determined to make the power of the law pay more dearly for their capture.

Sammy felt a cut, as of a hot-bladed knife, across his cheek, and a shower of crimson covered his shoulder at once. Someone else in the posse spun around and took a staggering step or two, and then went down. The rest dropped upon their bellies and began to worm their way forward.

"Who's up there on the left?" Cumnor called out as calmly as you please, while he sheltered himself behind an outthrust of rock.

"It's Jem Partridge."

"Partridge, damn it, what's the matter with you? Can't you angle some bullets down at them from where you are and roll them over for us?"

The side of the hill sloped sharply up, in this place, and with such an angle of fire it was most probable that Jem Partridge could send a few slugs of lead into the foes.

Presently a spark of fire glowed where Jem, without a word of reply, had opened fire.

And then: "Oh . . . damn it! Boys I got enough . . . lend a hand here . . . before I bleed to death . . . will you?"

"Tell your pal to stop firing, then!" called one of the hold-up gang.

"I'll see you damned first!" called another.

"Good Lord," whined the injured fellow, "you ain't gonna leave poor Thompson to lie here and bleed to death, are you?"

"You yaller-livered rat, Thompson. You was never no good. You was always a quitter. I dunno how the chief ever happened to bring you along for a job like this. No, you die there and be damned . . . but I ain't gonna. . . ."

The voice was cut short by the crash of the terrible rifle in the hand of Jem Partridge higher up the slope. And then they heard Jem say: "I guess that finished that sucker. You boys don't have to be afraid to go in and keep that there Thompson from bleedin' to death."

"Hurry up, boys!" cried Thompson. "I got news that you'll be mighty glad to have, I tell you. But I'm goin' fast. Oh . . . ain't none of you gonna come here and gimme a hand?"

But how dark and how open was that hillside. And who could tell if two of the three were really dead, or merely holding their fire in reserve to make it count the more effectively as soon as some one of the posse showed?

And then little Sammy Gregg thought to himself: *What good could I ever be with a gun in my hand for the shooting? But I can serve as well as the next fellow to stand out here and pull their fire . . . they can't know that it's only me.* So thought Sammy, with his knees turned very weak beneath him and barely strength enough to force himself to his feet and stand up in the brightness of the moonshine. But he made his way forward. He came safely through the perilous land between up to the rock behind which Thompson lay twisting.

"God bless you, partner," Thompson murmured, half gasp and half whine. "You're a brave man. You'll have your share of heaven for doin' this. It's right here . . . look how I'm bleedin'!" His voice was raising to an hysteria of terror.

But here were other men now coming hastily after Sammy—ashamed of themselves that they had let the little tenderfoot take the brunt of this danger. Cumnor and another were quickly at work bandaging the bleeding wound. And three of the men were sent back in haste to bring up the horses. The others bandaged their own badly hurt man, or examined the dead bodies of the two whom they had brought down out of the outlaw party.

The division of the spoils had already been made among the seven. And from each of the three captives, $32,000 was taken in fresh, well-crisped paper money—$32,000 for a single raid, a single half day's work.

CHAPTER THIRTY-NINE

They had learned from Thompson, in the meantime, what the probable plans of the leader of the bandits would be. He had intended to push straight in among the mountains, but, if there were any danger on the road and he were diverted from that purpose, he would turn straight about and take his men down toward the south, and past Munson, and so on until they were lost in the burning flats of the desert. This Thompson was sure of, because he had heard the chief speak of the thing several times.

"South is the trail, then," Cumnor announced. "He's had his check here. We'll ride south."

But Sammy, remembering something of the big, confident nature of Furness, broke in on this decision. "Go on toward the higher mountains, Cumnor," he begged. "You'll find him there. He'll never turn back from his way after a little defeat like this. He has himself and three good men with him. Besides, he probably knows that one of the three men he left behind may give away the news of the intended southern trail."

No doubt there was excellent good sense in this. Cumnor decided that it must be acted upon. The horses were by this time brought up. And the sound of the firing had brought in the vanguard. They carried with them the man who had been wounded by the first fire from the outlaws. So the wounded and the guard left behind were four members out of the party. Fifteen in all pushed on along the trail in the pursuit of the four fugitives. The odds were greatly altered. And on behalf of the pursuit the freshness of their horses spoke eloquently. Those of big Furness and his men had received a hard pounding during the course of this day and it would be very odd if they would be able to creep out of the range of the posse.

Indeed, they could not. With the silver clarity of the moon covering the mountains and showing them the way, Cumnor's party came momentarily upon fresher sign until they reached a point at which the trail turned off into four points, each followed by a single rider. It was the last desperate remedy to try to elude the pursuers by simply scattering—the usual vain attempt that children make when the constable takes after them in the orchard where they are enjoying stolen fruit. Cumnor instantly split his band into four sections. Three were of four each. With himself he kept only Sammy Gregg and another named Sid Lannister. And then each party hurried on its way.

Sammy Gregg, however, was none too content. So far all had been well enough. The rush of many horses, the creaking of much saddle leather, the oaths and the murmurs had kept up his courage to a fairly comfortable pitch. But this was now a very different matter—three riders on a trail that might be the trail of the lion—big Furness.

And when he considered that one of those riders—namely himself—was to his own knowledge perfectly incapable of handling weapons in a pinch—why, what would happen to them should it indeed prove that they were on the trail of the terrible Furness, and if he, Furness—his tired horse being pressed too hard—should turn back and strike at them?

That thought had barely formed in his mind when the wind blew faintly down the gorge through which they were riding the rattle of musketry, followed, at once, by the sound of exultant voices.

"That's Gavvigan and his boys. He started up that way,"

Cumnor said. "And by the racket they're making, they've got their man . . . yes, and he may almost be big Furness himself. Would they holler like that for running down any common man? I dunno. Push on, lads. We got to do our duty like the rest of 'em. There's where the rascal has turned to the right. We got him dodging now, and that's a pretty good sign that he's about played out and that he's not far away from us. Faster, boys! Wring the last stuff out of the ponies. The last that they got in them. We don't want to be the last of all to finish up our share of the job."

So they spurred recklessly through the dark woods just before them, Sammy with a terrible choked feeling of fear that made it hard for him to breathe. But he dared not give a warning, for the simple reason that it would make the others see his fear so vividly. And if they saw it, what report would go down toward the town and reach, at last, to the ears of Anne Cosden?

She would not be surprised. No, for he realized bitterly that this was merely what she would expect of him—cowardice, weakness, no manhood in body or in soul. So he said nothing but watched the mad onward rush of the two riders. They had forced their way ahead of him down the narrow trail—partly by their eagerness and partly by the superiority of their horsemanship.

They were, in fact, a full five or six lengths ahead of Sammy when they swerved for an instant out of his sight around a dense clump of saplings, and in that moment the thunder burst upon them.

Sammy heard a double report, as of two guns exploding in voice and answer. Then he whirled around the corner, plucking his six-shooter out nervously. He was in time to see big Cumnor grappling with the towering form of handsome Chester Ormonde Furness, while Sid Lannister was, even now, toppling from his saddle. In a trice, under the grip of Furness, Cumnor seemed to break in two in the back—then he was flung to the ground in turn—which left Sammy about five feet from the conqueror, with a loaded revolver in his hand, which was thrust out straight at the big fellow. Moreover, his horse was rushing him straight at his enemy.

He saw the glint of steel whipped into the hand of Furness. No bullet through the body would do the business, Sammy told himself. There was too much of this man. A cannonball through the midst might not dispose of him, it seemed to Sammy. So he chose the head as his target. And, with the pistol thrust out, he strode to keep open his eyes as he pulled the trigger.

The roar of the gun and the sting of the gunpowder smoke in his nostrils and in his eyes as he rushed past gave him a stunned feeling, almost as though he had received a bullet through his own body. Then one pull was sufficient to bring up his weary horse, and, turning about quickly, Sammy blinked in wonder at the sight of three saddleless horses behind him. Three horses without masters, and one of them the mighty and famous gray whose long-reaching gallop had kept his master for so long beyond the reach of the law.

But was big Furness down? Could it be that his puny hand—his—Sammy's—had dropped that famous chief? He got down off his horse at once. There was big Furness rising, swaying to his knees—Furness in all his hugeness of stature.

What happened in Sammy then he could not say. Propping himself upon a weak arm, Cumnor was groaning: "Your gun, kid. Use your gun on him."

But Sammy heard the voice and not the words or their meaning. A wild, hoarse cry burst forth from his throat. Such a sound he had never made in his life before—never dreamed of. He leaped in at the giant—and, behold, the giant crumbled before him with a groan and lay helpless at his feet.

There was an explanation of the miracle. All miracles can be explained, and this explanation was that the bullet from Sammy's lucky gun had clipped along the skull of big Furness and dropped him, stunned, to the ground. And, still weak from the shock, he had been unable to brace himself against even the light fury of Sammy's attack.

Furness was down, and now Sammy was on top of him, busily knotting the cord that was to secure the wrists of this famous robber and destroyer of men. Two had gone down before him. And then here came this wisp of a man and struck him to the ground. Oh, great was that monk who wisely invented the black powder that put the prince at the mercy of the commoner.

There beneath the trees he bound big Furness hand and foot—and then tied feet and hands together, so that he could hardly stir. After that he looked to his friends.

There was no use looking to Sid Lannister. He was dying before Sammy got to his side. He merely opened his eyes and stared vacantly into the face of Sammy Gregg, in answer to the anxious question of the latter. Then, with a stupid smile, he died.

With Cumnor it was a different matter. Two broken ribs and a badly bruised jaw were the effect of his grapple with big Furness, and now he was rallying fast. He even succeeded in struggling to his feet, and, gaining the side of Sammy, he rested a long, heavy arm across the shoulders of that little warrior.

"Think of it, Sammy," he said. "Once I was wanting to shoot lead into you. How was I to guess that you'd ever be out here saving my fool life and Sid's. . . ."

"Poor Sid is gone. Just see if that big devil is tied securely."

"Oh, say, you could hold a ship with less. How are you, Furness?"

"Well enough," Furness answered. "And now, lads, this is a lucky strike for you. There's more than sixty thousand dollars in my wallet, there. Take it and welcome. Divide it as you please.

Only let me get at that gray horse and away. I don't mind the wound . . . it's only a scratch . . . quick, friends, before the others guess that. . . ."

He was interrupted by the savagely crooning laughter of Cumnor. "Do but listen to him, Sammy Gregg. He thinks that we have been out to hunt for buried treasure, the dog. Oh, he's a grand man, Sammy. But a wee bit addled in the head."

CHAPTER FORTY

Cumnor was too badly battered to assist, but he could at least tell Sammy what to do. The little man, by his instructions, heaped up dried brush, and then a fire was lit that he was kept busy feeding as furiously as possible.

"They ought to see that signal, if any of them are still in the mountains above us, there," Cumnor said. "And they ought to file in down here to see the game we got in the bag. We'll have some of them here before morning."

Two of the parties were in before the night was three hours older. They had buried the men they had hunted down. And they carried with them from each the regular division of the spoil that the robbers must have made shortly after leaving Chadwick City. All had now been saved with the exception of one share of the loot. Of around $250,000 stolen from the Chadwick bank that morning and divided among seven pockets, a little over $220,000 had been retaken. And the remaining share might still be reclaimed if the party of four riders had any fortune whatever as they struggled somewhere through the mountains after their prey.

Of the seven bold men who had ridden into Chadwick City so bravely and so nonchalantly that morning, four were already dead, one was hounded across the mountains on a weary horse by four active pursuers, one was a wounded prisoner, and the leader of the whole crew was in the hands of the messengers of the law. Altogether a most discouraging day for crime and for criminals.

But Sammy was the hero. They turned to him with a respect that made him want to break into laughter, and when for the tenth time someone murmured that the thing he had done had been very fine, he could stand it no longer.

"Friends," Sammy said, "I can't let you go on talking like this here, because it won't do. The fact is that I was scared to death while we were chasing down the trail, just the three of us. I would as soon have gone hunting lions as I would have ridden down the trail of big Furness. Then I heard a crash. And the first thing I knew, there I was riding right straight at Cumnor and big Furness grabbing one another. I saw Cumnor broken. And then I couldn't do anything but pull the trigger of my own gun. My horse was carrying me right in at him. If I hadn't fired like that, I simply knew that I'd get a bullet in my back as I rode away. And then . . . I was simply lucky in having that bullet land. And there's the end of the story. But I hope that I'm not going to hear any more of this talk about how fine the job was. It was poor Lannister that rode in and took a bullet through the body that deserved most of the credit. And next to him, there was big Cumnor, who grappled with Furness . . . and then lived to tell about it afterward. They get the credit, and I had the luck."

He finished this speech with a deprecatory smile and a flush, as one by no means glad of his lack of greatness, but very eager that people should know him honestly for what he was, and not a scruple more. And he was answered by a grave silence and by curious, bright eyes fixed calmly upon him.

"Well," Cumnor said finally, "I'll be damned."

"And me, too," said another. "It seems that it was only luck, after all."

And a third said dryly: "Seems like all anybody needed was

to be there."

"But," said still a fourth member of the party in the same sarcastic manner, "that don't explain how you happened to run in at big Furness when he was on his feet."

"He was stunned," Sammy explained, frowning as he tried to remember.

"Cumnor didn't know that Furness was stunned. How did you know when you yelled and run in at him?"

"I was excited," Sammy said desperately. "I didn't know what I was doing."

The same solemn silence greeted him. And Sammy withdrew a little from his place in the circle of the firelight. The same grave, gloomy eyes followed him.

"You see what the little fool is worrying about?" Furness said, speaking up at the same time. "He's afraid that you're going to make a hero out of him and that then he won't be able to live up to that mark."

But that explanation did not make Sammy any less wretched. He only dreaded the manner in which Anne Cosden would laugh when she heard this thing.

They left a small party in the mountains to bring the wounded Cumnor to the other wounded, both friends and enemies. There they made a depot of all the provisions that they did not need and those who had been selected by lot started back on the pleasant journey to Munson.

Sammy did not wish to go. He protested that he knew a good deal about wounds and the dressing of them and that he should be detailed with the hurt men in the mountains, but they would not listen to him.

"I got to send in somebody who knows everything about what has happened," Cumnor said, "and you're the only man, Gregg. You got to go in and telegraph to the authorities. And I suppose that the bank over there in Chadwick City would be pretty glad if you was to wire to them, too. I think that maybe you could find out if they intend to offer any reward for the catching of the gents that walked away with their money. You run along, Sammy, and do the best you can."

So Sammy was forced to head the party that started on for Munson. No one talked about the work of the expedition to him on the way down, and no one asked him what sort of a report he was going to make. But now and again he knew that their eyes were upon him and that they were smiling.

So, when they arrived at Munson, he went straight to the telegraph office at the railroad station and there he sent off to Chadwick the following wire:

Party under Cumnor, of Munson, overtook and fought the raiders of Furness. Four raiders killed. Thompson and Furness wounded and captured. $224,000 recaptured. One bandit escaped so far as is known at present.

This was the legal truth, boiled down as small as possible. And Sammy, glad when that bit of duty was off his hands, started for the back room of the saloon to find out what had happened to the ruined, scorched feet of poor old Durfee. He went around the back of the saloon to escape the notice of the men whose voices he heard in the front, and just as he got to the open back door, he heard the happy voice of Anne Cosden crying: "And who really captured big Furness?"

"Sammy Gregg."

"Nonsense!" And her laughter ran like a thrill of poison through the tormented soul of poor Sammy.

"I don't mean that. I know that little Sammy planned the trip and I suppose that he planned it very well, indeed. But when Furness was captured . . . surely there was some sort of a fight . . . and I want to know what happened."

"Well, there was Lannister. He was killed by Furness."

"Poor Sid Lannister. He was a brave fellow."

"Then there was Cumnor. But he was smashed up in the hands of that Furness."

"Good heavens! What then?"

"Ma'am, there was only one left in the party that was trailin' Furness. Only three in that party to begin with, you see, and two of 'em had gone down before big Furness before the fight really got good and started."

"Yes? Yes? Why are you stopping? It was hand to hand, then, between Furness and the third man?"

"Yes. And the third man was Sammy Gregg."

"Are you ridiculing poor Sammy?"

"Him, I would be scared to ridicule him, ma'am, after what he's been seen to do on this here trip. He was the brains that started things going. And he was the hand that finished off the whole job that he had planned. He shot big Furness off of his horse. And when Furness got up, he ran in and grabbed him by the throat and knocked him down again and tied him up."

"Good heavens!" Anne Cosden cried. "Why . . . I have more strength than that little. . . ."

"Maybe you have right now, ma'am . . . but when he gets excited . . . he's apt to go sort of wild, I suppose."

"Stuff," Anne Cosden contradicted.

"But here he is himself."

Sammy stood at the door with a crimson face that showed that he had overheard too much of what had been said.

"Sammy," the girl said, "don't think that I've been running you down . . . only they're trying to tell me that you actually had the courage to fight hand to hand with Chester Furness. And of course I couldn't help laughing at that."

Sammy looked at her through a haze. His face was so hot that he felt that his hair must be scorching.

"Sammy," Anne Cosden said, "do you mean to tell me that it

is true . . . what they've been telling me?"

"It was all an accident, Anne," Sammy said huskily. "You see . . . my horse was carrying me right in . . . I couldn't do anything to defend myself except shoot . . . and luckily it clipped the side of his head."

"Oh," Anne Cosden replied. "But . . . no matter what you say, it was you who shot him off his horse? And then they said that you fought with him, hand to hand."

"He . . . he got up off the ground. I was a little excited. However, he was badly stunned, and so there was no danger from him at all. And that's all there is to it, Anne. And for heaven's sake let's talk about something else."

"We talk about nothin' else!" shouted a strong voice—the voice of old Durfee from the bed. "It was Sammy Gregg that bottled up them seven spiders that chewed me all up. God bless you, Sammy, say I."

Anne Cosden, however, stood as one entranced, staring at Sammy until he ducked suddenly away through the door and was gone. "But," she murmured in a troubled voice, "then it means that he really, after all, is *not* just . . . it means that he really is a good deal of a hero."

"Ma'am," a gruff voice said in answer, "when Cumnor comes in, you'll get the details. But this there Gregg is ashamed of what he's done. He's afraid that somebody is gonna find out about it and laugh at him. And I wonder if he's got you in mind."

CHAPTER FORTY-ONE

The jail that was created for the nonce in honor of Chester Or-monde Furness was simply a room in the hotel in the second story. To see that he was kept safely until he could be fetched away to another place of safeguard under the care of the federal marshal, who was at that moment traveling in the direction of Munson to take charge of the distinguished prisoner, the legs of Furness were secured with stout ropes and for a guard there was always one man sitting inside the door of his room and another man sitting just outside the same door in the hallway.

While Furness was detained, one of the former citizens of Munson was rushing west as fast as a train could carry him. And he came, among other reasons, to have the particular pleasure of giving testimony against Furness the moment that gentleman was brought to trial. The reason was that Barclay, for that was his name, had been among the victims of the industry of Furness in the days when that worthy had turned most of his attention to stealing horses on a large scale. Only three animals had been taken from Barclay, but one was a saddle mare he had had for ten years—a mare almost past the days of usefulness. But Barclay was one of the rare Western cattlemen who really loved his saddle string. And he had never forgiven the thief for this really minor robbery. Now he was coming to blacken the record of Furness as much as he possibly could, even if it required a special thousand-mile journey to accomplish his ends.

Before the train was half a day out from New York the conductor came to tell him that there was an old lady aboard the train who was bound for the same town that he was bound for.

Barclay was filled with wonder. "The same town I'm bound for?" he echoed. "Ain't there some mistake? Not the very same town that I'm headed for. Not for old Munson?"

"Munson is her stop, too."

"But, dog-gone it, you said that she was a lady."

"I did."

"But there ain't no ladies in Munson. There ain't no young ones to speak of, and there ain't no old ones at all." He stared almost bitterly at the conductor, adding: "Why, an old lady in that town would be a plumb calamity. What would the boys do with her?"

"How should I tell," the conductor answered, grinning. "I told her that there was a fellow townsman aboard and she's all set to see you. You better come back there with me right now."

Barclay groaned. "Look here, old son," he said, "now what would I be talking to a blooming woman about, will you please tell me?"

"Aw," the conductor said sympathetically, "I know what you mean, but this one is different. She's a regular lady."

What this mysterious difference meant, Barclay was very shortly to discover. He accompanied the conductor to a rear car and there he found that there was a little old white-haired lady seated at the end of the car with a white fluff of knitting in her lap. The conductor introduced him to Mrs. Fountain. She was the most dainty and delicate creature that Barclay had ever seen. And she made room beside her with such a smile that Barclay was actually glad to sit down there. A moment later she was telling him that she was going West to see her son, and to take him by surprise.

"Of course you know my boy, Chester Fountain?" she said.

Barclay admitted that he did not, and the little lady seemed enormously surprised.

"But," she said, "you haven't been there very long, I suppose. Perhaps you're just going there now for the first time?"

Barclay grinned. "I was in Munson," he said, "when there was no more houses there than nothing at all. I was in Munson when the trail was first called a street. And I was there when the boys dedicated the first saloon. That was Mortimer's Place. Oh, yes, I've seen about all of Munson there is to see."

"But," Mrs. Fountain said, "then you surely know my boy." He shook his head. "Not know my boy, Chester Fountain?" she cried. "Why, he must be almost as well known as the town, he and his farm."

At that last word, the ears of Mr. Barclay pricked a good deal. "Is his place near the town?" he asked.

"Oh, yes, very near," Mrs. Fountain answered. "You can see it from the train."

"Oh," said Barclay, for suddenly he understood. Of course there had never been more than two places that could be called farms. One was the little patch of cultivated ground around the shack occupied by old Hobo Durfee. And the other was that strange hodge-podge in the mountains that poor Cumnor called a farm and was trying to make into one—if the rocks and a thousand other hindrances would let him. But a place in sight of the train that could be called a farm? This precious boy of the old lady's had been lying in great style to her, on the chance that she would never, at her age, risk the long and wearisome train ride to the West. But here she was, coming gaily along.

Barclay could not tell in which way to be most moved—with pleasure that this gigantic liar should be exposed, or with sorrow when she learned what a hoax she had been made the victim of. But chiefly he was immensely sorry for the poor old lady. However, she was not the first to be bled by the devices of some rascal son who had gone West for the purpose of living on his annuity—which he found too small to keep him in liquor and pay his gambling debts. And here was some brilliant scoundrel who had created an illusory farm for the building of which he had no doubt drawn huge sums of money from his mother.

For there were signs of wealth about the woman. She was dressed simply. But it might have cost a small fortune to duplicate that gold pin at her breast—if the green gem in it were an emerald and not simply a bit of colored glass. And then, too, the daintiness of her hands, the tapered delicacy of her fingers, all spoke of a life in which there had at least been no labor. Barclay regarded these details with a critical eye.

"I suppose," she said, "that you begin to recall now?"

"Matter of fact," Barclay said, "you see how it is. Chester . . . of course I know him." He added: "But the last names . . . well, they aren't used very much. You know how it is out there . . . can't bother about remembering two names for every man . . . so it's just Al, Bill, Harry, Chester . . . everybody is in too much of a hurry to waste much time on two names."

"But suppose there are two men with the same name in town?" Mrs. Fountain queried. "The same first name, I mean. What do you do then?"

"Why, in a case like that, it's pretty easy fixed. Suppose there is two by the name of Bill. Then we'd call one Boston Bill, if he come from Boston, and we'd call the other just plain Bill. You see how it works? But mostly the boys don't stay long enough in town to be called by any name."

"How can they be remembered, then?"

"Mostly they ain't remembered. But if you're thinking back to somebody that had been in town, you speak about the gent that rode the Roman-nosed sorrel, or the gent on the cock-eyed gray horse . . . or him that had killed somebody some place or other. You see, people out there have a pretty good memory for the things that they've seen, but they haven't got any memory at all for the things that they've just heard."

She nodded, her head canted a little to one side as she drank in this information about the wild land in which her son was living.

Barclay went on systematically to draw what information he could from her. "Farming," he said, "is a great gamble, you know."

"Oh, is it generally considered so out West?" Mrs. Fountain asked.

"It sure is," he replied. "What with changes of weather and changes of prices, and such like things. . . ."

"How lucky my dear boy has been, then," Mrs. Fountain said. "But I suppose you know about his prosperity as well as I do."

"Humph," Barclay said, feeling that this was a tune that he could not follow so readily. "You see how it is with us. The boys are all pretty busy and they haven't got much time to talk about what they're making, and such like things."

"I suppose not," said Mrs. Fountain, "but then there are ways of telling even if a man doesn't talk about his own affairs all the time."

"I suppose that there are. . . ."

"And in Munson and the neighborhood I don't suppose that you have very many fifteen-room houses?"

Barclay blinked. A fifteen-room house in Munson was a thing to dream of, but not to tell. He could not even make an answer until finally he managed to gasp out that that was a pretty big house for any part of the country.

"And I suppose," Mrs. Fountain continued, "that a good many of the other men . . . the ranchers and the miners and the rest . . . will be wanting to follow my boy's example?"

"I suppose that people follow the leader pretty easily out there," Barclay agreed. But his mind was in a whirl.

"Ah, well," Mrs. Fountain said. "Money is made more easily now than it used to be. My husband and I waited a long time and he worked very hard, you may be sure, before he could get, even in years, what Chester earns often in a single deal."

"Is that so?" Barclay said huskily. And he wished with all his heart that he could get this monumental liar in a place where he could pommel him thoroughly and make him yell.

"Oh, yes," Mrs. Fountain said. "I don't suppose that Chester has even let the boys know that he has a mother. Nor that he has a mother who must look to him for everything. But, oh, I wish that the whole world could know what a genteel, thoughtful son he has been to me." And she shook her head. "And how he has showered me with far more than any woman in the world could really use."

Barclay was fairly downed by this last remark. This consummate liar who had told his lies while he was supporting his mother like a queen—and not drawing upon her bank account. It impressed him as being against all the rules.

And then little Mrs. Fountain, in her burst of fondness, snapped open a little locket that was suspended from a gold chain around her neck, and inside the locket Barclay found himself staring at a neatly painted miniature of none other than the handsome face of Chester Ormonde Furness.

CHAPTER FORTY-TWO

Chester Ormonde Furness! gasped Barclay to his innermost soul of souls. *Chester Ormonde Furness!* And then he cursed his stupidity for not having put the two together long before this. The same initials—the same first name. It was only wonderful that Fountain-Furness had dared to keep two of his first names the same as his true ones.

Moreover, Barclay told himself that he should have identified the wonderful son in another manner, because there was no one in Munson or its vicinity who could have pretended to a mother such as this fine old lady saving Chester Ormonde Furness.

"I think," said Mrs. Fountain, "that you have only placed him accurately in your mind since you saw this picture of him."

"Oh, no," Barclay said. "There's only one fifteen-room house at Munson." For he had become desperate, and he had sworn to himself that, no matter how profoundly he had to perjure himself, he would never take upon himself the painful duty of telling this poor little woman the facts.

Her son was in jail. Munson was congratulating itself upon the splendid performance of her citizens that had resulted in the seizure of the celebrated bandit. And he, Barclay himself, was now speeding West for the sole purpose of furnishing additional evidence to hang this very man.

Altogether, it was a nasty mess. He wished himself well out of it, of course, but since he could not be out of it, unless he left the train, he decided that he would go in for the wretched busi-

267

ness with all his might.

And in the days that followed, he was gradually ripening into an old friend of Mr. Fountain's. He was one of the boys who knew him best, in fact. And doubly delighted, therefore, to have had the pleasure of coming in contact with the mother of that gentleman. He could even recall pleasant little anecdotes that had to do with various exploits of her son. But, oh, what a check was put upon his imagination. How far he had to roam for the truth.

"Of course, my dear Chester has always loved the West," Mrs. Fountain declared one day.

"Sure," said Barclay. "It's rough, but sort of friendly."

"Rough?" Mrs. Fountain said. "Have you really found it so very rough after all?"

"Why, sort of," declared Barclay.

"That is odd," Mrs. Fountain said, "because do you know that my boy writes to me that the Western roughness is almost entirely the result of too much writing by Easterners who rush through the mining camps and similar places, and then have to write back to their papers to tell them about the wild sights and scenes that have come their way . . . turning old dogs into grizzly bears and sleeping Indians into drunken scalping parties."

"*Humph*," Barclay murmured. "Has he found it a pretty quiet place, speaking for himself?"

And through his mind in a long, shadowy procession, rushed the images of all the stories he had heard about Chester Furness, robber and warrior extraordinary—and it was like thinking back to a whole battlefield, in which every form was simply another silhouetted outline of the same man—Chester Furness. Oh, if the story of his doings were ever written out in full, what a tale it would make—what a history. But mere words could never tell it.

"Oh, yes, he has found it very quiet, of course," Mrs.

Fountain averred. "And he has written to me saying that he thanked heaven that he had never had to have a single gunfight since he entered the country and that he was sure he never would."

"Oh," Barclay said faintly. "Is he sure of that?"

"Because," Mrs. Fountain said, "he says that the trouble is nearly always with the people who drink too much and then hunt for excitement and find more than is good for them. Of course, my boy never drinks to excess, and he is so quiet and gentle that I suppose it is hard to imagine anyone desiring to do any harm to him even in that wild country."

"I imagine that it is." Barclay sighed. But he felt that his eyes were increasing in size with the passage of every moment and presently he escaped and stood on the observation platform of the train, wondering why this thing had to be, and why he should have been selected as the victim.

However, there was a sort of fascination about his torture, and he found himself wandering back to face it again, and receive long, rippling narratives about Chester in his infancy— how brave, how gentle, and how manly he had always been. And then there were stories about Chester in school. Oh, yes, there had been occasional storms. And Chester had been thrashed, on a time, by a large boy.

"After that, he learned to box," Mrs. Fountain said, "and a few months later he whipped the boy who had pummeled him. But as a matter of fact, the boxing went a little to the head of our Chester, and we began to get reports about Chester picking fights with other boys in the schoolyard . . . larger boys, or two boys at a time. It seemed hardly to matter to him. He had such a passion for fighting. I had to have the minister have a long talk with him. And after that, everything was all right . . . and there was never again the slightest trouble with my Chester.

And as he grew larger, he would never take advantage of his size."

Perhaps not, but Barclay could see the inward story of young Chester, with all the tyrant in himself repressed until the day when he found himself in the West, and at liberty to use his strength. And then the devil in him had come out, of course.

The train was approaching the town steadily. He was glad that they were arriving after dark. Therefore there would be no necessity to make explanations about the nonappearance of the fifteen-room house. Once the train got to the town, he decided that for his part he would bolt for the rear country and stay there until the poor old lady had left the place.

But how like a sneak he felt when the train pulled up at Munson and he helped Mrs. Fountain from the lowest step to the ground beneath and gathered up her suitcases.

"If Chester should see me . . . walking along the street like this," Mrs. Fountain said, laughing.

But Chester would not see. Several Colts were doing their duty and preventing that, of course. And Barclay thanked heaven for it. He escorted Mrs. Fountain to the hotel, where a dozen loungers stood up at attention, like soldiers when an officer enters. Some of them knew Barclay, but none of them spoke. One could never tell what to do when a friend showed up with a woman in tow, old or young. So they took no chances and did not speak at all—which was of course the surest way of being right in the matter.

Mrs. Fountain, therefore, found herself smiling cheerfully at brown, blank countenances, and there was a great flurry of cigarette rolling. And suddenly the hotel proprietor's face was a bright crimson, for this was the second time in the history of Munson that a woman had come to sleep in the hotel. The only other time was when Anne Cosden arrived. And she did not count, she was so big, and so hearty, and so like a man.

Mrs. Fountain was shown to an upper front room. It was the cleanest room in the hotel and always was reserved, if possible, for distinguished guests, such as mine owners. But still it could not be called in all respects a flawless room. One had to note, for instance, where a random pair of spurs had been raked a few times across the varnish of the door by way of demonstrating how a certain cowpuncher had handled a bucking horse. And then there was need of taking heed of the black spots along the window sill—some of them with little furry rags of brown paper still adhering to them, in token of the last cigarette butts that had been put down there and allowed to burn away, unheeded.

There were other slight tokens of wear about the chamber, such as the patch upon the matting that had been scrubbed through by the drumming of impatient spurred heels. And there was also a little board nailed across a spot in the center of the floor. The end of that little board was loose, and, if one turned it around, one could look down into the chamber below through a little hole just the size that a .45-caliber bullet is supposed to drill through planking.

But Mrs. Fountain overlooked these trifling imperfections with the blandest of smiles.

"You might say that this here is more or less of a man's hotel," the proprietor stated, redder than ever as he looked at his room and then at the lady who was to occupy it. "And out here in this part of the world, there ain't many accommodations for the womenfolk, you know."

Mrs. Fountain simply laughed. "Don't you suppose I know?" she said. "My son has written to me and told me what to expect, and if he has been able to live here and like the place, I'm sure that it is amply good enough for me."

So young Barclay and the proprietor found themselves outside of the door of her room. A sudden change passed over

271

the face of the proprietor.

"You pie-faced yap!" he said savagely. "Ain't you got better sense than to take your mother into a town like this?"

"You wall-eyed snake-eater," Barclay said no more amiably, "will you tell me what put it inside of your thick skull she was my mother?"

"Then why in the devil have you got her in tow?"

"Would you have me leave her to break her shins falling over the roughneck ways of Munson, young feller, without no assistance from nobody? Yes, I guess you would. You're that sort of a gent."

"Barclay," the proprietor said more gently, "leastwise you might have wired on to me from the train to let me know that a woman was comin', so's I might've swabbed down the room and got it fixed up a mite for her."

"If I didn't have nothing to think about but the sort of a room that she was to sleep in when she came to Munson, write me down for a four-year old unbroke bronco that never got no sense."

"What was you thinkin' about, Barclay?"

"Come along with me, son, and prop your ears open, because you are gonna hear some talk like there was never any talked before in this here town."

"What's the main lead, old-timer?"

"Come along with me. You ain't the only one that's got to hear it. The rest of the boys figure in pretty strong on it. Come along, low life, and get ready to listen in."

CHAPTER FORTY-THREE

When they reached the rude lobby of the hotel below, they found that new arrivals had come in, for the tidings that a woman had arrived in Munson had gone far abroad.

"All right, old sons," said Barclay darkly. "There is a considerable crowd here, but there ain't enough. I am missing some faces that should hear the news that I'm gonna spill in a minute."

"First, you poor old drunk," said a gentle voice, "will you lemme know what right you got to let live, after bringin' in your ma to a place like Munson?"

"If she is my mother, I am a pie-eyed pinto with no saddle on my back. You boys run out and collect in the rest of the bunch, because I feel that there is a speech coming over me. I got pains inside of me and words are sure to come forth. Go ramble and bring in the boys."

Moved by these injunctions, they hastened out from the hotel to spread the story through the town that Barclay had arrived with a story worth the telling. So presently auditors began to troop into the hotel and after a time that lobby was packed from wall to wall and all eyes were fixed upon Barclay.

The latter sat with his head sadly bowed and one hand clasping a half-filled whiskey bottle with which, from time to time, he moistened his lips and raised his spirits.

At length Jack Lorrain said gravely: "It looks like most all of the boys is in. So when might you be uncorkin' this here story that you got up your sleeve."

Barclay looked darkly around him. "This here ain't no joke," he said. "This here is a sad day for me and it's gonna be a sad day for the rest of Munson. I'm gonna start right in by telling you that the real name of the gent that you got in this here hotel, under guard, ain't Furness at all. Back in his home town, the skunk is called Chester Ormonde Fountain." He paused, rolling his gloomy eye and allowing this news to sink into the minds of his hearers. "Now that you got that idea put away in your head, I would like to have these here things percolate. That this here Fountain-Furness gent has come out here and that he has made a pile of money in . . . farming. That he has made so much money out here in farming that he couldn't think of nothing to do. So he sat down and built himself a little fifteen-room house, so's he could have a couple of decent rooms to live in, and so's the prairie dogs and the tree squirrels would have some place to go when they was tired of Nature." He paused and rubbed a languid hand across his brow.

There was a deadly silence in the room, but a great grin wrinkled every face.

"All right," Barclay said. "But that ain't all that I got to tell you. This here Chester Fountain-Furness was raised up plumb kind and gentle with a minister holding him by one hand and his ma holding him by the other. And this here Fountain, when he comes out West, he brung his gentle ways along with him."

He made another pause and the grins intensified. And the eyes shone brighter. But there was not a sound from that audience.

"And when he come out here," continued Barclay, "he decided that he would show folks in the rest of the world that there wasn't no real need, at all, for all the rough ways that some people had in the West, and that most of the roughness was caused by liquor and such. And so he made up his mind that while he was here in Munson and the neighborhood, he would never pull a knife or a gun."

The audience leaned forward in the same silence.

"And he never done it," Barclay said.

The audience leaned back again. And a groan of delight rumbled in their throats.

"It's funny, is it?" Barclay said harshly. "Well, gents, I am about to wipe that there grin off of your faces so hard that it won't never come back again . . . and don't you forget it. What I got to say next is that this here Fountain-Furness, he has been sending a pile of money back home to his folks, and he has been the single and sole support of his old mother."

The smile, indeed, had disappeared. In its place appeared a look of bewilderment.

"No, friends, I got to have you know that I'm talking to you from the heart, and, if I tell you a lie, you call me what I am. But I want you gents to recollect that I am not joking. And I tell you that the old lady that I put into this here hotel tonight is the one that give me the news about Fountain-Furness. It was from her that I heard all the news."

The gloom and the alarm in the face of Barclay was reflected, now, upon the faces of his auditors, and Jack Lorrain was heard to murmur faintly: "Old son, tell me the all of it mighty quick, will you? Tell me if this here old lady ain't some relation of his?"

"Gentlemen," Barclay said, "I can't tell you a lie. She *is* a relation of his. She is a relation of this here gent that you got locked up here in the hotel, guarding him with gents and six-shooters. And she has come out here to live for a while in the fifteen-room house that Fountain-Furness built out there on his ranch out of the money that he made from farming."

He waved a solemn hand. "Her and me sat at a window of the train and we strained our eyes through the dark tryin' to make out the outlines of her son's big house. And there was once that I thought I seen it. But the night was too dark, and I couldn't quite be sure. So I persuaded her a lot that the best way would be for her to spend one night at the hotel and the next day just to drive out with me in my buckboard and make a call on Fountain-Furness."

Lorrain said harshly: "Barclay, I don't like to say it about no friend of mine, but it looks to me like you have been encouraging that old lady to think that she was gonna live in a fifteen-story house out here. Almost like that there house was really built of stone?"

"It was built of stone, mostly," Barclay said gravely. "And it had marble fountains in the gardens, too."

The audience groaned.

"And now," Barclay claimed, "I aim to state that I have about finished up with my part of this here job."

"Son," said Lorrain, "you ain't even started with the explanation of why in the devil you didn't take part of the time that you was on the train with that there lady and tell her that she was wrong . . . and tell her that the reason you was on that train with her was because you was coming out here to try to help hang her son?"

There was a hoarse rumbling of assent.

"Well," said Barclay, "I am willing to tell you the reason why I couldn't very well talk too much to her about that. The reason, old-timers, was that I couldn't very well tell her that this gent was the world's greatest liar . . . him being her son." Here, upon his grand point, he made a long pause and ran a sardonic eye over the little crowd, as one who would say: *This is the poison. What can be done with it?*

And there was a long-drawn groan from the crowd, a groan from the very bottom of its heart.

"I dunno," Barclay went on, "how you gents may figure out these here things. I know that I came all the way from the East pretty much bent on finishing up with Furness for a dirty trick that he done to me a long time back. But I know that I'm not gonna bother with giving my testimony now. I'd rather that somebody else did the talking while that little old lady is sitting there in the courtroom listening."

Amazement and sorrow sat on every face.

"Howsomever," Barclay continued, "I guess that there won't be much trouble as far along as that, for by the time tomorrow morning comes and you gents have pointed out to her that there never was a fifteen-room house around here that her son built, I guess it will finish her pretty quick. And when you let her know that the money she's been living on has been stole from the poor suckers that live around these parts . . . I guess that won't be any more worse than kicking her in the face . . . but you gents is like me . . . rough and willing to say the worst you can. Only . . . don't ask me for no help. I aim to guess that they is enough able-bodied men in this here room to rope and tie and cut the throat of one old lady, if need be, without my hand being called for. Gents, I say . . . so long."

He slipped off the counter and wedged his way into the mass of men. But there was no further attention taken of what he had said by many of the crowd, who started eagerly for the doors. Then a loud roaring voice from the rear stopped them.

"You yaller-livered welchers and quitters! You ain't men! You're pigs! Would you turn away and leave a dirty mess on the hands of them that has to live in this here town?"

Shame, and the thunder of that voice made them turn around. It was Rendell, the storekeeper, who had checked their flight. And they turned back one by one, sullenly, sulkily.

"Yes," Rendell said with a sneer, "you are brave enough to come in here and shoot up the guards that is taking care of that reptile, Furness. You are brave enough to handle him and to take him out and hang him up by the neck in a pretty gay lynching party. Don't shake your heads and look at the other feller, because I know what was in your heads, and I've heard the talk that was going around. And I could name names, too, and darn my heart if I won't repeat 'em, unless there are a lot of orders showed around here. You could hang this here Furness mighty slick and smooth and manly, but you ain't got the common manliness to stand up to one little old woman. But I tell you that you're gonna stay right here with me until we get an idea of how we're gonna handle this here mess. And you're all gonna help." He paused and looked around for suggestions.

Lorrain said: "Boys, it looks to me like one of the best brains in the mountains is going to waste right here in this hotel. I mean Sammy Gregg . . . which by a manner of speaking, Sammy got us all into this mess, I guess."

Here no less a person than big Cumnor spoke—Cumnor recuperated from all of his wounds. "Boys," he said, "nobody has got more respect than I have for the brains of Sammy Gregg, but right now I sort of have an idea that he's got worries of his own." He said this with a gesture of his thumb over his shoulder toward the back room of the saloon where Anne Cosden was nursing old Durfee back to health and happiness. And by the sudden grin that spread over the faces of the men in the room, it was plain that they understood what Cumnor meant. "But," went on Cumnor, "there is another that we could ask for a few suggestions, and that is Fountain-Furness himself."

CHAPTER FORTY-FOUR

This idea, as the saying goes, struck them all where they lived. Instantly the mutter of assent went around and in another moment Rendell and Cumnor had been selected to go and confer on the matter with Furness.

So they passed the guards and entered the chamber to find the big fellow stretched upon his bed, smoking a cigarette. He looked up from his ten-day-old newspaper and smiled at them. "Well, boys," he said, "you look so solemn that I suppose you have come to lynch me?"

"And what have you got to say," Cumnor said, "ag'in' that?"

"I have nothing to say against it."

"Furness, you're a cool gent, and a sort of brave one, in your own rascally way. But will you be telling me, now, if there is any message that you would like to send to your folks . . . maybe in the part of the country that you come from when you left for the West?"

"Why, gentlemen," said Furness, alias Fountain, "you are very kind, really. I think if I had known how extremely decent most of you fellows are, I would never have given you such a good cause for wanting me hung. But as the matter stands I can assure you that I have been forethoughted enough to prepare for that matter. In the hands of a certain lawyer there is now lying a letter, and, if he does not hear from me within a certain number of days, he simply communicates that letter to the people most concerned, and they know that I have made my exit from this vale of tears, so to speak. Now, if the necktie party is all arranged, I'll be only too happy to walk out with you boys."

"Fine and handsome," Rendell said. "Well, Furness, all I say is that it is a shame that you wasn't born honest. But I wonder as to why none of your folks ever come out here to visit you, seeing how well you've done."

"Naturally not," said Fountain, "when they don't really know where. . . ."

"Oh," Cumnor interrupted, taking up the idea from the storekeeper, "they might have heard about a gent that made as much out of farming as you've done."

"And built a fifteen-room house out of a part of the profits," put in Rendell.

Fountain turned perfectly white with emotion as he started to his feet. "Friends," he said, "will you tell me what this means?"

"She's here," said Rendell. "She's here in this hotel."

Fountain sank slowly back upon the bed. "I never thought there would be a way to hurt me like this," he said at last. "But this is it. Are you going to bring her in here to see me like this?"

"What else d'you deserve?" Rendell asked in a terrible voice.

"Nothing," Fountain admitted. "I deserve nothing. But for heaven's sake, men, take me out and put a bullet through me. Don't make me face her like this."

Cumnor found it necessary to turn away. And the guard at the door assumed a sick look. Because it is not a pleasant thing to hear such a man as big Fountain beg, as he was begging then—with a drawn face and with tremulous voice.

So Rendell cut the torture short. "We're not gonna do it, man," he said. "Heaven knows that we ought to do anything that we can to make you suffer. But we ain't got it in us. All we want out of you is to suggest a way out . . . so start thinking.

She's right here in the hotel, and in the morning she wants to be taken out to see your fifteen-room house that can be seen from the station."

The outlaw thanked them with a single eloquent glance. Then he was lost in thought.

"The house was burned down," he announced suddenly. "It caught fire a week ago. . . ."

"But there would have to be a lot of ruins for a stone house. . . ."

"The stonework was sold to the railroad to build a station farther down the line."

"Even the marble fountains?"

The bandit smiled faintly and nodded.

"But there was your farm," Rendell reminded. "What are we going to show her in the way of a farm? We can show her the place where the stacks burned down out on the edge of town and say that was where your house stood. But what are we going to do by way of a farm?"

Fountain buried his face in his hands, lost in thought, but it was Cumnor who had the next good idea.

"There is only one farm around these parts that deserves to go by the name. That is my place. This here house of yours was just your town house. And besides that, you had your ranch house up on the farm in the hills. My place has got to do for your place tomorrow when we show the old lady around."

"Cumnor," Fountain said, "you're a gentleman. And I'd like to thank you."

"Leave the thanks be. One time or another, all of us has some sort of an experience with a mother, I guess."

Then the face of big Chester Furness became illumined. "I have it, boys," he said. "Take me out in the woods, here, and put a bullet through my head. That will simply shorthand what the law would have done to me. Put a bullet through my head.

And then let on to her that I had an accident, and that while I was shooting . . . you know what I mean. There is always an accident handy. People don't seem to realize how really hard it is to turn a gun around in your hand and shoot yourself in the face with it, even if you want to do it. Tell her there was an accident. She'll be happy and have a chance to take me back home and bury me. And the law will be satisfied . . . is that fair?"

"It sounds fair to me," Rendell said to Cumnor. "What more could be asked out of him?"

"All right," said Cumnor, "but at the trial a lot of things would be proved about the crooked things he did. And if they had a chance to get a confession out of him. . . ."

"Boys," Fountain said, "I'll be glad to write out a full confession."

"A true one?"

"Yes."

"Then start now. There's the ink and paper on that table. You got from now until sunrise to finish it off."

With those words, Cumnor herded his companion out of the room and they went gravely down to the room below. Not a man had left it. All were waiting calmly there in expectation of the return of their committee.

"It is all decided," Cumnor announced, looking steadily at them. "We got the suggestions from Furness himself. In the morning we'll take the old lady out and show her the place where the stacks burned down a few weeks ago, and we'll tell her that is the place where the fifteen-room house stood. Y'understand? Then we'll drive her out to my farm in the hills and show her that, telling her that it belongs to her son . . . who is away on a trip. And when we come back to the town, we'll get the sad news that her boy has been accidentally killed by his own hand while riding through the woods just outside of town.

And then she'll have, as Furness says, the pleasure of taking him back East and burying him."

This recital was received with a slight stir.

Then Jack Lorrain asked gravely: "Did Furness himself suggest that we take him out in the woods and shoot him?"

"He did that," Cumnor answered without comment.

"H-m-m," said Lorrain. "I would say, speaking personal, that was sort of abrupt . . . on his own suggestion."

But the rest of the crowd maintained the same stricken, depressed look that it had worn before. And in that humor they broke up and started for their bunks.

Some of them, wandering through the streets, met a small man skulking in from a ride through the country—a little man riding slumped in the saddle, with a hanging head. They looked sharply askance at him, and when they spoke, they heard a voice of one who had recently become very familiar to the men of Munson.

It was Sammy Gregg, who had taken his troubles off to the dark of the night, to commune with them in silence. He made no rejoinder to the hails that he received beyond a single terse word, and so he passed on down the street, a lonely form. And he entered the hotel and passed wearily by a big hulk of a man—Rendell.

"Son," Rendell said, "did you ever hear of the old proverb . . . Nothing ventured, nothing gained?"

Little Sammy Gregg turned around upon his heel. "Now what do you mean by that?" he barked out.

"I mean what I say," Rendell said.

"But why should you say it to me?"

"Think it over, son, and you'll see. You ain't so darned mysterious as maybe you would like to think you are." And with this, he hobbled out of the hotel and left Sammy standing, blinking, behind him, with his thin hands hanging helplessly at his sides.

And then, turning a bright crimson, Sammy hastened out of the hotel and rushed to the back of the saloon and tapped softly at the door that opened upon the room where the injured Durfee was still kept.

In answer to his tap, the door was opened at once, and tall Anne Cosden towered above him. The red in his face became more fiery still.

"Anne," he whispered. "I just came to see . . . how . . . how Hobo Durfee might be this evening."

Anne Cosden, who had seemed to stand there quite expectant a moment before, now sagged wearily against the side of the door. "Oh, he's all right, I suppose," she said. "I wish that somebody would ask how I felt once in a while."

"But, Anne . . . how do you feel!"

"Tired," groaned Anne.

"I expect you are," Sammy said.

"Tired of all the men in the world," groaned Anne Cosden. "They're all such fools."

Sammy sighed before blurting out: "Anne, I love you! Will you marry me?"

"I've been an idiot," Anne said. And then there was nothing more said just then. Sammy looked foolishly happy, and Anne was radiant.

CHAPTER FORTY-FIVE

On the next morning, Cumnor and Rendell were the official guides. Jack Lorrain went along with the party. But the nice young man who had known dear Chester so well and who had traveled with Mrs. Fountain all the way from the East—he was not anywhere to be seen.

But the three chosen worthies were seen bundling the good old lady into a buckboard. And a hundred pairs of awe-stricken eyes watched her settle herself.

They heard her say: "You are all so kind to me. But I knew that it was sure to be this way. Chester has never gone any place without making himself loved by everyone."

Then they drove away.

Afterward, they were seen by covert scouts who sneaked in the rear and made observations where the buckboard paused in front of the charred remains of the old straw stacks that had burned down recently on the edge of the town. They made their observations and they saw Rendell, walking with a limp that in nowise interfered with his eloquence, striding about the plot and making large gestures to indicate the handsome structure that had once stood there. But most of all he distinguished himself when he came to a small hollow in the ground.

"And here was one of the fountain pools," big Rendell announced. "It was lined all around with marble that must've cost a mighty lot of money. And there was a bronze lion a-standing up."

"A bronze lion!" Mrs. Fountain cried. "Why, how extravagant my dear boy has become!"

"Money don't mean nothing to a gent like him that picks money right out of the ground, you might say. There was the bronze lion up there, lolling out its tongue and lolling water out, too, and the water it run down into the pool where there was a whole lot of goldfish swimming around, as sassy as ever you seen."

"All destroyed by that frightful fire." Mrs. Fountain sighed.

Then they went on out to see the farm, and the country house of Mr. Fountain.

They spent most of the day out there. Cumnor pointing out the possibilities of the farm until the eyes of the good old lady glistened.

"You seem to know almost as much about it as Chester could," she said.

"I'm only his foreman," said Cumnor. "But he says that I know enough to run the place while he's away."

And so, in the late afternoon, they started on the road back and were encountered, miles from town, by a dusty rider who communicated to them the terrible news.

"There has been a tragic accident." the messenger said. "And Chester Ormonde Fountain has killed himself."

Of course the poor old lady fainted, but when she came to and was told the whole story, she took it all bravely enough. Not that she was told what actually happened, for she will never know that her son deliberately took his own life to save her from a great misery. She believed that it was all an accident that he was killed in the manner that they had so minutely described to her.

But the truth of the matter was that Furness was not shot by the boys who took him out in the woods, according to his own suggestion, but that they gave him a gun and he brought about his own end.

Later, they found that Furness had left a number of checks that were drawn on different bank accounts that he had. By one of the checks he left $20,000 to old Durfee to take care of the poor old codger the rest of his life. And old Durfee said that the price was the money that he lost and a little over $12,000 more. He hired a Negro to work for him and went back to his shack in the hollow and started in making strawberry preserves. He said he never would have known how many friends he had if it all hadn't happened, and so he's pretty happy.

There was about $80,000 more that Furness left behind to go to pay back the bank the rest of the money that it had lost. All of which goes to show how much Furness appreciated what the men of Munson did for him in the end.

ABOUT THE AUTHOR

Max Brand is the best-known pen name of Frederick Faust, creator of Dr. Kildare, Destry, and many other fictional characters popular with readers and viewers worldwide. Faust wrote for a variety of audiences in many genres. His enormous output, totaling approximately thirty million words or the equivalent of five hundred thirty ordinary books, covered nearly every field: crime, fantasy, historical romance, espionage, Westerns, science fiction, adventure, animal stories, love, war, and fashionable society, big business and big medicine. Eighty motion pictures have been based on his work along with many radio and television programs. For good measure he also published four volumes of poetry. Perhaps no other author has reached more people in more different ways. Born in Seattle in 1892, orphaned early, Faust grew up in the rural San Joaquin Valley of California. At Berkeley he became a student rebel and one-man literary movement, contributing prodigiously to all campus publications. Denied a degree because of unconventional conduct, he embarked on a series of adventures culminating in New York City where, after a period of near starvation, he received simultaneous recognition as a serious poet and successful author of fiction. Later, he traveled widely, making his home in New York, then in Florence, and finally in Los Angeles. Once the United States entered the Second World War, Faust abandoned his lucrative writing career and his work as a screenwriter to serve as a war correspondent with the infantry in Italy, despite his fifty-one years and a bad heart. He was killed during a night attack on a hilltop village held by the German army. New books based on magazine serials or unpublished manuscripts or restored versions continue to appear so that, alive or dead, he has averaged a new book every four months for seventy-five years. Beyond this, some work by him is newly reprinted every week of every year in one or another format somewhere in the world. A great deal more about this author and his work can be found in *The Max Brand Companion* (Greenwood Press, 1997) edited by Jon Tuska and Vicki Piekarski. His next Five Star Western will be *The Wolf and the Man*. His Website is www.MaxBrandOnline.com.